ASSASSINS

A RYKER RETURNS THRILLER

ROB SINCLAIR

BLOODHOUND
— BOOKS —

ALSO BY ROB SINCLAIR

~

~

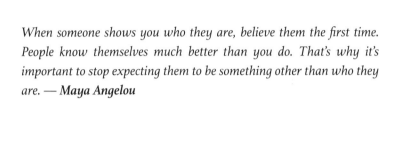

*When someone shows you who they are, believe them the first time. People know themselves much better than you do. That's why it's important to stop expecting them to be something other than who they are. — **Maya Angelou***

1

Ten pm, but still over thirty degrees Celsius, with choking humidity that sapped his strength with every step, and made his limbs heavy and sluggish. Sweat covered his brow. Thick droplets ran down into the small of his back. His attire didn't help much. Black tie. The top button of his shirt clung to his neck like a creeper. The fitted cotton stuck to his body all over like armour, weighing him down.

'Over there,' Elliott said.

Ryker looked off into the darkness in the direction Elliott had indicated. All he could see across the grass was the line of shrubs that gave way to the road, and the bright street lights beyond. Traffic hustled along, though in this part of the city, at this time of night, the road was far from busy.

'I don't see anything,' Ryker said.

'Behind the bushes. Sure I saw someone.'

Ryker stared as they continued to walk through the dark. No. There was no one there.

'I should go and check,' Elliott said.

Ryker nodded. Elliott set off at pace and Ryker took a wider arc in the direction his colleague was headed for.

Moments later Elliott gave his answer, his voice echoing in Ryker's earbud. 'Nothing.'

'Better safe than sorry.'

'What's taking you two so long?'

Another voice in Ryker's ear now. Nadia Lange.

'We'll be there in thirty seconds,' he responded.

It wasn't a bad estimate. Elliott regrouped with Ryker and they carried on across the dark grassy area. They reached the edge of the red stone wall twenty-eight seconds later. Ryker had counted each one of the seconds in silence, a basic aid to keep his breathing and his heart rate and his mind steady in anticipation of the task that lay ahead.

They pulled to a stop at the wall and Ryker looked around. All clear. There was no one following in the park behind them. Why would there be? Ryker listened to the sounds drifting over from the other side of the wall. Still distant. They were necessarily entering through a quiet corner, though he could still make out chatter. String music. The chinking of glasses. One or two voices louder and more boisterous than others even though it was still early – relatively.

'We're good,' Ryker whispered to Elliott. They moved a few steps along until they reached the door in the wall. Elliott went one side, Ryker the other, neither standing too close to the wood, just in case. Both had one hand inside their suit jackets, at the ready.

Ryker reached out with his free hand and knocked. Lightly, yet loud enough for anyone standing on the other side to hear.

There'd better bloody be someone standing there, Ryker thought as he waited.

A clunk. A click. The door was pulled open and light surged out from within. Enough to reveal the face of the lone man who'd opened up. Khadri. Not one of the crew, but a worker here. A worker who'd been paid handsomely – and had his arm twisted more than a little – for this small yet crucial role.

The team for this operation, including Ryker in the lead, numbered seven. Four would be on the inside tonight with Ryker, but there had simply been no feasible way to get all five of them on the official guest list. Only two were. Plus they had their 'chauffeur' with them. Ryker and Elliott would make their own way in. The remaining two would stay outside.

'Thanks,' Ryker said as he moved past Khadri who was practically shaking from nerves. 'You've done your part. Get on with your night.'

Khadri nodded and scuttled off.

'You trust him?' Elliott said.

'Doesn't matter now.'

'About time,' Lange said. She was one of the two on the outside. Not just backup, but an extra set of eyes and ears. Lange was in charge of the drone, which was high enough in the air for its rotors to be silent from the ground, but remained close enough for her to keep watch on below with the craft equipped with both a night vision and thermal camera. Ryker glanced up now, but could see nothing of the machine.

Assisting Lange, in the back of the van two hundred yards away, was Joey Weller. The technology guy. In charge not just of the team's comms, but for monitoring their positions with their trackers. He would also keep a close eye and ear on the airwaves and, if needed, do what he could to hack into and disrupt the host's security system.

'Has anyone seen Alpha yet?' Ryker asked.

'Yes,' came the reply from Penny Diaz. 'He's with the posse from the ministry.'

The ministry being the Ministry of Energy and Industry, responsible for handling a significant element of Qatar's burgeoning economy. The guest list for this shindig, in what was essentially a state-run palace which had been given over to tonight's foreign host for the duration of his stay in the emirate, included not just the bosses from the ministry, but several other high-ranking politicians from Qatar and further afield. Not to mention a large number of expats – predominantly from Europe and Asia – who were here to wine and dine and, over the course of their dealings here, make themselves and their friends a hell of a lot richer than they already were.

'Security?' Ryker said.

'As we expected on the outside,' came the gruff voice of Ali Salman, who was Diaz's better half tonight – at least to onlookers. Salman was the 'local' among them, and a genuine employee at the Ministry of Interior, even if for the past six months he'd been taking instructions from Ryker. 'I've spied six so far on the inside too.'

'Alpha's?'

'No doubt, judging by the look of them.'

Ryker checked his watch. Five past ten. They had to be on the boat at midnight – Salman included. There was no way he could stay in the country after tonight.

The boat was a forty-minute drive away. They didn't have long.

'Okay, let's get to it,' Ryker said.

He and Elliott moved off from the dark corner at the service side of the palace. Nothing salubrious here, although the scale of the palace was already apparent, rising tall and wide in front of them. They casually moved across the bland and quiet space at the back, around a corner and into the manicured gardens, then along a twisting path toward the hubbub. No one here, but they soon had some of the partygoers in their sights – stragglers who'd come outside for a quick smoke. Men only, all wearing identical-looking suits to those that Ryker and Elliott had on.

'Evening,' Elliott said with a nod to a group of three who glanced their way.

The men nodded in return before getting back to their nicotine and champagne. Ryker and Elliott headed up the stone steps to the side entrance the men had come out of: a wide, arched and vaulted space that wouldn't have looked out of place at the front of a glorious five-star boutique hotel. Here, in a country where space and money often seemed endless – at least for the few – the entrance was a little-used afterthought.

'We're moving in,' Ryker said.

'Okay. We're at the top of the central gallery,' Diaz said. 'Alpha is by the... I don't know. Some bloody big gold statue.'

'It's a Heckler,' Salman said.

Ryker smiled. He glanced over to Elliott who was looking a little less enthused.

'Suck it up,' Ryker said. 'And remember the role you're here to play.'

Ryker could tell by the look on his colleague's face what the problem was. The overt wealth, the hypocrisy and dodgy dealings that accompanied it. But tonight they had to pretend to be a part of it. Elliott nodded and his face softened as he got into character.

Just in time, as they turned a corner and were suddenly among a throng of people. They both grabbed a glass of champagne from a white-gloved waiter and Ryker looked around to take in the people, and the grand space they were there to fill.

A sprawling gallery. Three storeys, though with the extra-high ceilings it was tall enough for ten. Over a hundred guests, Ryker estimated, though they were swallowed up here. High above them the roof was a gold-encrusted dome. There were crystals and splashes of gold everywhere. The building was undoubtedly modern, breathtaking and expensive, with Arabic flourishes throughout.

The guests, on the other hand, were something of a clash. At least eighty per cent of the people Ryker could see were male – not surprising in a country where females were generally discouraged from socialising at all, and particularly if they were not chaperoned. Westerners were, in general, given much more leeway, depending on the setting. Like here, behind closed doors, where money was as important, if not more important than religious culture. More than half of the men here were in black tie. The rest were in traditional Arab dress. The groups were mingling, and there were smiles all around, despite the divide in culture that was as obvious in the choices of dress as it was in the choices of drink: champagne versus orange juice.

'Come on, this way,' Ryker said.

He and Elliott set off again, all the while scanning around them, taking in the guests, looking for anyone who stood out – covert security belonging to either Alpha, the other guests or the Qatari government. They had to expect all of those to be present tonight, and those harder to spot individuals would be the biggest stumbling block to them achieving their aim; to kill Alpha.

Yet getting to their target during this high profile and busy gathering was still a far more straightforward proposition than doing so any other time. Of course, for a simple assassination they could have just had a sniper on a rooftop. But this wasn't just a simple assassination. They needed information from Alpha too, and for that they had to get face to face with him. That was far easier to achieve here. The sheer number of people, and the relaxed nature of the proceedings, was the perfect cover.

Ryker and Elliott moved for the grand spiral staircase. They were halfway to the next floor when Ryker spotted Diaz and

Salman, now chatting to a group of four others. Needless distraction, but they all needed to blend in, and be capable of holding their own in this crowd.

'That's Pavel Grichenko there, isn't it?' Salman said, jovial and chatty, to the man to his right. 'By the Heckler statue?'

Ryker heard this through his ear from fifty yards away. As he spoke, Salman caught Ryker's eye and ever so slightly indicated to his left.

'Yes, you haven't met him before?' came a more distant reply from one of the men Salman and Diaz were talking to. The conversation carried on, but Ryker wasn't paying much attention. He was now too busy watching Alpha – aka Pavel Grichenko.

Then, 'Shit.'

A pause. 'What?' Ryker said.

He tapped his earbud and glanced to Elliott who gave a slight shrug. They stopped on a landing midway to the next floor, Alpha and Diaz and Salman remained in view. No outward signs of alarm from any of them.

'Aldern?' Ryker said.

No reply now from Aldern – Salman and Diaz's chauffeur, who was keeping watch by the front entrance.

'Wait a second...' Aldern said. 'This... this isn't right.' His voice was patchy, the line breaking, though the rustling sound also suggested he was walking. To where?

'Aldern?'

'Out here. There's a...'

Then nothing.

Ryker stood and waited. 'Aldern?' No reply. 'Lange, Weller, help me here?'

'His feed's down,' Weller said. 'Give me a minute.'

'Do you see him?' Ryker said.

'He was by the car five seconds ago. I saw him walking away, toward the trees, but... he's out of view now.'

'His tracker.'

'Offline too.'

Not good. Ryker stared at Elliott for a couple of seconds, trying not to show any concern. Despite the passive face, he knew his colleague was doing the same. They had a problem, and that didn't just mean the chances of their mission being a success were diminishing by the second.

So, too, were the chances of them walking away from this alive.

2

'Okay. Everyone keep on track,' Ryker said. 'I'll go and find him.'

An uneasy silence in response. Ryker turned and headed back down the stairs. He eased his way through the guests, nodding and smiling, then stepped outside the main entrance, out of the air-conditioning and back into the sultry heat.

He'd clocked eight security guards dotted about the place, including four who were on the outside. None were Alpha's core crew. These were just guys hired in for the night to provide a visual deterrent, to stop people coming in who weren't invited. Well, they'd failed on that one then. Still, Ryker was cautious as he headed past them.

He continued down the steps and to the sweeping gravel drive that was filled to bursting with the most extravagant collection of cars Ryker had seen in his life.

'You're moving in the right direction,' Diaz said in his ear. 'Our car's seven along on your left, one row back.'

Ryker found it. The gleaming Mercedes S-Class that Aldern had driven in with Diaz and Salman as his passengers was parked between two hypercars – a Bugatti and a Pagani – that together were probably worth twenty of the top-of-the-range Mercedes. Even extreme wealth had its extremes.

He moved around the Mercedes. The driver's door was ajar. Ryker whipped his eyes about. There was no one here. The nearest people he could see were the two security guards either side of the bottom of the steps. Twenty cars between them and him.

'His feed went down just to the north of where you are now,' Weller said.

Ryker looked over in that direction. The driveway and adjacent gardens were lit by low-level glowing bulbs, but beyond was a cluster of trees that was drenched in darkness. Why the hell had Aldern gone over there?

'What does thermal show?' Ryker said. He opened the door further and ducked down into the driver's seat. No sign of the key fob. Aldern hadn't left his ID or his phone or anything else. Ryker checked in the glovebox. No weapon.

'Weller? What does thermal show?'

'There's... there's no one over there as far as I can see.'

He sounded surprised.

'But you're sure you saw him head in that direction?'

'Positive.'

'Okay. I'm going to check. Keep a lookout.'

'Alpha's on the move.' Diaz now. 'Me and Salman will follow,' she added.

No one intervened. That was fine. Ryker had wanted to be on the inside with them, but he had trust in his team. At least that part of the night was still on track. The plan had always been to wait for Alpha to move away from his guests. Either with or without his chaperones or the staff from the ministry. They needed him away from the crowds so they could confront him and get what they needed before they took him out.

'Is Alpha alone?' Ryker said as he approached the black edge of the treeline.

'No. With one of the ministers, plus someone else I don't recognise. I'll try to get a snapshot to Weller.'

Where were they going?

Ryker moved into the darkness, slowing his pace as he did so. He stopped for a second and stood and listened. Nothing, except for the murmur from the palace behind him, and the distant hum of traffic in the other direction.

'Weller, what do you see?' Ryker said, his voice not much above a whisper as he looked into the darkness.

No response. 'Weller? Do you still see me?'

Ryker spun around. He didn't know why. A noise?

'Can anyone hear me?'

No answer.

Ryker took his bud out, pressed the reset button. The little light blinked blue to show it was connecting. Green to show it was working. In theory at least. He stuck it back in.

'Anyone?'

A noise behind him. Ryker ducked and twisted and could see nothing but a wispy shadow coming for him. Not a shadow. A figure. A glisten of metal. A blade.

Ryker shimmied as the knife swooshed toward him. A scratching sound as the tip of the blade flashed across the side of his jacket.

He went to grab for the arm holding the knife, but in the darkness he miscalculated and grabbed nothing and nearly lost his balance in the process.

He righted himself. Was crouched down, at the ready to counter, to attack, but all was silent and still once again. Ryker spun on the spot. He couldn't see a thing in the darkness.

Another rush of air in front of him. Ryker didn't try to move out of the way this time. Instead, he rooted himself. Saw the blade. Used his forearm to block just in time. He smashed his arm into the wrist of the hand holding the weapon as it came toward him. The knife stopped only inches from his face.

Ryker reached out with his other hand, grabbed the arm, twisted. As he did so he swiped a leg away and pulled the off-balance figure to the ground. Ryker forced his knee into the attacker's neck. Pushed the out-turned arm down so the elbow and shoulder were at bursting point.

'Drop the knife,' Ryker said, absolute calm and command in his voice as his eyes continued to slowly adjust to the darkness, and the black-clad figure below him took shape.

No response. Ryker pushed down further on the arm and the knife came free with a yelp of pain. A man. But the man wasn't alone. Ryker saw the movement in front of him before he heard it. He let go of the arm and grabbed for the fallen knife, but in the dark he missed it and instead burst upward empty-handed. He was facing toward the palace, and this time at least the distant lighting cast the moving figure in a silhouette. Ryker connected under the jaw with a ferocious uppercut that sent the figure flying backward. Ryker planted his feet back down. Rooted around and found the knife.

He was about to get down to search and interrogate the mystery attackers...

Bang.

A gunshot. Not near Ryker. Inside the palace. Then another gunshot rang out. Then a cascade of rat-a-tat gunfire in response. Shouting, screaming.

'What's going on?' Ryker said, pushing the bud in his ear as though the skin contact would solve the connection problems. No response.

He growled in frustration. Each of his team were carrying weapons, but the plan hadn't been as overt as barrelling in there and shooting all and sundry to get to Alpha.

Knife in hand, Ryker dropped down to the ground, landing on top of the first man. His friend, the one who'd taken the uppercut, remained sprawled and unmoving next to them.

Ryker yanked the balaclava from the man's head, though still could see virtually nothing of his face in the darkness. He pushed the knife onto the man's neck.

'Who are you?'

No answer. But a second later an alarm blared over at the palace. Then bright spotlights burst to life, their reach from the gardens enough to light up the area Ryker was in. Ryker found himself staring down into two dark eyes of a man who didn't look in the least worried about his predicament.

'Who are you!' Ryker shouted.

Guests were piling out of the palace. The security guards were dashing about, unsure what to do. Inside intermittent gunfire continued. Then, *BOOM*. An explosion. Glass shattered and a fireball and debris erupted from somewhere high in the palace.

With Ryker glancing up to the palace, the man beneath him took the opportunity. He bucked and threw Ryker up. Hauled a knee to Ryker's groin. Grabbed Ryker's arm and tried to wrestle free the knife.

He was trying to turn the blade around, both his hands clasped over Ryker's. He roared in effort. Threw his knee up again. The tip of the knife edged toward Ryker's chest...

Ryker didn't plan what happened next. His intention was only to push the knife away. With a burst of effort, he achieved his aim. It was simple misfortune that momentum took the knife back down and straight into the neck of the man below him.

His eyes went wide. He gargled for breath as blood flowed out. Ryker let go of the weapon and climbed back to his feet. His eyes flitted between the soon-to-be-dead attacker under him and the chaos in front. He spotted Elliott, alone, edging through the dispersing crowds, but a second later he was out of sight again. No sign of Alpha. No sign of the rest of his crew.

What he could see were two suited guards – Alpha's guards – coming down the steps. They looked over in Ryker's direction. They spotted him.

Ryker turned and ran. There was shouting behind him. He ignored it. Didn't look back at all as he sprinted along, zigzagging through the trees until he came to the outer wall. A gunshot, close behind him. The bullet smacked into the wall, inches from Ryker's back.

He still had his own holstered weapon. He could stand and fight, but that wasn't the mission. Instead, he clambered up the wall as the shouts behind him got louder and closer.

His leg scraped across the edge of the wall, tearing a hole in his suit trousers. He reached the top and swivelled and dropped down the other side as two more bullets thwacked into the stonework. His ankle twisted and a shock of pain shot up his leg. No time to think about that. He hobbled along, doing his best to keep going at pace. Took off his jacket and tossed it. No point in having that now. Not in this heat, not when he was trying to move fast.

He was on a pavement, next to a four-lane boulevard. Traffic was light here at night, in the financial centre of the city. There were no apartments in this part of town, no pedestrians at this time. A good thing.

Ryker glanced behind him just as one of the guards jumped down onto the pavement. Ryker darted left, into the road. Dashed across and into a side street where modern office blocks towered over him.

He rushed along, looking over his shoulder every few steps. He scuttled behind one of the tower blocks, along a security fence, beyond which a half-built skyscraper loomed high, the construction site quiet at night-time.

Should Ryker lure the chasers into there to attack them? Or should he just try to lose them? Neither option was perfect, particularly in this largely unfamiliar city.

He came to a stop behind a skip. Listened. Could hear nothing.

'Can you hear me?' he whispered, fully doubting that he'd get any response in his ear. His doubts were well-founded.

But then he did hear a growling car engine. Not far away, and getting closer. He looked over the top of the skip and beyond to the main road. The guards chasing him down?

Ryker set off in the opposite direction, looking behind him every few steps. He was fifty yards away from the next street. If they turned onto here from behind they'd mow him down before he could reach the end.

Forty yards. Twenty-five.

He looked behind again. There they were. The car stopped as it passed by the end of the street. Then it turned in a moment later.

They'd spotted him.

The car's bright beams stretched down to Ryker like tentacles. He ran. But the lights wrapped around him, he couldn't shake them off. He sprinted as fast as he could. The sound of the engine behind him filled his ears.

Twenty yards to the end of the street. Fifteen. Ryker pumped his arms and legs. Ten yards. Five...

A van sped into view in front. Ryker flinched as it screeched to a halt. He slowed his pace, went for his gun, a fraction of a second before he processed what he was seeing. The side door of the van slid open with a clank.

'Get in!' Lange shouted.

Ryker launched himself forward. The van was already moving off again before he was fully in. Was already accelerating heavily as Elliott opened fire on the chasing car with an assault rifle. Bullets thunked into its bonnet. Enough to stop it?

The van door was slid shut. Ryker turned over and pulled himself onto the bench, chest heaving, sweat pouring. He looked around the van. Weller was driving. Lange was up front with him. Including Ryker there were five in the back. Elliott was by the door, gun in hand. He looked pissed off, though was still smartly dressed in his suit. Diaz was in the far corner, hovering over Salman who was crumpled by her feet. Blood streaked down her face and over the bare skin of her arm. Her designer dress was ruffled and torn, her hair and make-up a mess. Salman was bleeding from somewhere on his side. His hands clasped over the patch of red on his white shirt.

Over in the other corner was Aldern. Suit mangled. Mucky streaks of brown and red across his clothes and his face, which was hard as stone. Probably a similar look to Ryker, whose shirt was speckled with the blood of the man he'd killed in the trees.

Seven people in the van. All of the crew. Not unscathed, but all alive at least.

'What the hell happened?' Ryker said. He looked over all of them, but his eyes settled on Elliott.

'There was nothing we could do,' Diaz said, shaking her head. She was rattled.

Salman groaned in pain. No one else said a word.

'What happened?' Ryker said again, looking around his crew. 'What happened to Alpha?'

Ryker's eyes found Elliott once more. 'We got him,' Elliott said, no hint of satisfaction on his face. 'Alpha's dead.'

3

Ten years later

Ryker made his way across the square in the Smichov district of Prague. The temperature was steadily dropping. The early morning rain had turned to ice on the pavements. He took short and heavy steps to avoid slipping, and hunkered down in his thick coat to protect him from the chilling breeze. The dark clouds above him suggested snow was on the way.

He passed by the curious Golden Angel building, a curved structure with sleek lines whose tall glazed facade was delicately etched with the image of an angel among clouds. The oversized figure looked down on the square below as though a protector. Ryker was far from religious, though he'd often wondered if he'd had some higher power looking out for him during his troubled and violent life. After all, despite everything, he was still walking, still free.

Or perhaps the opposite was true. His troubled and violent life was in fact a punishment.

He shivered as he glanced up to the angel, the thick and low clouds that filled the sky up above giving her a sinister edge.

Ryker carried on across two blocks, to a smaller and quainter square. He'd been here three times before in his stay in this city. Two weeks. That's how long he'd been in Prague. Longer than he'd originally intended, but this intriguing city – and some of its equally intriguing inhabitants – continued to draw him in.

Why was that?

Ryker had arrived in Prague alone, and would leave here alone. He'd been intermittently on the move for several months, across several different countries. Everywhere he went it was the people he paid closest attention to, always from afar, as though his new quest was to analyse strangers to determine their life stories.

But what was he looking for? Perhaps more importantly, why did he care?

He headed up to the door of the bar-cum-restaurant and pushed the creaky fixture open. The wood-clad space inside was dark and dingy. A heavy varnish odour was just about drowned out by the far nicer smell of freshly cooked food. One of the reasons Ryker was here.

He took a seat at a table for two by the window, and looked around him. A variety of familiar faces. Two weeks in this city. His fourth time in this place, yet he already had a good grasp of the schedules of some of these people it seemed.

Ryker scanned the menu and made his order at the bar, deciding on an ice-cold local beer to help wash down the stew he ordered.

Back in his seat he continued to look around, flicking his eyes between the people and the TV screen up behind the bar that was showing rolling national news coverage with subtitles in Czech. Ryker had only a basic grasp of the language, though could gain most of the key facets of the mostly gloomy news items from the images.

A few minutes later the door to the kitchen opened and out came the waitress who'd served Ryker each time he'd been here. Dyed black hair, nose ring, figure-hugging leggings and a thick woollen jumper, she carried the casual look not just with understated elegance but with confidence and a *don't mess with me* attitude that drew Ryker in. She brought the food over, holding Ryker's eye the whole way.

'*Dobrý den*,' she said with a warm smile as she put the food down onto the table.

'*Dobrý den*,' Ryker said in return, trying his best to get the pronunciation of the basic greeting correct.

Her smiled widened. She glanced over her shoulder but remained standing over him.

'You're back again,' she said in pretty decent English.

'I am.'

'You like the goulash?'

'The best outside of Hungary, right?'

She looked over her shoulder again. Ryker followed her line of sight to the table of three men in the opposite corner. Two of them were eyeballing Ryker. When she returned her gaze her smile had dropped a little. Agitation, but also wariness. Across the other side of the space, the sole barman, who was wiping a glass, also had his rabbity eyes flitting back and forth.

'What's your name?' Ryker asked. It seemed appropriate enough to do so now that he was a regular.

'Simona.'

'I'm James,' he said.

'You're from England.'

'I am.'

'Just visiting?'

'Yeah.'

'Business?'

'Pleasure.'

'On your own?'

'So far.'

A coy smile.

'I'd be lying if I said the only reason for me coming back here again was the food.'

'Yeah. So what else?'

'You could sit with me, have a drink, and I could tell you all about it. But I don't think your friends would appreciate it.'

Her smile flickered again, but not for long. There was an awkward pause. Awkward for her at least.

'Not while I'm working, but... perhaps a drink after I finish?'

'Here?'

'No, how–'

'Simona,' the barman called over, before rattling off a command in their native tongue.

'Sorry, I've got to go.'

Nerves now. Her tough exterior wavered.

She turned and strode over to the bar where she and the barman exchanged a short but agitated tirade before Simona disappeared into the kitchen. She didn't reappear over the next ten minutes as Ryker ate most of his food.

Finally the inevitable. It had taken four visits. Was that more or less than he'd expected?

But then why did it even matter to Ryker?

He thought again of the angel. The protector.

The man sat down without asking. He thudded his arms down onto the table, crossed them over as he glared at Ryker. He was the youngest of the three. Probably late twenties, though his bushy beard made him look several years older. He wasn't the tallest guy, nor the most muscled, but the way he'd swaggered over clearly showed he thought he could handle anything and anyone. Most people who felt that way eventually realised their mistake quite abruptly.

'Why are you here?' he said. English, though not as good as Simona's.

'To eat.'

The sides of his jaws pulsed from him clenching his teeth.

'Why are you here? Again.'

'It's a restaurant, isn't it?'

'You shouldn't talk to her.'

'Who?'

'Don't talk to her. And don't come here again. We don't need your money.'

He picked up the notes that Ryker had placed on the table, scrunched them and threw them in Ryker's face. The paper bounced back onto the table. The man stood and headed back over to his friends, who were both glaring at Ryker.

Message understood. Ryker finished his beer. Wiped his mouth clean, then uncrumpled the money before neatly laying it back on the table again. Then he got up to leave.

Still no sign of Simona.

Ryker headed on out.

But he didn't go far. It was cold outside, but Ryker hung on the edge of the square, pulled into the foyer of a closed-down clothes shop, then waited. And waited. He looked around the increasingly familiar buildings here. A mishmash of apartment blocks, five to seven storeys. Far from the most luxurious living spaces in Prague, but also nowhere near the bottom either.

Ryker remained where he was for more than an hour, seeing barely any passers-by, before the three men emerged from the bar. They headed across the square to two parked cars. They didn't go anywhere. Instead, they remained standing, smoking, chatting, checking their watches.

Ryker slid further back.

A few minutes later another car entered the square directly across from where Ryker was standing. It parked up. Two men got out. Older than the three. Gruffer-looking. The five began a conversation, but it wasn't long before eyes were turning in Ryker's direction. He'd hardly tried his best to stay hidden.

The exchange ended. The two older men got back into their car and drove off. The other three remained standing, staring over to Ryker. Would they simply head away too?

No. Of course not.

Shoulder to shoulder in a battle line, the three moved toward Ryker. He peeled off from the front of the building he was standing by. Thought about turning and striding away. Something held him back from doing that.

The men were ten yards from Ryker when Mr Beard shouted over angrily.

'I told you to go.'

Ryker raised an eyebrow. 'You told me to leave the restaurant. I did.'

'Leave here. Now.'

The men stopped. They were still several steps in front of Ryker. A stand-off. What were they going to do? All had their arms by their sides. Hands empty.

Then the door to the restaurant clanked open. Simona burst out. All eyes turned to her. Overcoat on, she stormed toward the men, gesticulating, shouting. There was fire in her all right. Ryker smiled. Mr Beard peeled away and went to intercept her. She took her phone out. Waved it in front of his face. A warning? She held the phone aloft. He grabbed her wrist. Ryker twitched. The two other men flinched as though ready to attack if he tried to intervene.

He didn't. Not yet.

Simona's angry rant continued. She whipped her arm away and stomped over to Ryker.

'Come on,' she said.

She grabbed his arm and pulled him away. He went with it. Turned to see the three men regrouped and staring, but they weren't following.

Simona took Ryker around a corner.

'You shouldn't make them angry,' Simona said.

She sounded pissed off.

'I wasn't trying to.'

'Are you sure about that?'

He glanced at her. Couldn't read the look on her face. Somewhere between incredulous and amusement, if those two things could ever go together.

'I'd like to think you only came back for some goulash, and to see me,' she said. 'I saw the way you looked at me the last time. But now I'm not so sure.'

Ryker didn't say anything to that. They carried on walking, their pace slowing.

'What did you say to him?' Ryker said.

'It doesn't matter.'

'So where are we going?'

'For a drink. Away from there.'

She led the way and two minutes later they arrived outside an Irish pub.

'Does every city in every country have one of these?'

Simona looked a little confused by that question.

'After you,' he said, indicating the door.

They headed inside, got a drink each and took a seat at a booth. As well as harps and Irish flags everywhere, the pub also had a multitude of TVs. RTÉ news, BBC World Service, golf, football, all at once.

'I don't get you,' Simona said before taking a sip from her wine.

'Why not?'

'You hang around like you want something. So what do you want?'

Now there was a question. What did Ryker want?

He took a long drag of his beer.

'Tell me about yourself,' he said. 'I'm guessing one of those guys is a relative. Your brother?'

She laughed. 'No. Not that. I think you've got the wrong idea. But I can tell you're as interested in them, as you are in me.'

'No chance,' he said with a smile.

And while she didn't give any explanation as to her relationship with the men, she did then begin to talk about herself. Twenty-eight years old. Unmarried, no kids. Never lived anywhere but Prague. Ryker was paying attention to every word. And he was engrossed by her.

At least to start with. But as drawn to her dark eyes and her feisty attitude as he was, he couldn't resist flitting his gaze up to the TV screen behind her when there was a flash of red. The BBC news channel going to its headlines.

Ryker's eyes remained fixed there as he read the scrolling bar of the breaking news over and over.

And over.

Russian oligarch Pavel Grichenko found murdered in England.

Impossible.

'James?'

Long thought dead, Grichenko officially missing for more than ten years.

24

'James? Are you even listening to me?'

No. He wasn't.

Ryker rose up from the table. Looked down to see anger and disappointment on Simona's face.

'I'm sorry.'

And he really was, but there was nothing else he could do.

'I've got to go.'

Which was exactly what he did.

4

MARBELLA, SPAIN

'Take my offer. Two million dollars... I know I'm asking a lot of you. A betrayal... Weigh it up. Two million and you live. Or you get nothing and you die... I can tell you love him. He loves you too. But let me put it another way. How much for him to betray you instead?'

She buried the near two-decade-old memory as she rode along. Even in the midst of winter, and with a cold snap covering most of Europe, the sun remained beaming in the sky on the Costa del Sol. Leia Devereaux hated it. Her light and freckled complexion hated it. Despite the warm temperature she wore jeans and a jumper and a thick leather jacket that was zipped up to her neck.

She pulled the motorbike over to the side of the road and shut the whining engine down. Off to her right the Mediterranean glistened and twinkled. Off to her left the Andalucian hills rose up to meet the blue sky. Hills that were dotted with some of the largest, most exclusive and most expensive villas on the continent. The man she was meeting here owned one of them. Though the place they were meeting at today was a far cry from that. There was no way he'd invite her into his home, where his wife lazed by the luxurious heated pool and his children played.

So instead it was here, again. The abandoned meat factory that had an unusually prominent position on a bluff overlooking the sea. Prime real estate undoubtedly, and Devereaux wondered why no developer had ever tried to make a mint from it by razing the old brick building and erecting a hotel or high-end apartments. Perhaps it was the blood and death that drenched the earth here that put people off. Each time she'd been she could smell it, could taste it, could hear the cries of the animals still.

She stepped from the motorbike and slipped the helmet from her head. She propped it on the handlebars and looked over to the entrance where five-foot weeds sprouted up from the remnants of tarmac. Two men stood in wait, casually dressed. Both were part of Khaled's crew. Both were young and dumb, and both had handguns in the waistbands of their jeans.

She adjusted the backpack on her shoulders then headed over.

'You're late,' the taller and more handsome of the two said when she was two steps away. His T-shirt showed off his slender physique, his hair was heavily styled with neat lines cut to the skin. His dark-brown eyes were like two beacons of brooding intensity.

'I'm worth the wait,' she said.

The two men exchanged a look.

'Arms in the air,' the shorter one said. Shorter, but more muscled. His face was squashed as though his parents had dropped him more than once as an infant – the closest she'd ever seen to a human version of a bulldog.

Devereaux did as she was told. Brown Eyes came over while Bulldog took out his gun. He kept the barrel pointed to the ground as Brown Eyes bent down and patted her legs. When his hands reached just below her crotch he glanced up and seemed taken aback by the sultry smile she was giving him.

He hesitated for a moment then carried on.

'What's in the bag?' he asked when he was finished feeling over her figure.

'Nothing yet. Hopefully my money soon. Take a look if you want.'

He did. Moments later he was finished, though Bulldog didn't look satisfied, as though he couldn't believe his friend hadn't found anything on her other than her phone, the key for the motorbike, and the thumb drive – all of which he kept.

'Okay, follow me.'

'My pleasure.'

They set off. Brown Eyes in front, Devereaux in the middle, Bulldog behind. The factory loomed high in front of them. Three storeys of decay. Stuck out on this bluff the wind howled across from the sea, despite the warm and bright day. Or was that just the ghosts again?

Two cars were parked to the side of the crumbling factory. A big black BMW X5, and a big white Mercedes S63. Nice motors. Both were comfy for five decent-sized adults. So together with the two chumps she was walking with there could be up to a further seven others with Khaled here, although she doubted her illustrious host would have travelled all squashed up against his henchmen.

Two more sentries were stood in wait at the open loading doors to the factory. They didn't say a word as Devereaux and her chaperones passed, though Devereaux held the eye of the one on the left for a few beats. Badger. For some reason his actual nickname, not a silly name she'd given him because of his looks.

They headed into the lofty loading area. Three ramps led down into gullies where animals would have been shepherded from the vehicles that transported them, and crammed together awaiting their final painful and pitiful moments. Was it ironic or apt that Khaled and the other two men with him were clustered together down there, at the bottom of the middle ramp?

Khaled was standing arms folded. Loafers, no socks, cream trousers, white shirt, sunglasses atop his frizzy black hair. *Miami Vice* on steroids.

Brown Eyes and Bulldog stepped either side of Devereaux as she continued forward. So four men behind her, two men plus Khaled in front. Seven in total.

'You don't trust me?' Devereaux said, flitting her eyes across the assembled muscle.

'Why would I?'

Devereaux shrugged.

'You were quick,' Khaled said.

'It was easy.'

'No problems?'

'Why would there be?'

'Do you have it?'

'No,' she said, turning her head to Brown Eyes. 'I don't.'

He nodded to Khaled and moved forward. He put the backpack on the floor in front of Khaled and handed his boss the phone and the thumb drive.

'You have my money?' Devereaux asked.

'It's not your money,' Khaled said. 'Not until I make sure I have what I need.'

Devereaux rolled her eyes and looked around again. Two of the minions got to work. One folded out a small table, the other grabbed a laptop computer from a leather satchel in the murky far corner and placed it onto the table. Then the other took the thumb drive from Khaled. Everyone was silent for the next few minutes, the only sound the light tapping of fingers on the keyboard and the groan of the wind through the dilapidated building.

'It's here,' the minion said.

Khaled looked to Devereaux. 'You really did it.'

'You sound surprised. Now can I have my money?'

A smile spread across Khaled's face. 'Well, about that.'

Without warning, Bulldog grasped Devereaux around the neck, pulled one of her arms into a hammerlock. The other men rushed into positions, an arc around her, five handguns pointed in her direction.

Khaled walked forward, a sickly smile on his face.

'It's a shame, it really is, because I actually like you.'

Devereaux said nothing.

'And honestly? I was surprised at just how well you did. I was told you were good, but...'

He stopped when he was only a few inches from her face. His coffee breath wafted up her nose. His aftershave tickled her sinuses. She squirmed against Bulldog's muscly grip.

'But your reputation precedes you.' Serious now. 'Unfortunately, in your line of work, reputation means problems. Your success means enemies. And when it came down to it, I had a simple choice. Pay you. Or get paid for killing you.'

'Money talks,' Devereaux choked out.

Khaled smiled and laughed. 'Indeed. As a sign of respect, I will make this quick. I hope you'll appreciate that.'

'Just... one question.'

Khaled thought about that for a moment, as though trying to decide whether he'd allow it or not.

'Who paid you?' Devereaux said.

Khaled laughed. 'Sorry, my beauty. That thought will have to go with you.'

He took two steps back. Badger came forward. He stood to the side of Devereaux. Placed the barrel of his handgun an inch from her temple.

Silence.

Then... *BANG.*

A thud as Badger dropped to the ground. *BANG. BANG.* Khaled crumpled.

Bulldog released the hammerlock as he went for his gun. Devereaux grabbed the arm around her neck.

BANG. Another shot. Another hit.

She stooped down as she heaved and pulled Bulldog off his feet. She flung him over and landed by his side. An elbow knocked the wind from his lungs. A second elbow strike split his nose. She manoeuvred on top of him.

BANG. Another gunshot. Then another. Two more thuds.

She looked down at Bulldog. Panic and surprise in his bleary eyes. She grabbed his head and smashed it into the concrete ground below with a roar of effort. Three, four times, until the back of his head was mushy and sloppy.

She jumped to her feet. Looked around. Six bodies on the ground. Two still standing.

She calmed her breathing in an instant.

'Good shooting,' she said, looking to Brown Eyes as she wiped a smear of blood from her face.

Chest heaving, he smiled. Though it wasn't all that convincing. He'd just killed five men. He wasn't as used to this as she was. She could see the terror in his eyes. But he'd done it for her nonetheless.

She looked around the space. No. He hadn't killed five men. Not quite. Khaled was crawling away.

Devereaux sauntered over to him, staring down at him

curiously. She picked up a gun from the floor on the way. The bullet that hit him had torn through his side and out through his back. She could tell from his raspy breaths that one of his lungs was done for. He didn't have long.

When she reached him she used her boot to turn him over. He groaned in pain then lay there, prone and pathetic like a turtle on its back.

She kneeled down to his side. Waved the gun in his face.

'You said yourself, you didn't trust me. How could you have made such a stupid mistake?'

He said nothing. Could barely breathe. Could barely keep his eyes open.

'Tell me who paid you. I'll make this quick for you. I hope you'll appreciate that.'

Still not a word. She pressed the gun barrel into the wound on his side. He grimaced and moaned.

'Leia. We need to go.' Brown Eyes. He sounded panicked now.

'Tell me,' she said to Khaled, her voice still absolutely calm.

But he didn't say anything. He couldn't now. He wasn't breathing at all.

She straightened up, trying to push that final disappointment to the back of her mind.

'You weren't supposed to kill him,' she said, unable to hide her irritation.

Brown Eyes stepped toward her. 'I'm sorry. I tried. Come on we have to go.'

He reached out for her hand. She took it, and relaxed a little at his touch. He put his gun back in his waistband and gently caressed her face.

'We did it,' he said.

He wrapped his arms around her and she reciprocated. She closed her eyes for a few moments. Enjoyed the embrace, the sensation, the chemistry of their bodies so close. Their hearts beat in time, inches apart. Their chests rose and fell in unison.

A scene from *Bonnie and Clyde* flashed in her mind. She loved that movie.

'We need to go,' he whispered into her ear.

BANG.

The embrace continued. But only for a couple of seconds before his hands flopped to the side. Devereaux let go and his body slid down, slow motion, until he was on his knees, open-mouthed, eyes wide.

She looked down on him then reached out and ran her fingers gently across his beautiful face.

'You should have listened to Khaled. He knew me too well. He knew I couldn't be trusted.'

She lifted the gun. Barrel against his eyeball.

She fired once more.

Then she turned and walked away.

5

The journey from Prague to Ryker's native England took just over a day. Air travel would have seen the journey over in a few hours, but Ryker was always reluctant to travel by such a security-restricted method if he could avoid it. So it was trains and buses for him, at least until he reached the British Isles, at which point he organised a car from a local rental shop near to the Eurostar terminal in Ashford. He spent the night in a basic guesthouse midway across England, and the following morning had only a two-hour drive to the south-western county of Gloucestershire to complete his journey.

In the early throes of winter, the days here were short, night-time arriving a little after 4pm, and following several hours of surveillance, Ryker called it a day.

He made his next trip to Upper Slaughter – a tiny village in the Cotswolds – the next day, just as darkness was on the horizon. The village was nestled across the slow-moving River Eye, and comprised of a collection of handsome limestone homes. Some were small and modest, others large and elaborate, and most dated back to the sixteenth and seventeenth centuries.

Ryker had heard of the village before, and its neighbour Lower Slaughter, though had never been to either before this trip. He wondered how the villages had got their names, the imagery conjured in his mind bloody and violent. The names seemed apt given why he was here now.

He kept his head down as he walked along the twisting streets. There weren't many people about. Not on a cold afternoon at this time of the year. Ryker imagined in the summer that the stone houses, with their decorative mullion windows and projecting gables, and all surrounded by the greenery of the British countryside, would be glorious. On a day like this the whole scene was bleak.

Ryker turned a corner. The river tinkled a few feet to his side. He crossed over a stone bridge, edging toward the last properties in the village. He headed on past a row of terraces to a stone wall that at just under six foot gave little clue as to what lay beyond. At least until he came to the wide wrought-iron entrance gates to the property. A police car remained stationed on the outside. A solitary policeman in a thick hi-vis jacket stood arms folded at the closed gates. Ryker nodded at the copper who responded in customary fashion.

He kept on walking.

In the brief glimpse beyond the gates he'd also spotted another marked car further up the driveway by the house, probably another police officer there. Not a problem. Just the two police squad cars. When he'd been here yesterday it'd been a hubbub of activity with vans and cars and a mini army of people jostling about, many of them in their white forensic suits.

The wall veered left, away from the pavement, and Ryker veered with it, heading onto a dirt footpath that was frozen solid. The wall continued on for fifty yards before it veered left again. The footpath didn't. Ryker went with the wall and headed on through the tall grass of the field that stretched into the distance.

He moved another ten yards before stopping to quickly look around. No one in sight. He couldn't even see a single building from this spot. He scaled the wall and jumped down into the back garden of Hawthorn Cottage.

Although the plot of land encircled by the stone wall was a good size, perhaps half an acre, the home in the middle was quaint rather than extravagant – a three-bedroomed house, Ryker had found from his search on the internet, where he'd identified the property's selling particulars from when it was last sold eight years previously.

There was no view from this angle of the front gates, or of either of the police cars or the sentries. Still, Ryker moved cautiously up to the back door of the house.

He had the tools in his pocket to pick the locks, but he could see through the small square panes in the door that there was a deadbolt both at the top and bottom. He wasn't getting in through there unless he broke the glass to reach in.

He looked across the back wall of the house. The windows were original. Metal-framed, with lead running across the glass to add strength to the brittle single-paned glazing. It would take little effort to smash through, though doing so wasn't ideal given the closeness of the police.

He wouldn't need to do that anyway. The ageing frames were badly warped. The window closest to Ryker had a near quarter-inch gap between window and frame at the bottom-left corner, and he could see through the glass that it was only held shut by an equally ageing clasp.

With a gloved hand, he took the screwdriver from his pocket, stuck the end into the gap. Took a breath. Then yanked across.

Snap.

Ryker held his breath a few more seconds. Silence.

He pulled the window open fully then slithered inside. He landed on a stone floor. Through a combination of the disappearing daylight outside, and the property's small windows, the room was poorly lit, and he remained on the spot a few beats to let his eyes adjust. Some sort of sitting room. Decked out exactly how Ryker envisaged an English country cottage would be. Big old fireplace with a wood basket next to it, worn sofas, a few knick-knacks. A small TV in the corner was the one mod con, but it wasn't the dominant fixture like in the vast majority of twenty-first century living spaces.

The more he saw, the more the questions and doubts tumbled in his mind as to how Pavel Grichenko – a man Ryker had long thought dead – had come to be here. Had come to be the person who called this home. A far cry from someone who ten years ago had been a multi-billionaire oligarch.

Ryker spotted a cluster of photo frames on a dresser in the corner. He moved over and glanced across the pictures without picking them up. His heart beat a little faster in his chest with each picture he took in. There'd still been plenty of doubt in Ryker's mind as to whether Grichenko had been here at all. Whether the whole story in the press was a hoax or just an incredible tale of mistaken identity.

Not now.

In the pictures, Grichenko was a little older, a little thinner than the last time Ryker had seen him in Doha, but the main facial features; his pinched eyes, his prominent nose, were absolute giveaways. Grichenko had lived here all right.

What was very different in the pictures, though, was the woman Grichenko was with. When Ryker had 'known' Grichenko, he'd been married to a former Russian opera singer – rich and famous in her own right in her home country. They'd had two children together. She and the young kids hadn't been in Qatar that fateful night, when, as far as Ryker was concerned, his team had completed their mission and eliminated Grichenko.

The official story in the aftermath was that he was missing, but Ryker had always seen that as Kremlin spin. His own crew had confirmed that Grichenko was dead, and plenty of checks had been carried out since on his widow and children, who continued to live alone in Russia.

Yet it appeared now that Grichenko had very definitely survived that night in Doha, and had found a new life, and a new wife in England.

The press reports Ryker had seen stated the woman had been found dead with him, in this very house. Most likely collateral damage, whoever she was, and however she'd come to meet a man who, as far as the rest of the world knew, had been missing since an assassination attempt a decade previously.

Ryker carried on through the house, those thoughts still whirring in his mind. The press reports, although naming Grichenko, had been sketchy on details of the crime here, and there was no sign downstairs of where the bodies had been found. No evidence that this was a crime scene at all, really.

He headed upstairs. Found the master bedroom.

So this was the room.

The bedsheets remained ruffled. Clothes were on the floor. Forensic markers were placed all around the room. This space had been searched, tested, recorded. For what? There was no obvious sign of a crime here. No blood. No signs of a struggle. Yet the press had been very clear that this was a murder investigation. Husband and wife found dead, together, in their home.

So what had led the police to so quickly conclude this was murder?

Tabloid speculation suggested poisoning, though Ryker believed that was most likely a leap based on past form for Russians dying in suspicious circumstances on UK soil. The authorities wouldn't have been able to conclude toxicology tests so quickly after the event. Unless the police weren't being forthcoming on certain aspects. Could the murder have happened earlier than was being reported?

Ryker did know, for absolute sure, that if there was any doubt as to whether Grichenko had been killed using a radioactive poison, like some of his countrymen before him, then this crime scene would have been a different beast altogether. Likely the whole village would have been on lockdown.

So what was the story?

Ryker continued to survey the room. Continued to think. He was in the en suite bathroom, looking over the pill bottles in the mirrored cabinet above the sink, when he heard tyres crunching across the gravel drive outside.

He closed the cabinet and listened. A car engine shut down. A door opened. Then another. Both were closed, then he heard softer footsteps across the gravel.

Ryker slunk out of the en suite and to the bedroom window. He carefully peeked down below. A man and a woman. No uniforms. No forensics gear. These were plain-old detectives. The two arrivals moved out of view below Ryker, and started a brief conversation with the policeman on guard by the front door.

A few moments later and the wooden floor beneath Ryker's feet shuddered as the front door was opened and then closed with a thunk.

He stepped back from the window. Crept across the wood to the open bedroom door. The two detectives were in conversation below, though they were too far away, and their voices too low for him to make out any of the words.

He was about to step out onto the landing when he heard footsteps on the stairs.

Ryker slid back inside the bedroom and edged behind the door.

Just one set of footsteps coming up. Getting closer by the second. Ryker's hands hung by his sides, at the ready. He really didn't want a confrontation, and certainly had no interest in hurting these two... but if he was left with no choice he'd have to do something.

A creak on the floorboards at the head of the stairs. Soft footsteps on the thick landing carpet. Another creak. Right outside the door now. He could hear short, shallow breaths the other side of the wood. Ryker breathed too, as silently as he could, as his brain rumbled with how he'd tackle the detective if they stepped over the threshold and spotted him.

Non-lethal. Subdue them and run.

What were they doing? Just standing there, staring inside?

Ryker clenched his fists.

Did they know he was there?

'Adam, get here, now!'

The female detective. Downstairs. So it was the man who'd been standing there.

Footsteps heading away now. Ryker slowly exhaled. He waited a few more seconds. Unclenched his fists, then ever so carefully crept out onto the landing. He peered over the bannister. Could hear the heightened conversation below. He knew exactly what they were talking about. They'd spotted the broken window.

Time to go.

But then, as he glanced back into the bedroom, a silvery object caught Ryker's eye. Coming from the wardrobe across the other side of the room. The left-hand door was slightly ajar. The metallic object just visible beyond. Ryker strode over. Pulled the door further open. A safe. Built into the wall behind a cut-out in the back of the wardrobe. The safe door was open.

Nothing left inside.

Ryker didn't dwell. He straightened up, spun around and legged it out of the room. A creak here. A creak there. Too late to care about that now as he could already hear the female detective shouting to the two uniforms outside. Soon there would be four coppers inside, searching, and perhaps more on the way.

He didn't move toward the stairs though. Instead, he headed to the door for the bedroom in the opposite corner. He hadn't yet had a chance to look in there, and as he pushed open the door he saw it was a box room with nothing but a single bed and small wardrobe. And a window, which Ryker knew from the orientation looked out to the side of the house. Probably as good as he could hope for right now.

Ryker unclasped the lock, swung the window open and quickly peered down below. No one there, though alert voices travelled upward to him. Ryker didn't hesitate a second longer. He grabbed the window ledge and climbed out, then eased his body down so it was dangling. He let go and dropped to the ground with a soft thud.

No time to take stock, he turned and sprinted for the wall.

'Hey, you! Stop! Police!'

Ryker didn't stop. He drove forward. Practically ran up the wall, flung himself over, spinning around to land on his feet the other side. He turned left, heading the opposite direction from which he'd arrived and into a wood. He ran on, snaking between the trunks, until he reached the treeline at the far edge, and then looked back. There was no one in sight behind him.

Content that he was on his own, Ryker slowed to a brisk walk when his feet hit tarmac. No one around here, though the not-too-distant sounds of sirens drifted over the rooftops.

Ryker found his car, sank down into the driver's seat. He fired up the engine and pulled out into the road. No one on his tail. A few turns later and he was on the A429. About as busy a road as there was in this rural area. Traffic moved freely. Ryker was soon hitting sixty. He spotted flashing blue lights approaching on the opposite side of the road, but moments later the police car whizzed past. He watched it disappearing in his rear-view mirror.

A close call, and far from ideal, but for now he was in the clear, and left with plenty to think about from his visit to Grichenko's murder scene.

One thing was for sure: he still didn't know anywhere near enough about what had happened there.

Those two detectives on the other hand?

That was his mind made up. The police were Ryker's next focus. First up was finding out who they were, and then he'd do whatever he could to figure out exactly what they knew.

6

A night in another basic hotel, paid for in cash, and a few hours of online research later, and Ryker had what he needed for his next move. All told, it had been relatively simple to find the identities of the two police officers from the previous day; DS Adam Hennessey, and DI Jennifer Alessi. What Ryker was still trying to figure out was how the hell Pavel Grichenko had ended up in England.

Ten years ago Ryker had been working for the Joint Intelligence Agency, a secretive intelligence service originally set up and funded jointly by the UK and US governments. Black ops, under the radar, outside of public scrutiny, and with the most plausible of plausible deniability, should operations ever go haywire. Which was exactly what had happened back in Qatar.

The mission brief that night had been to assassinate Pavel Grichenko, and to steal information related to his arms sales to terrorists. Not the first time Ryker had had such an objective, and not the last. Grichenko was known to the world as a Russian oligarch, loyal to the Kremlin, but he'd branched out, using his billions and his expansive social circle to seed terrorism, drug running, people trafficking, political assassinations and even on the odd occasion all-out military conflict, such as his helping hand in funding rebel groups in Georgia in its war with Russia in 2008.

He was a bad apple. A rotten human being who'd caused death and misery indiscriminately, and who deserved to be put on trial and spend the rest of his life in jail. But such a fate had been an impossible dream given his political ties, and so someone, somewhere in the UK government had signed off on his assassination.

And, while the night in Qatar hadn't exactly gone to plan, they'd still got their man. Or so Ryker had been led to believe by his crew from that night. His crew. A disparate group of individuals from within the JIA and beyond who Ryker had seen and heard nothing of following the briefest of debriefs the morning after the event, when the mission was closed as a success.

Except the mission had been far from a success. Grichenko wasn't dead at all. Someone in Ryker's crew had lied to him, and ten years later the Russian had somehow wound up living a quiet life with a new partner in the English Cotswolds. A life which had ended abruptly a few days ago.

None of it made sense. Who had lied to Ryker that night? Who had covered up Grichenko's disappearance? Who had ordered his death this time around? The UK? Russia? Some other party altogether?

Why did Ryker even care? After all, he'd left behind his life with the JIA for good.

He cared for one very good reason; self-preservation. Someone had lied about Grichenko's assassination ten years ago. Someone had covered it up. The lie was now exposed, at least to the few people who'd been involved in Doha. The conspirator, or conspirators, would be more dangerous now than ever, and more determined than ever to keep their lie under wraps.

Ryker had to believe he was at risk.

Plus, he hated the idea that someone had bettered him so underhandedly.

Despite the jumble of conflicting theories in his mind, Ryker was absolutely positive he'd get to the bottom of it all, but first things first, he had to know more about the circumstances of Grichenko's death.

At 11am the sleet finally stopped. Another cold day, though at least the slushy white on the ground brightened the dull scene a little. Ryker stepped from his car, put his hood up and walked down the street. In the Coney Hill suburb of Gloucester, the road was lined both sides with traditional 1950s to 1980s semi-detached homes. Just like Upper Slaughter, Ryker had never been to Gloucester before, though he knew it as a traditional English cathedral city with a rich history. This area, however, could have been any suburb in any city in the country.

Gloucester was one of two small cities, along with Cheltenham, within the remit of Gloucestershire Constabulary – a modest-sized police force, given the relatively small and mostly rural nature of the population of the county.

Gloucestershire Constabulary had a single major crimes team that covered the whole county. DI Alessi was one of only two at her level within the force who investigated murders, which rarely reached double digits in the county in any given year, from what Ryker had found through simple online searches.

The murder of Grichenko and his wife, therefore, was a big deal for this police force, and given the high-profile nature of the victim, and his chequered past, Ryker felt sure that the Gloucestershire police would be looking to pull in help from other forces.

Would that help or hinder him? Just because Alessi and her colleagues weren't up to their eyeballs in murders day in, day out didn't make them any less competent, Ryker knew.

Regardless, first things first.

He had been mulling over how to get access to the police's case files. Despite the UK police forces operating apart from each other, with different power structures, different budgets and different focuses, a lot of crime databases were managed at a national level, and every force in the country used the same electronic system, known as HOLMES 2, to record crimes. Ryker didn't need direct access to Alessi's local police station to find records for the Grichenko crime scene, he simply needed access to any of her devices that she used to access HOLMES 2.

He took a left turn and three houses later arrived outside number fifty-four. There were no cars parked on the drive. Alessi was at work. So, too, was her husband, an accountant for a local manufacturing business. Her two kids were both at school. The house was unoccupied, as were most others on the street at this time during the week, judging by the few cars Ryker could see dotted about on neighbouring drives.

He didn't break stride as he turned off the pavement and up the driveway for fifty-four. He quickly looked over his shoulder to make sure there was no one in sight before he reached into his pockets and took out the torsion wrench and pins to pick the lock on the door. For a lock like this he'd need only a few seconds.

He got to work. Five seconds. Ten. Nearly there.

Car engines. High revs. Moving fast. Strange, in otherwise quiet streets like these. Ryker kept his hands moving as he glanced over his shoulder. Couldn't see anything or anyone. He faced the lock again, but the car engines continued to get louder and closer.

He did it. The lock released. Ryker put his tools away. Put his hand to the door.

Screeching tyres. At the corner of the street Ryker had just come from.

No. He didn't like this. Ryker left the door, turned on his heel and strode back down the drive toward the road. He spotted the two cars, big and black, shooting his way. Ryker turned onto the pavement, away from the cars. Tried to stay calm. Willed the vehicles to blast on past. But in the distance he could see two others, racing down the street toward him.

Ryker stopped. Hands at the ready. But as the first two cars came to a rocking halt, and six figures quickly jumped out, all dressed head to toe in black, all carrying heavy-duty weaponry – M4 carbines – Ryker knew the game was up.

The six figures crowded toward Ryker. One of them barked instructions at him. *Get down. On your knees. Hands above your head.* The other two cars came to a stop. Another half dozen figures emerged. Twelve versus one. And Ryker was unarmed. Even for him, escape was beyond impossible.

Then came number thirteen, out of one of the cars to Ryker's left. His eyes were drawn in that direction, initially because this person wasn't dressed in tactical combat gear like the others, but in shiny black shoes, suit trousers, and a long and thick winter coat. Yet it wasn't the clothing that really set this man apart; it was the fact that Ryker knew him. Kaspovich. An MI5 agent. A man Ryker had never liked much.

'James Ryker,' Kaspovich said, a grin on his face that Ryker wished he could wipe off for good. 'Welcome home.'

7

'What the hell do we do now?'

A man. Panicked. She couldn't see him at all as she was in complete darkness, and she didn't recognise the voice.

'Stick to the plan.'

A woman. Her voice wasn't panicked. It was warm, almost comforting, and equally unfamiliar.

'The plan? Fuck the plan. Fox is dead. He's dead!'

'I know he's dead. I saw.'

'We shouldn't have left him there.'

'We had no choice.'

A sigh. Then silence. Except for the constant whoosh of the tyres on tarmac. Where were they taking her? She didn't know. She didn't move. Just sat huddled in the corner, in the darkness, shivering with cold and with fear. Wondering how she'd possibly get out of this alive.

Devereaux fired up the motorbike and headed back onto the road, the pile of bodies behind her already out of mind. No one in that slaughterhouse meant anything to her, not even Brown Eyes. He'd been a play, nothing more, nothing less.

Yet two things irked her. She didn't have her money, and she didn't know who had paid Khaled to kill her. The former was easier to solve. She'd do it right now.

The drive up into the hills took only twenty minutes. She may never have been on the inside of Khaled's villa complex before, but she was hardly unprepared and had analysed and memorised every detail of the layout of the place from afar.

The first that could be seen of the property from the road was the pool, the edge of it jutting from a rocky outcrop. Water gently lapped against the glass side and shimmered in the winter sunlight. She rounded the corner and all she could see was rock, rising up, then took the turn onto the long private lane that led to the entrance gates.

No one was stationed outside the gates. On occasions there would be, but most of Khaled's closest men were lying in pools of their own blood in the old abattoir down by the sea.

She pulled the motorbike into the dirt at the side of the tarmac and shut the engine off. Empty backpack over her shoulders, she jumped up over the gates and landed on the gravel driveway beyond. A glimpse of the pool off to her right. No sign of the children. That was good. The glorious whitewashed villa took up most of the rest of the view in front of her. Two cars were parked outside the home. One was Yasmin's convertible. The other was a more generic Opal. So she wasn't home alone. The last remaining chumps from Khaled's security detail most likely.

Devereaux was a few steps from the entrance when the door opened. She barely paused. Gun out. Aim. Pull trigger.

Man down.

She carried on inside.

A shadow flicked left to right. A figure darted into view from the kitchen.

Point. Shoot. Man down.

A panicked shout now. 'Pietro?'

A female. Yasmin. Downstairs.

Devereaux rushed forward. There she was. Standing by the open patio doors. Bikini under a sheer shawl. Her phone out of reach on the coffee table.

Their eyes met. Then Yasmin's flicked to her phone.

She'd never make it.

'Who are you?' Yasmin croaked.

Devereaux smiled but said nothing. Yasmin screamed as Devereaux lunged forward.

The master bedroom was the pinnacle of opulence. Everything about the overt display of wealth disgusted Devereaux. Yet here she was doing all this for what? Money. But there was a difference between flaunting material wealth like this, and getting what was deserved. What was earned.

Yasmin was splayed out on the Persian rug at the end of the four-poster bed. One ankle was tied with a length of rope to one of the bed legs. The other ankle was tied to the leg of a chest of drawers on the other side. One arm lay on the rug. The other was trussed and suspended above her head. Her eyes stared up at it in horror.

'You like it?' Devereaux asked.

No answer. Just a murmur of disquiet.

'I only tried this once before. It works well in here. Don't you think?'

'W-why are you doing this?'

Devereaux moved over and kneeled down by Yasmin's side.

The rich bitch wouldn't meet her eye. Of course not. Devereaux wasn't in their social league.

'Your husband owes me a lot of money. I need it. I already know there are two safes in this house. One in here. One in the office. I only need the codes to open them. And I'll only take what I'm owed. You have my word on that.'

And she did like to keep her word. Well... of course, there were exceptions to every rule.

Yasmin said nothing. Devereaux had never met Khaled's wife before, but her first impressions weren't good. Arrogance. Self-entitlement. Still, for some reason she didn't hate Yasmin as much as she'd expected.

'Tell me,' Devereaux said.

'I... I don't know!'

Devereaux sighed and rolled her eyes.

'Then let me explain this to you very clearly. Because you won't get many chances to find the right answer.'

She straightened up a little. Hovered over Yasmin. She reached out and put her finger delicately onto the bound wrist.

'Think of it like a tourniquet. Except this tourniquet won't ever stop. It'll only get tighter. And tighter. And tighter.'

She ran her finger along the wire that was twisted around Yasmin's wrist, and then along to the turnbuckle. A simple tightening device that she'd found outside, used to tighten a sunshade sail above the patio by the pool. She'd also taken the rope from there, which was used to secure Yasmin's ankles, and to tie this turnbuckle to the doorknob. The other end of the wire led to another turnbuckle, which was in turn roped to one of the posts of the bed. The ropes and the wire were taut enough to keep Yasmin's arm held in the air, but not yet tight enough to cause her any damage.

Overall, a neat little contraption, Devereaux thought, and it had only taken a few minutes to assemble.

'You see, all I need to do is turn this here...' She turned the buckle a full three-sixty and the tension on the ropes and wire noticeably increased with a *twang*. Yasmin squirmed and squeezed her eyes shut. '...and the wire is pulled tighter around your wrist.'

'Please!'

'How many turns will it take, do you think, before it cuts into your skin?' She paused. No answer. 'How many turns before blood pours? How many before the wire slices through your flesh.' Devereaux laughed. 'And how many before you hand is chopped off completely?'

Devereaux turned the buckle another full circle. Yasmin screamed, long and hard. Genuine agony or just the thought of what was to come?

'Tell me how to get into the safes.'

Another turn. Then another. Yasmin moaned and begged and writhed on the floor. But she didn't answer the question.

Devereaux turned the buckle again. This time blood seeped out along the wire and dripped onto the rug below.

'No one is coming to help you. They're all dead. Please don't think your delays will make a difference.'

Yasmin's shouts turned to sobs. At the thought her husband was dead, or at the thought that she was all alone?

'But you *will* be fine. So will your children. If you just give me what I need.'

Yet still she didn't. So Devereaux continued on, and soon the wire was sunken out of sight, wedged deep in skin and flesh that oozed with blood.

But then: 'Okay!' Yasmin bellowed. 'Please, stop! Please!'

Devereaux did. For now. 'Go on.'

'I... I don't know the combination. I've n-never used the safes. But... You'll find what you need, i-in his office... Notebook. B-Bottom desk drawer.'

Devereaux frowned. Her fingers twitched on the turnbuckle. Not many turns were needed now before the wire was slicing through bone. 'You never used the safes before, but you know where he wrote down the combination? Sounds like bullshit. But hey, it's your hand.'

Another half turn.

Another scream. The most harrowing yet. Harrowing to anyone who gave a shit at least.

'Wait!' Yasmin bellowed with a surprising show of strength. 'I did open the safes before. When I found the codes. But I don't remember the numbers. I just know where they are. Please.'

Devereaux stared down at the captive for a couple of seconds. Yasmin had lied. And she could have just told Devereaux all this from the start. Devereaux did want to believe her, but a small part of her couldn't ignore that this could be a trap of some sort.

One way to find out.

'Try to move, try to do anything at all, and I won't stop with chopping off your hand.'

She started a video call with Yasmin's phone, then carefully propped the device on top of the drawer unit. She really didn't expect Yasmin would have the wherewithal to escape the binds holding her, but better safe than sorry.

Devereaux headed out of the room, down the stairs and into the office. Modern, clinical. Not a bookshelf in sight. In a way, that was a refreshing change to Devereaux, who'd been in plenty of expensive homes. This was the office of a rich businessman who didn't feel the need to have a vast array of old books he'd never read, to try to pretend that he was more intelligent than he really was. Khaled, for all his faults, had understood exactly who he was.

The bottom desk drawer was locked. A letter opener from the desktop was all she needed to pop it open. The leather-bound notebook was on top of a pile of papers. Devereaux flicked through. It only took her a few seconds to find what she was looking for. A long list of what was obviously passwords. No identifier as to what each was for, but definitely passwords given the jumbles of letters, numbers and symbols. Some appeared random, but others were obviously made up by Khaled and contained various fragments of the names of his family members.

There were four passwords which contained only numbers. Devereaux moved over to the cupboards in the corner of the room. She opened the doors to reveal shelves stacked high with all manner of paperwork. A big square space in the bottom corner was taken up by a metal-fronted safe with a classic dial in its centre.

A faint whirring noise outside the window. Devereaux glanced across. What was that?

She couldn't see anything. Couldn't hear anything now.

She looked to her phone screen. Yasmin remained in place. Not even moving. Sensible.

Devereaux put her phone on the floor and got back to work. The first code did nothing. The second one…

Clunk. She pulled open the door. Bingo. Cash. Not enough to satisfy her debt, but very nearly enough. A passport. Fake name, of course. A handgun. Didn't need that. Some bank statements. Devereaux whistled as she skimmed over the amounts. But she wouldn't touch those accounts.

Two watches. Bloody expensive ones. Nice. A diamond necklace, the chain encrusted with stones. Even nicer. Into the backpack.

Job done.

She left the door hanging open. Picked up her phone from the floor.

A creak upstairs. Devereaux stared at the screen. Yasmin was still there. Still not moving.

Devereaux moved with a bit more caution, gun in hand, as she edged back up the stairs. Had there been someone else in the house all along? A third security guard? A cleaner?

She reached the landing. All was quiet. A whoosh of wind caused the slightest strain in the window behind her. Just the wind. Still, she whipped around on instinct.

Nothing there.

She carried on to the bedroom. Took a step inside.

And found herself staring down at the empty space where Yasmin should have been.

There was a small blood trail on the rug, heading right over to where Devereaux was standing. But that was where it ended. So where was Yasmin?

Devereaux looked over to the drawers. Two phones there now. One propped just in front of the other. She grit her teeth in anger – and just a sliver of embarrassment – as she moved over. She picked up the second device. So whose phone was this? She stared at the screen. A picture of Yasmin on the floor, taken right from where the first phone was. Clever.

No wonder it had looked like Yasmin wasn't moving.

Devereaux quickly fought against the tide of anger. That wouldn't help her here. She didn't like to be made to look stupid, but she did like games.

She would win this one.

A crunch outside. Feet on gravel.

She spun on her heel and stormed for the bedroom door. Pounded down the stairs. Across the marble to the front door which was now wide open.

Out onto the gravel. No one there. Both cars remained.

A whir above her. She looked up. She should have known

the first time she'd heard it. The miniature drone was all of twenty yards above her.

Thwack.

The dart stabbed into her neck. Her hand reflexively went there. She was already on one knee as she pulled the pointed object out and tossed it angrily to the ground. She tried to get up again but there was no way.

Moments later she was sprawled on the ground, two sets of shoes – all she could see – gathered in front of her.

'Get her in the car with the other one.'

A man. A voice she didn't recognise.

Gloved hands dug under her armpits to lift her up, though she was barely aware of the touch.

She closed her eyes and was out.

8

The drive lasted nearly an hour. At least that was what Leia thought as she sat crumpled in the back of the vehicle, nothing but darkness around her, nothing to hear except for the drone of the engine, the tyres on tarmac, and her own panicked breaths that filled the sack with thick moist air each time she exhaled.

Finally, they came to a stop. Doors opened and rough hands dragged her out.

'No! No!'

But her screams did nothing to help as she was hauled across jagged ground and into an echoey building. Once inside, she half shuffled, was half pulled along, until she was tossed down to the corner of a room she could see nothing of. Cold floor, cold walls. Where was this?

The hood remained over her head, though she could hear the two of them in the room with her. Moving about. Talking.

'He's not answering.' The man.

'Keep trying.' The woman, still calm.

'I've called ten fucking times already. He's not answering. This is bad.'

'Keep trying.'

'What's the point? We should just run.'

'Leave her here?'

'Fox is dead. We just killed her mom. Now Remi's not answering the phone. This wasn't the plan. We need to drop everything and go.'

'No. We'll find a way.'

'Damn it!' There was a loud bang. Something hard against metal. The guy thumping something? 'I need some air.'

Banging, then silence.

Or near silence. Feet shuffled lightly toward her. Leia froze. She could hear breathing, right in front of her. She flinched when she felt pressure on her neck.

Finally, the sack was removed.

It took her eyes several seconds to adjust and to properly see the dank room. Some sort of storage room? In a warehouse? Everything looked and felt industrial.

'You want something to drink?'

Leia nodded. The woman crouched in front of her was casually dressed, but with a balaclava over her head. Her eyes were blue and intense.

'I'm not going to hurt you,' the woman said. She held a bottle of water out. Leia took it. Drank two mouthfuls. 'I'm sorry about what happened.'

'My mum...'

The woman said nothing for a few moments. Leia knew what the silence meant. Her mother was dead.

'I couldn't stop him.'

'That's why you shot him?'

Leia had seen what had happened. The other man. The one she'd heard them call Fox. He'd shot her mum when she tried to wrestle the gun from him. This woman had seen it. Had pulled Fox and her mum apart then blasted her own accomplice through the chest when he'd been about to turn the gun on her. An inner squabble between this woman and Fox. Whether that was because of the heat of the moment *or tension that had already been brewing, Leia had no idea. End result; one dead on both sides.*

Before the sack had been pulled over Leia's head, she'd seen the woman place a gun in her mum's limp hand. Perhaps for the cops to find, or perhaps so she could lie to her partner about what had gone wrong. Possibly both. Judging by the look of worry in the eyes of this woman now, Leia didn't believe she'd told her partner exactly what had happened with Fox, and perhaps hadn't realised that Leia had seen everything too.

Did that make Leia even more vulnerable, or was it the opposite?

'How old are you?' the woman asked.

'Fourteen.'

A strange question, under the circumstances, and there was no follow-up, though the woman hovered, as though waiting for Leia to say something else, or thinking through what else she would say herself.

'Why am I here?' Leia asked.

The woman shook her head. 'This will all be over with soon. I promise.'

Then she stood up and walked away across the room, the sack that had been over Leia's head dangling in her hand.

Devereaux awoke from her drug-induced sleep inside a helicopter. A civilian helicopter, the back cabin of which was separated from the cockpit by a glass divider. Devereaux was on a cushioned bench. There was room for four in the back, and there were three others with her. A man and a woman – to her left, sitting opposite each other – who were dressed in combat gear and who had semi-automatic weapons in their hands. Plus the man sitting across from her. He was more casually dressed. Nice shoes. Suit trousers. An open-necked shirt. Unarmed, as far as Devereaux could see. With a newly trimmed beard he had a youthful and not altogether unhandsome face.

Devereaux's wrists, on her lap, were zip-tied, but she wasn't otherwise secured or held down. No gag, no hood. Nothing particularly threatening really, all things considered.

Except for the two armed commandos, that was, but Devereaux had certainly been in worse positions before. Even before anyone said a word she was already planning different scenarios for how to attack these people and escape. She could see out of the window that they were currently over water. It wouldn't be that hard...

The man was smiling at her.

'You've got nothing to say?' he asked. English. A very neat accent too. More authentic than hers. She wasn't quite sure if he was a native or not.

Devereaux shrugged. 'Where are we going?'

The man chuckled. He glanced to the two grunts who remained stony-faced.

'That's your first question? You're not wondering who we are or why we took you?'

'Those were my next questions. I thought it rude to ask all at once.'

The man said nothing now, though the amused look remained on his face.

'So?' Devereaux prompted.

'You want me to take those off?' he said, indicating down to the plastic on her wrists.

'Do as you please. They don't bother me too much.'

'I had wondered whether we needed to make you more secure. I decided not. I didn't want you to get the wrong impression when you woke up. But others...' he looked to the two grunts again, '...were a bit more cautious.'

Devereaux shrugged. 'Sometimes the impression of control is more important than control itself.'

The man looked like he didn't get what she meant. She was fluent enough in English but sometimes expressions didn't quite translate properly.

He pulled a knife from the sheath on the belt of the man next to him, leaned forward and drew the blade effortlessly through the plastic tie.

'Thanks,' Devereaux said as he replaced the knife. 'But you didn't answer my question. Where are we going?'

'That wasn't the question I wanted to answer.'

'Fine. So why am I here?'

'Better. You're getting good at this. You're here because of what you did in England.'

'I drank tea and ate fish and chips?'

He chuckled again. 'I like you. No, not that. You've caused, how can I say this, a *big fucking headache*. For my employer.'

'I'm sorry to hear that.'

'But he's the forgiving type.'

'So I can see. And who is your esteemed employer?'

As the words passed her lips there was a notable shift in the helicopter's trajectory. They were no longer headed straight ahead, they were going down.

The smile on the man's face widened.

'You're about to see. Welcome to Cyprus.'

The helicopter touched down less than two minutes later on a prominent stretch of land that jutted out from a rocky coastline. Given the sun's position Devereaux thought they'd come down somewhere on the south side of the island. There was no sign of a town or even a village within the near distance.

They landed in a field of green grass. The edges of the field fell away into the sea. There were no markings for a helicopter here, nothing to suggest this was anything other than a regular field.

The rotors were still whirring at full speed when the man leaned forward and opened the door.

'Come on,' he said.

He jumped down to the ground. There was no welcoming party. Devereaux glanced over to the two grunts but they remained in place. Not even looking at her. Disinterested. She was tempted to lunge for them and attack just for the reaction.

She didn't. Instead, she jumped down onto the grass, and the din from the rotors filled her ears and the blast of air caused by their relentless spin nearly sent her off her feet. She only realised now, as she tried to take a step, just how disconnected her muscles and her limbs remained from the after-effects of the sedative.

'Follow me,' the man said as he kept low and scuttled away.

Devereaux set off with him. She was only a few yards from the helicopter when she sensed it was already pulling up and away. Several more steps and she could barely feel the wind from its rotors at all.

'Your army chums aren't coming with us?'

'Not army.'

'Then what?'

'A helping hand. They did their job. You won't see them again.'

'Their job being capturing and sedating me?'

'Precisely.'

'Interesting.'

With the helicopter vanishing in the sky, Devereaux and the man walked more casually through the short grass. They headed over the top of a small hill and a rocky outcrop was visible below, the cool blue of the Mediterranean beyond it. A villa sat quietly there. White-washed, just like back in Andalucia, except this one looked so different. Smaller, understated, it somehow blended with its surroundings like it'd been there as long as the cliffs themselves.

They carried on down the hill, over a fence, until they were onto a manicured lawn with flower borders.

'This way,' the man said. He checked his watch. Devereaux got a glimpse. Just after 4pm. The winter sun was creeping down toward the horizon. Nightfall would be here before long, and the temperature was already dropping because of it. At least Devereaux still had her jacket.

Her backpack though...

'You took my things,' she said.

Her money. Everything she'd gone through today – the last few days, in fact – was all for nothing.

'I'm sorry,' the man said. 'But please just wait to hear what my employer has to say about that.'

'Your employer who has no name.'

'He has a name. I just haven't told you it yet.'

They headed around the side of the villa. Up close, Devereaux could see that the white walls were cracked in places, paint was peeling, some of the render was powdery and crumbling. Not in complete disrepair but this building needed some TLC. They rounded a corner and the garden opened out, leading directly to a rocky edge that gave way to the sea. There was a small swimming pool over in the far corner, though it was a classic sunk-in-the-ground affair, not a glass-fronted infinity like Khaled had. The fact this pool was covered over with an ageing tarpaulin suggested it was off limits for the season, perhaps because it wasn't heated.

Under a striped fabric awning at the back of the property

was a dining table. A large rustic wooden table big enough for more than a dozen people.

A man sat there alone. A bottle of red wine and two glasses – one half-filled, one empty – were on the table in front of him, along with a large bowl of olives. The man was middle-aged. Thick grey hair hung over his forehead and his ears, and he had heavily tanned and lined skin. He wore a loose-fitting short-sleeved shirt over what was obviously a portly figure.

He reminded Devereaux of her long dead grandad.

The man rose to his feet when he realised he had company.

'Ah, Paulo, you're back. And you must be Ms Devereaux. It's a real pleasure.'

Devereaux and Paulo continued up to him. Paulo stepped forward and shook his employer's hand and whispered something into his ear which caused a raised eyebrow, but he was soon all smiles again as he turned his attention to Devereaux. He held out his hand. She stepped forward and took it, and he held hers gently, clasping his other hand on top.

'And you are?' she said.

'My name's Kyriakos Anastopoulos,' he said, before laughing. 'Just call me Kyri, it's what most people do.'

He took his seat and a sip of wine.

'Please,' he said, indicating the chair adjacent to him.

Devereaux hesitated for a second. She glanced to Paulo who was now standing behind his boss, arms folded. On guard, but hardly threatening. The relaxed nature of this whole set-up was making Devereaux all the more unsettled.

She took the seat. And the offer of some wine.

'Cypriot wine,' Kyri said. 'My own grapes.'

She took a sip. Ever so slightly chilled. Probably straight out of an underground cellar. She was no wine connoisseur but she would say it tasted damn good.

'You like it?'

'I prefer Italian.'

That knocked a little bit of his friendly facade away. A deliberate attempt on her part.

'You're probably wondering why you're here,' he said.

'Something about you having a headache.'

The smile was back. 'Indeed. That's right. I do have a headache. And I'm afraid to say, my dear, that you are the cause.'

'So you invited me to your home for wine.'

'This isn't my home.'

She didn't know how to take that.

'No. Seriously. It isn't.'

Devereaux shrugged. She couldn't care less really.

'Tell me about this headache,' she said. 'And why you drugged me, stole my money, and flew me thousands of miles across the Med.'

'Your money?'

Devereaux nodded.

Serious now. 'The way I understood it, you were helping yourself to that money. After torturing a poor, defenceless woman to get it.'

'Ah yes. Yasmin,' Devereaux said. 'And where exactly is she now?'

'Not your concern. But she'll be fine.'

'I'm glad to hear it.'

'I like your attitude,' he said. 'It's cute. If a little grating. You don't take murdering and torturing and stealing too seriously. That's quite unusual.'

Devereaux said nothing.

'I should probably explain why you're here. Why you're still alive. Because you do realise that the fact you are still breathing is through my choice and nothing else?'

Still she said nothing.

'There were plenty of places in Spain where we could have

left your corpse. Places where your remains would never have been found and your bones would have disintegrated into the earth.'

'Thank you, I guess.'

He smiled again, but it faltered more quickly this time. 'Let me tell you a story. Do you like stories?'

'Depends on the ending.'

'This one doesn't have an end yet. But it starts a long time ago. In Russia. With a man named Pavel Grichenko. You know that name?'

'I think we're both well aware that I do.'

'Good. This man, he had a very good friend–'

'Kyri, by any chance?'

'That's right. And the two of them together were very successful. They made a lot of money. Made a lot of people happy. We did good in this world. But success has a habit of breeding contempt in others. Unfortunately for my friend, he came from a country which has far less allies than mine. At least in the West. So rather than being celebrated, he was maligned for his success. He became... an enemy.'

He paused for a moment and took a large gulp of wine.

'Do you want an olive?' he said, pointing to the bowl in the middle of the table.

'Let me guess. You grow your own?'

'How did you know?'

'I'm fine, thanks.'

'Do you know this next part to the story?' he asked as he chewed.

Devereaux shook her head. Kyri followed suit. 'I really don't get it. I understand the need for people like you. After all, you get these dirty jobs done. But do you not even care *why*?'

'I only care for the details that are needed.'

'What if you kill a good person?'

'Let's move on.'

'As you wish. So, my friend, he's now an enemy of the West. Although I say the West like several hundred million people all think the same. He became an enemy of certain people, is more accurate. A very small number of people, really. But people who could make a difference. They wanted him dead. But my friend found out. He tried to fight back, in his own way. He succeeded, to an extent. I won't bore you with every detail, but he survived, and he was able to start a new, quieter life. Quieter for his safety, mainly. Now not many people knew that he survived. But I did.'

He stopped talking again and held Devereaux's gaze, as though expecting her to say something.

She decided to play along. 'And next?'

'And next, ten years later, he's dead. Because a few days ago, in England, you killed him.'

'Sorry,' she said.

'I'm not sure you are. But I am sure you're still asking yourself why are you still alive, if you've hurt me so badly?'

'That's true.'

'You said yourself you didn't know, or was it didn't care, why he was a target. But I found who ordered this. And from there I found you.'

Devereaux clenched her fists. '*You* paid Khaled to kill me?'

Kyri nodded.

'But now you're inviting me over for wine?'

'I'm sorry to say I acted on impulse when I made Khaled that offer. I will admit I was driven by revenge. But now I've had time to think. I only saw after just how good you are. How useful you could be to me.'

'You want me to work for you?'

'There's something you need to do for me, yes.'

'That depends on the price. I'm already down, because your friend here took my money.'

'My price, my offer, is your life.'

Devereaux clenched her teeth. Kyri stared at her. In that moment she thought, not for the first time, about getting up and jumping across the table and breaking his neck.

What was stopping her?

'You owe me,' he said. 'You owe me a lot. Yet you can make amends. And you'll get your dirty money back, the money you stole from Khaled.' He said the last words with real disgust. 'But only when I'm satisfied.'

He reached into his pocket and took out a folded piece of paper. He held it up then tossed it across the table.

Devereaux picked it up and straightened it out and looked down at the scribbled words. Names.

'I still don't know how Khaled knew of my friend's new life in England, or why he wanted him dead. It's going to be harder to get that information now that you've killed him. So we'll come back to that. But the people on that list? They're all involved, one way or another. They all need to go. That's your job. As quickly, and as cleanly as you can.'

'And if I say no?'

Kyri huffed and he and Paulo exchanged a look.

'Would you like another story?' Kyri said.

'Not really.'

Kyri got to his feet. Slowly, achingly, like it was a real effort. He downed the rest of his glass of wine.

'This one is easier to show, rather than tell.'

He turned and moved to the back doors of the house. Devereaux hesitated but was soon following. Paulo moved in behind her. Kyri opened the doors and stepped into the dim interior. Devereaux glanced over her shoulder to check Paulo remained at a safe distance before she headed inside too.

The smell hit her. A copper, iron twang. Unmistakeable. Fresh.

Her body tensed. She followed Kyri through the country-style kitchen...

She stopped just past the doorway of the lounge. Her heart pounded against her ribs as she looked around, though she tried to remain absolutely calm on the outside. Devereaux looked over her shoulder again. Paulo was causally leaning against the door frame, a sickly smile on his face.

Devereaux's eyes flicked across the room. There were three bodies in total. One was only a child. Propped up in the far corner of the room. A bullet hole in his forehead from which blood wormed down his lifeless face.

The knot in her stomach tightened.

The other bodies were a man and a woman. At least what was left of them suggested that was the case. They were naked. Hacked apart. Skin peeled back in places. Limbs severed. Blood drenched the walls, the windows, the stone floor. The child's death had been quick, painless. The man and woman...

'This one is a short story,' Kyri said. 'I can be your friend. Or not. This is what happens when not.'

Devereaux didn't fully think through what she did next. It was more instinct than anything else. Not just survival instinct, but an instinct for justice. Strange, that such an instinct was still buried somewhere deep inside.

She spun and lunged toward Paulo. Grasped the bloody knife from the sideboard as she moved. She'd gut him. Rip his insides out. Do the same to the old man. See if they liked that story.

Paulo reacted as she moved in for the kill. But not quick enough. Devereaux swooshed the knife through the air.

And made perhaps the biggest mistake of her life.

Paulo hadn't been slow to react. He'd read her move precisely. Why had she underestimated him so badly?

He whipped into action at the last moment. Deflected the

blow. Grabbed her arm and twisted it outwards with force until the knife fell free. He grabbed her, threw her up face first up against the wall, her arm pressed out onto the stony surface.

The knife was in his hands...

Chop.

Devereaux screamed. The top half of her middle finger fell to the floor.

Paulo knocked her feet away, she fell to her knees. He twisted her arm the other way. Held it aloft, at bursting point, as his foot pressed into her back to keep her bent forward. She felt the tip of a blade pushed into the back of her neck.

Devereaux tried to hold the pain in as blood dribbled down her hand and her arm. She breathed heavy breaths.

Kyri sauntered over.

'It's just a finger,' he said, picking the digit up from the floor and inspecting it. 'You have nine others.'

He threw it across the room then pulled a handkerchief from his pocket. Devereaux grimaced as he grasped her hand and tightly tied the fabric in place around the stump.

'You should see a doctor. But you'll be fine. You'll be able to complete this job for me still. Won't you?'

Devereaux didn't answer. She was too focused on the pain.

Her arm was twisted further.

'Won't you?' Kyri said again.

'Y-Yes!'

'Good.'

Her arm was freed. Paulo kicked her hard in the back and she smacked down onto the floor.

'We'll speak soon.'

And with that they turned and left, leaving Devereaux crumpled and bleeding in the pool of cold blood.

9

Ryker had no watch on, and there was no clock on the wall of the room, but he thought he'd been in here, alone now, for coming up on three hours. It was a bland room, all in all. The type of room seen in countless police stations the world over. Four walls, no window, a single door. A basic interior. Though there wasn't the ubiquitous one-way mirror here. Just a camera near the ceiling, right in front of Ryker, the lens looking down on him as he sat on the chair in front of the table, his hands cuffed together and secured to a metal rod attached to the tabletop.

He hadn't tried to fight. What was the point? Instead, he'd let the men cuff him outside DI Alessi's home, and stuff him into the back of one of the cars. He'd been blindfolded, and they'd driven at speed to this place. A nearly thirty-minute drive. The blindfold had only been removed once he'd been placed in this room, on this chair, with his wrists shackled. The men who'd brought him in had promptly left. No words said. And Ryker hadn't seen or heard from anyone since.

Curious, all in all. Particularly the drive time to this place, which certainly narrowed down where he could be.

It was three hours and twelve minutes, at least to Ryker's count, when the metal door to the room finally opened and in stepped Kaspovich. Alone.

The door was swiftly closed and locked behind him by someone on the outside. Gone now was Kaspovich's overcoat to reveal a typically smart look. Kaspovich was early forties, and although his hair was thin and receding, he looked younger than he was. He was also full of himself, his role in life, and even though he and Ryker had only ever come across each other once before, Ryker knew the MI5 agent had an intense dislike for him. The feeling was mutual, though that was beside the point. The point wasn't even how Ryker had been tracked since he'd arrived in England. The point was what on earth did MI5 have to do with any of this?

'I'd say it's nice to see you, but...'

Kaspovich plonked himself down opposite Ryker without finishing the sentence.

'How's Winter getting on?' Kaspovich asked. Ryker was sure he saw the slightest of smirks on his face at his question.

Winter, Ryker's old boss at the JIA, back when Ryker had been an agent there. No, not really an agent. Not in the end. At one time, long ago, yes he'd been an agent. Had worked for his old mentor Mackie for years, carrying out orders without question. Including in Doha ten years ago. But following Mackie's death, following more than one time when Ryker had been betrayed, had very nearly lost his life, and had come to question more and more what his life really was, he'd left the JIA behind. Or tried to. Except it had proved impossible to fully escape the clutches of his past. More recently, he'd worked for Winter – Mackie's successor – on an ad-hoc basis. A helping hand. A freelance consultant. Including last year when Ryker had worked alongside Kaspovich. That job had hardly gone smoothly, and Ryker had since cut all ties for good.

Or so he'd finally hoped.

'I haven't seen or spoken to Winter in months,' Ryker said.

'Is that so?' Doubt. 'You mean, since your careless actions caused such a furore that the JIA basically imploded.'

Such a smug look on his face still.

'The way I see it, I got the job done. Despite your incompetence.'

A flash of irritation at Ryker's accusation. 'Try telling that to all your former colleagues who are out of work now.'

Ryker sighed. 'I'm pretty sure you didn't haul me in here just to revel in the misery of others.'

An arrogant laugh. 'No, of course not. We're here to talk about your continued cock-ups.'

'So where are we exactly?'

Kaspovich held Ryker's eye though he didn't attempt to answer the question.

'My best guess would be GCHQ,' Ryker said. 'Given how long it took to get here from Gloucester.'

No tell on Kaspovich's face.

Government Communications Headquarters, the UK's permanent intelligence and security organisation, was housed in the awkwardly known Doughnut building, in Cheltenham. The Doughnut was the UK's ultra-modern and ultra-expensive equivalent to the world-renowned Pentagon building and was shaped like... well, a giant doughnut.

'But then, I'm not sure you're operating quite as officially as that, are you?' Ryker said. 'I mean, I haven't actually been arrested, have I? I haven't been charged with anything. And this place...'

'What do you think we should be charging you with exactly?'

Now it was Ryker's turn to stay silent.

'Even disregarding your past,' Kaspovich said, 'we caught

you today in the act of breaking into the home of a police officer. Yesterday, you were spotted breaking into and then running from a crime scene.'

'So why aren't I in the local police station then?'

'I think we're both well aware of why not. The murder of Pavel Grichenko raises issues of significant national security. And you know that, don't you?'

Ryker shrugged. 'I've no idea why that would be the case.'

Kaspovich sighed. 'No need to play dumb with me, Ryker. Like you said, you're not under arrest. This isn't a police station. We don't have to give you a phone call. We don't have to release you in twenty-four hours if we can't charge you. You're here for as long as it takes. And we don't have to be nice. Our place, our rules.'

'You need to work on your threats. That was pretty pathetic, even for you. Or is it just that you know you really have nothing, and can do nothing.'

Kaspovich's face creased in anger and he banged his fist on the table. Ryker didn't bat an eyelid at the outburst.

'Yes, because you'd know all about threats, wouldn't you?' Kaspovich sneered. 'Know all about the lengths the intelligence services really go to for queen and country.' He let those words sit, as though they would have an effect on Ryker. They didn't. 'Don't forget I know about you, Ryker. I know the sort of man you are, the things you've done and would do.'

'You think you know me?'

'Yeah. I do. You're pitiful. But let's not make this personal. Let's just do what needs to be done. I don't know where you've been these last months, but you came back here. You made a big mistake. Now you're in my hands. Tell me, because I am curious, why didn't you just leave the country again?'

'Sorry?'

'You went back to the house. What for? What did you miss? What were you trying to cover up?'

'No, you've lost me.'

Kaspovich shook his head. 'Ryker, don't take me for a fool, I'm really not in the mood. You went back to Grichenko's house yesterday. You were seen there. That's why you're here now. We were able to use ANPR to track you after you left. It was the most idiotic move imaginable, even for you. I'm just curious as to what made you do such a stupid thing.'

Ryker's brain whirred. ANPR. Automatic Number Plate Recognition. A clever system, but hardly one that was so widespread that the authorities could use it in real time to track someone's every move.

'Fine. You don't want to answer that. I get it. No one likes to be made to look stupid. Still, I can't fathom it at all. I mean, you head into there, do your thing. Your thing is killing people, right? Perhaps you actually think it's impressive that you're so experienced at that. But it's not impressive. It's obscene. So you killed Grichenko and his wife. But you didn't scarper for foreign shores. You bloody went back to the scene two days later for a little look around, broad daylight, with four police officers on site! Come on...'

'You think I killed Grichenko?'

Kaspovich reached down to his side, to the satchel by his feet, then plonked a manilla folder onto the desk. A few of the papers inside spread out. Ryker's eyes flicked across what he could see.

'Think? No, Ryker, I don't think you killed them. I *know* you did.'

10

The silence that followed Kaspovich's blunt statement lasted an age, both men unblinking.

'I'm guessing you want me to take a look at those papers,' Ryker said, nodding to the folder. 'If you'll just uncuff my hands...'

A sarcastic laugh. 'A comedian too. Wonders never cease with you. Here, let me help.'

Kaspovich reached forward and lifted the front cover of the folder. He neatly arranged four pieces of paper across the desk for Ryker to see. Basic crime-scene analysis, but not enough to give Ryker anything of use. No mention of Grichenko's cause of death. Some initial forensics results on blood traces and fingerprints. A profile of James Ryker.

He said nothing.

'Your fingerprints were found in several places at the scene of the murder,' Kaspovich said with a solemn shake of his head. 'I really thought you were more intelligent than that.'

'You're lying.'

'You can see the results for yourself.'

'I never set foot in that house before yesterday.'

Plus he'd worn gloves. Plus the reports here were for prints found right after the murder, not yesterday.

'Oh, but you are admitting now that you were there? That's a start.'

'You're setting me up.'

'You've done a pretty good job of that yourself.'

'Why?'

'No one's setting you up. This is what we have. What the police have. The days are gone when people like you could run around this country, circumventing laws, hurting and killing people under the auspice of working for the greater good.'

'I didn't kill them.'

'No? So who did?'

Ryker said nothing.

'Unless you can give me an alternative explanation for being there. For your interest in a murdered man and his wife, for your fingerprints at the scene of their murders...'

Ryker still said nothing. What was this? A fishing exercise so Ryker would spill all as to his link to Grichenko? But then why would Kaspovich even care about what happened in the past?

Or was Ryker really being set up here? Had his fingerprints been planted all over that house? If that was the case Ryker had an even bigger problem than he'd first imagined. There were very few people in the world who would even think to link him to Grichenko's death. And the biggest question was, why would they do so?

Perhaps the answer was sitting right in front of him. Was it all Kaspovich?

'I need to speak to Winter,' Ryker said.

Kaspovich glared at him. 'Peter Winter has nothing to do with this. He has no authority over me, or over this investigation.'

'Still, I want to speak to him. You want answers? Let me talk to Winter.'

Kaspovich seemed to mull that one over. 'No. You're playing by my rules now. You don't work for him. There is no JIA anymore. There's no one to bail you out. This time you'll answer for your actions.'

'Then I'm done. No more talking.'

'You're done?'

Ryker held his tongue.

Kaspovich's forehead creased. Not anger. More annoyance. The silence went on. And on.

'I don't know why I even gave you the chance,' Kaspovich said. 'Just don't forget, this was your choice. It's time to take things up a notch, wouldn't you say?'

He got up from his chair. Moments later he was gone.

Several more hours passed with Ryker still chained to the table. No food, no water. No toilet break. No semblance of his captors following any official regulations for holding prisoners. For all of his talk of despising men like Ryker, of despising the cloak-and-dagger life that Ryker had once led, Kaspovich was the biggest hypocrite of them all, holding Ryker like this. And Ryker was increasingly apprehensive about what would come next. He wasn't unused to ill treatment, to being subjected to torture, from the psychological to downright barbaric and brutal. But did Kaspovich really have that in him? Who within MI5 would even sign off on that? Or was Kaspovich rogue?

Ryker's eyes were half shut from tiredness and boredom, his head flopping forward, when the door opened next. Four men strode in, Ryker jerked upright. He'd lost track of time. His brain was weary. His arms and shoulders ached from having been stuck in position for so long. He was thirsty, his belly ached, and his bladder was on the verge of giving up.

A bottle of water was thrust forward by one man. Another pulled Ryker's head back. His brain flashed with memories. He awaited the cloth over his face. His body tensed. He'd been waterboarded before. A horrific experience.

Though there was no cloth this time.

'Drink,' one of the men said before a burst of water was sprayed toward him.

The water smacked into Ryker's face and dribbled down his chin onto his clothes. He opened his mouth and did his best to take the water in. Most of it splashed away, but he knew the paltry amounts he managed to drink would help his depleting reserves.

The bottle was still half full when it was pulled away and the man plonked it onto the table. A moment later a sack was yanked down over Ryker's head.

Pressure on the back of his skull.

'You know what that is?'

Ryker was about to retort with a quip but decided against it.

He nodded.

'Let me be clear. We will shoot you if you try to fight us. Don't kid yourself that we won't.'

'I'm going to release your hands from the table now,' came another voice. 'We'll move them around to behind you, then you'll follow us out of here.'

'Got it?' The first voice again. Just off to Ryker's left. So was he in charge? 'Do you understand?' More stern now.

'Yeah.'

Ryker flinched as strong hands grasped both of his arms. He wanted to fight, but this wasn't the right moment. Even if he wasn't sure these men – whoever they were – would shoot him dead for simple disobedience.

His hands were released from the table, but there was no chance for respite, and with two hands on each of his arms, the men were able to quickly re-cuff Ryker's hands behind him. He was hauled up to his feet.

'Walk.'

A prod in the back. Ryker got moving.

He remembered the sequence of turns, the number of steps, from when he'd first been brought here, and he was intrigued when it appeared they were retracing the exact same path. Wherever they were holding him, they were now leaving.

'So where are we going?' Ryker asked, when they were only one turn away from where the exit to the outside should be. 'I'm pretty hungry. Could murder a steak.'

'No talking.' A smack to the back of his head. Ryker clenched his teeth.

He heard a door opening. They were definitely heading out. They were transporting him somewhere else. Was this just Kaspovich's lame attempt to scare Ryker, or was this ordeal genuinely about to get a whole lot worse?

'Where's Kaspovich?' Ryker said.

A harder smack to his head this time. 'I said no talking.'

Ryker already really hated that guy.

A whoosh and clunk – the sound of a van door sliding open. Just a few yards from where Ryker was.

'Mind the step,' another man said, a moment before rough hands grasped him either side and pretty much hauled him up and into the van.

'Sit down there.'

Ryker was pushed down onto a hard metal bench. His hands were secured to some sort of metal bar behind him. The side door closed. Then the driver's door opened and closed. So there hadn't already been anyone in the front. Did that leave just the three other men in the back then?

The engine started and they were on the move.

'How long's the journey?' Ryker asked after a few minutes.

No answer. Not even a clip around the ear this time. In fact, none of the men had said a word to each other thus far.

'You guys are crap company.'

Nothing.

'Too dumb for MI5, I reckon. So what are you? For hire mercenaries? Ex-army?' Nothing. By now he had no clue if he truly believed this was MI5 or not, but he would fish for clues as best he could. 'Probably just steroid-junky ex-nightclub bouncers who think they're smarter and tougher than they really are.'

'Why don't you just shut the fuck up.'

Him again. The one who'd clipped Ryker before. And he was sitting directly in front of Ryker.

'Or what?'

'Or this.' A different voice.

A blow to Ryker's left kidney. Despite the discomfort he smiled under the sack. So that was two he'd figured the positions of. A third driving. Was there a fourth man in here, or had he been left behind?

Either way, Ryker had enough to work with. He'd already been playing out the possible moves in his head, and now that he knew exactly where two men were, he knew what to do.

He waited for the next sharp turn. Knowing that each of them would be slightly off balance as the van rounded the corner. When it came, Ryker bucked upward. Planted his hands behind him on the bench he was sitting on. Elongated his body like a worm as he twisted sideways. Used all the strength from his core to lift his legs up, knees bent...

He thrust his feet out with force. Hit home exactly where he expected the head of the man opposite to be. There was a horrific squelch, then a vibrating boom as the double sidekick full in the face smashed the guy's head back against the panel side of the van. A thud a moment later told Ryker he'd keeled over, out of it.

Ryker didn't hesitate. As soon as his feet touched the floor in front of him, he twisted and spun upward, his bound hands on the bench like a gymnast's on a beam. He swivelled, and his knee pounded into the head of the guy next to him, driving him down. Ryker completed the turn and ended up with his body laid out across the bench, facing down, the man underneath him, his head clasped between Ryker's thighs.

Ryker squeezed his legs together with everything he had. He drew his legs up into his body to drag the man forward, closer to him. The guy coughed and spluttered and choked.

'I've got you... in a sleeper hold,' Ryker said through laboured breaths. 'Your carotid artery is closed off. In a few seconds you'll lose consciousness.'

'Let... go!' His voice was weak and muffled under Ryker's heavy body.

'It won't be long until you suffer irreparable brain damage. Not long after that, you're dead. Reach for the keys. Uncuff me now.'

Ryker squeezed harder still and the man tapped the side of the van as though this were a wrestling bout and he was bailing.

Not this time.

'The keys,' Ryker said. 'Before it's too late for you.'

The man was fumbling by his side. Ryker willed him to do the sensible thing, and not reach for a knife or other weapon. If he did that, he wouldn't get a second chance. Ryker would hold on for good.

No need. Ryker heard the tinkle of the key chain. Released the hold just a little to let the man reach up. He scrabbled around trying to find the spot while smothered under Ryker's torso. Ryker tried to make it easy for him.

Click.

Ryker squeezed his legs harder than ever. There was a muffled cry from underneath him. He pulled his hands free. Dragged the sack from his head and took a deep lungful of air. The van screeched to a halt. Ryker jumped to his feet a moment after the man beneath him went limp.

He looked around. Blood poured from the nose and mouth of the man he'd smacked in the face. Both he and his colleague were out of it. Both would be fine though. Ryker couldn't see up front to the driver because of the central divider, but clearly the guy had realised something was up given they were now at a standstill.

He grabbed the M4 that was lying on the floor next to him. The driver's door opened. Ryker grabbed the man who'd released him and pulled him up, held him by the neck as he waited.

The side door slid open.

'Drop it,' Ryker said, pointing the gun at the driver, who was in turn pointing his weapon at Ryker. Except Ryker was hidden behind the unconscious man.

The guy with the gun looked to his other friend, bleeding all over. He was obviously trying to stay strong but Ryker could see the doubt in his eyes.

'Drop the weapon,' Ryker said again.

The guy released one hand. Pulled the barrel away to the side.

Good enough for Ryker.

He pulled the trigger. A single shot. The bullet glanced across the man's shoulder. He yelped and reeled back.

Ryker shoved the man he was holding out of the van. Drove forward and slammed into the driver and both men clattered to the ground. Ryker headbutted the driver on the nose. His fight was all but gone.

Ryker grabbed the key fob from the driver's pocket. Grabbed his phone too. He jumped back to his feet. Pulled the bloody man from the van then shut the door. He rushed to the front, sank down into the driver's seat.

Seconds later he was racing away.

11

Ryker drove on for only five miles before he dumped the van. His only intention in taking it had been to get away from the men; he knew he couldn't stay in the vehicle for long if he wanted to evade whoever it was that would undoubtedly now come looking for him. The police? MI5? A government hit squad?

When Ryker had first driven off he'd been on a quiet B-road on the outskirts of Swindon, and after leaving the van, he headed the couple of miles into the centre of the town on foot. On his way he used a simple hack to gain access to the stolen phone, and once in the town was further able to use the stored card details to buy a change of clothes and some food. In a quiet café he spent some time browsing the device for clues as to the identities and loyalties of his captors, but there was nothing that jumped out at him on there, other than confirmation of the man's name, and from his social media profile that he was indeed ex-army – that in itself was of little help.

A quick search through breaking news and social media didn't pull up anything of interest. There were no reports of Ryker being a wanted man. No reports of his violent escape from custody. That was good. It meant there wasn't a full-on nationwide manhunt for him.

The big question though, was why not?

He left the phone behind in the café. He had no further use for it, and before long Kaspovich would be able to trace Ryker's whereabouts if he kept it on him.

Instead, Ryker found a Western Union shop, and after using one of their terminals to transfer five hundred pounds to himself, he was soon on his way back to Gloucestershire to pick up his belongings. A risky move perhaps, but a necessary one under the circumstances as Ryker was now officially on the run, and he wouldn't get far without quick access to cash or his collection of IDs.

It was a risk worth taking, and one that went without any hitches, and Ryker was soon on the move again, heading out of Gloucestershire in another newly rented vehicle. His trip to the Cotswolds had gone far from plan. He still knew little about the circumstances of Grichenko's murder, and he knew little about how and why Kaspovich was not just involved, but had Ryker in his sights as a suspect.

Turning the tables and tracking down Kaspovich himself, and putting some pressure on him, was an option which Ryker seriously considered, but it was an alternative route that he decided on eventually.

Grichenko had survived the assassination attempt ten years ago, despite Ryker's crew confirming he was dead. Whoever had killed the Russian days ago in England, the simple fact remained that at least one of the team from Doha had lied to Ryker. The cover-up of the failed mission had to have some connection to Grichenko's new life, and his eventual death.

It was time to go back to the beginning.

⌇

The drive north and east took three hours and it was deep into the night before Ryker made it into Lincolnshire. After the day he'd had he needed to rest up, but he decided against a hotel, and, instead, spent the night huddled in the car in a lay-by next to a farmer's field. He shivered through the cold night and woke up with the sunrise the next day with a splitting headache and a grumbling belly. But at least he was only a couple of miles from his destination.

The converted barn was a good half mile from the next nearest building, nestled among rolling fields that were barren in winter and dotted with patches of white where previous snow and sleet hadn't fully melted. It remained cold outside, though at least the sun was shining for once.

Ryker parked up on the road outside the property, scaled the gate, and headed along the driveway on foot. Smoke plumed out of the single chimney pot to the stone-built structure. There was one car on the drive – a banged-up Land Rover Defender. An almost omnipresent vehicle choice in these rural parts.

He moved cautiously, not knowing exactly what to expect from the owners if they spotted him approaching. He reached the oak door without seeing or hearing anyone, and knocked three times then stood back.

Footsteps inside. Ryker braced himself. The door was opened and two timid eyes stared out to him.

'Can I help you?' the woman said.

'Mrs Aldern?' Ryker said.

'Yes.'

'I'm an old friend of Wes's. Is he in?'

She looked even more apprehensive now.

'Is he home?'

'An old friend, huh?'

'We worked together.'

'Did you? Then I'm surprised you don't already know.'

Ryker slumped a little. He understood. 'He's dead.'

Not the introduction he'd hoped for. Yet Ryker still found himself sitting in the cosy lounge minutes later. Paula Aldern was through in the kitchen next door, as the kettle boiled away. Ryker looked around as he waited. Several pictures on the wall were of Aldern in his military uniform when he'd been a much younger man. There were also pictures of two children, although there was little sign of them in the house. Aldern was only a few years older than Ryker, but perhaps the kids had already left the nest.

Paula came back in carrying a tray of tea and biscuits. Ryker wanted to smile at the hospitality, but the mood of his host was understandably sombre.

'What happened to him?' Ryker asked.

She placed the tray on the coffee table then perched herself on the edge of a threadbare armchair.

'Straight to it, right?'

'I'm sorry, I just–'

'It's fine. I know the type. The truth is, I don't know exactly what happened to him. They didn't tell me.'

Certainly work then, rather than natural causes, Ryker could only assume.

'When?'

'Three years ago.' An awkward pause. 'You say you worked with him? I'm guessing not in the army.'

She looked at Ryker with something between pity and disgust as she said that.

'No. Not in the army. I was never in the army.'

'Those were his best years. He was a good man back then.'

Ryker nodded.

'Until he became... like you.' She wasn't making any eye contact with Ryker now.

'Like me?'

'I know what you are. I see it in you. Your eyes. Just like his at the end. It was like living with a ghoul. A shadow with no soul.'

Was that how some people saw Ryker? Given the things he'd seen and done in his life, it wouldn't be a surprise. The trauma he'd suffered, the trauma he'd inflicted, it all took its toll. Though it was unusual to be called out on it so openly, and so soon after meeting someone for the first time. And it didn't make him feel good in any way to know that that was the way some people saw him.

Was it justified?

'We worked together just one time,' Ryker said. 'In Qatar. Ten years ago.'

She did make eye contact now, though showed no particular reaction to Ryker's words.

'He'd only been in the job two years at that point,' she said. 'There was still some of the old him left.'

Another interesting comment. Ryker hadn't known Aldern well, but what he had known of him was that he was loud and boisterous – in a jovial way. A strong-willed man who said what he meant, and was as tough as nails. But they'd only ever worked together on that one job, and it had been far from perfect. Aldern was supposed to have been a lookout. He'd strayed from position, gone to that wooded area having been spooked and had been attacked there, likely by the same men Ryker had grappled with when he'd gone looking for his crew member. The next Ryker had seen of Aldern was in the back of the van as the crew made their escape. Grichenko dead. Mission messy, but complete.

The team had taken the boat to Oman, and had separated on the docks after a perfunctory debrief. Ryker hadn't seen or heard anything from any of them since. He'd moved on to his next mission, as he expected the others had – doing whatever, for whoever. Yet Ryker had always had a niggle in the back of his mind as to exactly why that night had strayed from plan. Why Aldern had left his position and ended up incommunicado. Who'd opened fire first indoors, and why. Who the mystery men were who'd attacked Aldern and Ryker.

'Did he ever talk about Qatar? About what happened there?'

'I didn't even know he'd been there. He never talked about any of it. I take it you're not married?'

Ryker shook his head.

'No, of course not. Who could be married to someone like that. So many secrets. So many lies.'

A tear rolled down her cheek. They sat through a few moments of silence. Ryker could tell her brain was racing. He waited for her to open up.

'The thing is, to start with I got the sense that he *wanted* to talk to me about it,' she said. 'He was so excited when he was approached to join. He wanted to tell me about it all. But he couldn't. His hands were tied. He was too loyal. I got that even from when he was in the army. I knew the new job was for the government, and that that was all I'd ever find out. But...'

'But?'

'But after a while he... just became numbed to it all. His whole being was numb. He said nothing, felt nothing.'

Ryker closed his eyes for a few seconds. He knew exactly how that felt.

'And then came the call.'

Ryker held her eye now. Again waited for her to expand. She didn't. 'The call?'

'All they told me was that there'd been a problem. Abroad. He was dead. They were working hard to repatriate his body. They'd put on a ceremonial funeral when he was home.'

'And did they?'

She nodded.

'So they got him home?'

She nodded again.

'You saw his body?'

She screwed her face in disgust. 'What is this?'

'I'm sorry. That was inappropriate.'

'Who sent you?' Paula said. Her tone was stronger now. The accusation all too clear. She saw Ryker as a threat, not a friend.

'I don't work with anyone. I left that life. That's the truth. I'm not a threat here.'

'No. Everything and everyone from that life is a threat. Even if you don't see it, you bring it.'

He felt he knew what she meant by that.

'I needed to ask about that night in Qatar, that's all,' Ryker said. 'And I needed his help. But I can see you're not comfortable with me being here. I'll go.'

Ryker made to get up. That was when he noticed Paula's eyes flick behind him. Ryker followed her line of sight, then jerked upright, spun around.

He was staring into the double barrel of a shotgun. The guy holding the weapon snuck up quiet as a mouse.

'Time for you to leave,' the young man said.

All of twenty years old, he was tall and beefy. Well, flabby, and looked exactly like a younger but fuller Aldern.

Ryker held his hands up and glanced back to Paula. The tea and biscuits lay untouched still on the coffee table. Clever. To offer that, trying to keep Ryker at ease while she awaited her saviour.

'I'm not a threat to you two,' Ryker said. He sounded way more calm than Aldern's son had. The shotgun quivered in his grip now. Which actually made Ryker all the more nervous. One twitch and he'd have a bunch of shotgun pellets in his chest. This was a time for treading carefully.

'You don't want to shoot me,' Ryker said. 'And you don't want me as your enemy. Believe me.'

'Just go,' Paula said.

'I think that'd be best.' He stepped to the side. The gun barrels followed him. He remained staring at the metal as he continued to step sideways, then backward toward the door. He opened it without looking then back-stepped outside. The gun and Aldern's son followed him out.

'I don't want to see you here ever again,' the guy said.

That was fine by Ryker. 'You won't.'

There was nothing for him here anyway.

12

'Get down and stay down!' the man barked a moment before there was a thump right next to her. Leia's eyes sprang open, wrenching her from an unlikely sleep, and she jolted and shuffled back, even further into the corner.

She looked to the groaning lump next to her and her eyes widened. Even without seeing his face, without him saying a word, she knew who it was.

The sound of him breathing. His smell. Both so familiar and comforting.

'Daddy!'

'Leia?'

She clambered over to him. Sank down next to him as he lay in a heap on the floor, on his side. His wrists and ankles were zip-tied together. His head covered by a sack, like hers had been.

'Daddy.'

She nestled into him and sobbed.

Dubai felt surreal to Devereaux. A fantasy land with no real soul. The image of a metropolis thought up by a thirteen-year-old, with skyscrapers in every direction, as far as the eye could see, some as tall as the sky itself, but most with no real purpose. There was no true centre here, there was no warmth or feel that Devereaux could grasp. There was a lot of money though.

She sat in her rented BMW a hundred yards from the school gates. The Faisal Ahmed International School of Dubai. Devereaux had no idea who Faisal Ahmed was, or had been, but his school was clearly decent enough given the vast array of expensive cars that were here for the end of day pick-up. Mostly big cars. Diesel-guzzling four-by-fours, driven by the home help because Mummy and Daddy were too busy working or too busy not working.

Despite the obvious wealth of the families who could afford to send their children here, the school itself was a nondescript affair. A sprawling, three-storey, sandy-coloured stone structure that looked like it had one day simply risen up from the desert that surrounded this city. A far cry – and almost refreshingly so – from the usual glass-rich sleekness that dominated much of the inner city and felt so out of place.

Devereaux checked her watch. Fifteen minutes until home time. Her eyes flicked from her watch to her hand. Her still bandaged hand. Two days later and the stump where her finger had been sliced off remained painful and swollen and bloody, despite her best efforts to cauterise the wound with a glowing red spoon she'd heated on the gas stove in the bloodbath house in Cyprus.

At least there was no sign of infection yet. She'd re-dressed the wound every few hours to keep it clean, and she'd give it a few more days like this. If it wasn't looking any better by then, she'd have to seek a doctor. A last resort really, and she didn't know any that she could trust in this part of the world from previous experience.

She pushed the thoughts away. She wouldn't dwell on what had happened in Cyprus right now. Wouldn't dwell on the man who'd called himself Kyri, who she'd been able to find so little about, but who reminded her so much of another man, from a long time ago. For now she'd go along with his game. She liked games. She'd do what he'd asked.

Eventually she'd figure a way to play by her rules.

Another glance to her watch, then she pushed open her door and stepped out into the sunshine. Even in winter the weather here was hot and sunny – at least it was hot to Devereaux – though she still had on a smart jacket. Not just to hide a holstered gun and a sheathed hunting knife, but to give her pockets to hide her bandaged hand. No point in inviting questions or arousing suspicions.

She headed up to the school gates where there was already a gathering of adults standing in wait – mostly carers, rather than parents. Mostly female, mostly from the Indian sub-continent or the Philippines. Many wore uniforms – simple cotton dresses that were blue or red or green – that showed their lowly status as general dogsbodies. There were a few men too, though they were quite different. Black suit trousers, white shirts, designer sunglasses in the main. Chauffeurs-cum-security guards, for the kids whose parents felt that was necessary.

She carefully looked around. No, he wasn't here.

A few minutes later the caretaker came out of the front entrance, down the steps, across the path to the entrance. He unlocked the gates and the bell rang moments later. Teachers and their pupils emerged, though there was no mad rush. The kids waited patiently with their tutors at the steps until there was a nod and a wave and the little ones scurried over to their adults.

One by one the number of kids in wait dwindled. Car engines fired and the street slowly emptied. Devereaux spotted her. A tiny little thing. Five years old, in a red-and-white uniform dress. She was slight and skinny. A bag of bones and must have been as light as a feather. Her silky black hair reached down to her waist. The teacher had her hand on the girl's shoulder and the two of them were searching. No luck, so the teacher moved on to the next child. Kept going until the girl was the only one remaining. Devereaux shimmied past the last few straggling adults and kids and headed over to the teacher.

'Mrs Vallance, I'm so sorry, but Mahmoud got held up.'

The teacher looked at her with a hint of suspicion, but despite the protocols here this wasn't Fort Knox, and as she looked around there was obviously no one else to pick little Tanya up. Why would she suspect anything untoward?

'Sorry, I haven't seen you here before. You are?'

'I'm Leia. I'm pretty sure I was added to the list recently. You can call Mrs Wilkins to check if you like? I'm happy to wait,' Devereaux checked her watch, 'though we're quite late already.'

Next, she proffered her phone but the teacher shook her head then looked out across the entrance again where it was clear there was no one else for the little girl.

'No, it's fine,' she said. 'Off you go, Tanya.'

Devereaux smiled then held out her hand to the girl who seemed unsure but took it nonetheless.

'Did you have a good day?' Devereaux asked as they walked out through the gates and toward the BMW.

Tanya nodded. 'I haven't seen you before.'

'I'm new here,' Devereaux said.

'Here?'

'At the school.'

'You're a teacher? But I thought you said...'

The girl trailed off, like she couldn't quite remember.

'I just started. I'll be taking your class next term.'

'Are you taking me home? Where's Mahmoud?'

'He's running late, that's all. You'll see him at home.'

The child looked a little puzzled, but didn't question it anymore and was soon tucking into the sweets Devereaux had brought with her. Were all kids this easy to confuse and manipulate? Or was it more that people were so unsuspecting of Devereaux's bright and breezy appearance?

They reached the car. Devereaux looked over her shoulder. The teachers had all headed back inside. One or two adults remained chatting by the gates.

A gleaming black Mercedes raced down the street.

Devereaux sighed inwardly. Change of plan.

'It looks like he made it after all,' Devereaux said, tugging lightly on Tanya's hand to pull her back toward the school.

Once again, the girl didn't question her as she chomped away. They reached the gates just as the car screeched to a halt and a man jumped out of the driver's seat. He took one look at Tanya and darted over, the expression on his face somewhere between worry and anger.

'Tanya,' he said, 'I'm so sorry, I had a problem with the car.'

Devereaux would have asked 'what problem', except she already knew.

Mahmoud took the girl's hand and she edged into his side. Both he and her looked to Devereaux.

'Not to worry,' Devereaux said. 'I was just about to drop her back at home myself.'

He didn't seem too pleased about that idea.

'Oh, how rude of me,' she said, before holding her hand out to him. 'I'm Mrs Devereaux. I just started working here.'

'She's going to be my teacher.'

He didn't look impressed but he took her hand anyway and she gave him a sultry smile as she gently held his hand.

'I'm Mahmoud. I work for–'

'I know. Tanya explained. It's really nice to meet you. I guess we'll be seeing a bit more of each other soon.'

He smiled back at her now. He'd read the signals just fine. And he was confident. She liked that.

'I guess we will,' he said.

She finally released his hand.

'What was your name again?' he asked.

'Leia. Perhaps...' She laughed coyly. 'If I had your number, you could call me next time you're going to be late.'

He seemed to weigh that one up for a moment. Devereaux took her phone out, only too happy to be eager. As she opened up the screen she discreetly took a photo of both Tanya and her chaperone.

'We can do that,' Mahmoud said. He read out his number. Devereaux typed it in and rang. His phone buzzed.

'Just testing,' she said, with a cheeky chuckle.

He smiled again. She put her phone away.

'It was nice to meet you, Leia,' he said. 'And thanks for helping with Tanya.'

'My pleasure.'

He held her eye a moment longer before he turned and took Tanya back to his car. Seconds later they were in the Mercedes and driving away.

Devereaux moved back to her car.

Then set off after them.

13

No mistakes. In her line of work that had long been a rigid ethos. Yet it was even more apt now, Devereaux felt. She had reason to be wary working for a man like Kyriakos Anastopoulos and his curious henchman Paulo. She'd seen what the two men were capable of, and really didn't want to lose any more fingers, or any other part of her body for that matter. Which was why she was being careful to make sure she had this right.

She sent the pictures to Paulo as she drove. Four pictures in total that she'd sent now. Mahmoud, Tanya, and her parents. Better safe than sorry, particularly as she was on the hunt here for a target whom, from the little Paulo had given her, had spent years living under aliases, even if he did only look like he was in his early thirties at most.

Hopefully she'd get Paulo's response in time. Otherwise she might just have to make the call herself.

The drive from the school to the gated residence was five miles, but as the route passed through the centre of the traffic-heavy city, the journey took nearly half an hour. At least the traffic made it all the more easy for Devereaux to blend as she remained within touching distance of the Mercedes.

Finally they arrived, and as she drove past the entrance gates, Mahmoud's car was just disappearing beyond. She kept going, then did a U-turn and pulled her car onto the verge at the side of the road. They were right on the edge of the city here. The road was lined on either side with exclusive residences, all blocked off from the street by high walls and trees. In front of her the city skyscrapers rose tall, but in every other direction there was little more than desert.

She turned the engine off though remained in the car. She scrolled through her phone as she waited. How long would it take for Paulo to respond? Of course, she had no idea what he was up to right now. Butchering another family somewhere? In a helicopter having taken another hostage for wine and olives with Kyri? Or was he sitting in the sun somewhere drinking an ice-cold beer?

The truth was, she was fascinated by Paulo. Even more so than Kyri. Whatever Kyri's story, which she did want to find out more of, she'd already decided he was most likely just another in a long line of men who believed their wealth and power made them a demigod. Old story. Devereaux was a bit bored of it to be truthful.

Paulo though... who was he? *What* was he? Because she'd seen that look in his eye. Had admired the way he moved when he'd attacked her, and she was damn sure the handiwork in that villa was down to him, too, rather than the old man.

Devereaux didn't know whether she hated him and wanted to cut his balls off and slit his throat, or whether she wanted to–

Her phone buzzed on her lap. She picked it up. Didn't even need to unlock the screen to see the extent of the short message she'd received in response.

An odd response, as far as she was concerned, but what did she know?

At least her work here would be quicker this way.

She put her phone down, slipped on the thin leather gloves – being careful of her bandage – then stepped out. The temperature had dropped a couple of degrees since she'd arrived at the school earlier. Night-time wasn't far off. Would she be out of this weird city by then?

She strolled up the cracked pavement, the grass on the verge was brown and wispy and in need of care and attention. For all the money here, and on this street in particular, pavements in residential areas were a notable deficiency it seemed. Nothing more than an afterthought. Perhaps that was because the car was king here. Why walk out of your house when you could have someone drive you? And so why bother with nice pavements and neat verges if no one is going to walk along them in the first place?

The street was deserted. Not a car or anyone in sight, all the residents who were home were safely holed up behind their outer walls and closed gates.

Devereaux reached the wall for the Wilkins' residence. Another quick look around, then she jumped up and grasped the top ledge and pulled her body up and over. She landed in a bush the other side and brushed the stone dust from the wall off her clothes before carrying on. Yes, this family were wealthy, yes, they were security conscious, but this wasn't the home of a mafia don or a drug kingpin. There were no patrols of armed guards here. Just a standard residential security system to cover the large estate, plus a few house staff, the most notable and likely dangerous of which she'd already met.

No one was in sight and she cautiously headed toward the house. One of the houses anyway, because off to her left, in the far corner of the plot, was a second building that could have been a mansion in its own right, but here was just a pool house. Or perhaps a garage. Or maybe both.

She didn't go that way, but toward the main building. Mahmoud's Mercedes was parked up on the circular driveway in front of the mansion. Two other pricey cars were there too. Tanya's parents were home? Or were those just spare cars for the weekend?

Devereaux kept on moving and soon reached the house. She didn't go to the front door but headed around the side. Found another entrance. A plain-looking door. She could hear water gently lapping in the near distance – a pool, she guessed – though the quiet noise suggested no one was using it right now. She tried the handle on the door. Locked. She could pick it easily enough. Instead, she kept moving, around to the back of the house. Yes, it was a pool. A pretty nice one too. Somewhere in between the one in Spain and the one in Cyprus, in terms of extravagance. The filters whirred away, water trickled. Peaceful.

No other sounds out here. No signs of anyone either.

She crouched as she passed under a window. Pulled up alongside some closed bi-fold doors. She peeked in. A lounge of some sort.

She jumped back when she spotted Tanya dashing across the open doorway at the far side of the room. She listened as carefully as she could. She didn't think anyone was in the room. Peeked again. Empty. She reached for the handle. Then spotted the patio doors further along the back of the house. One of them was ajar.

Devereaux quickly moved across the bi-folds and to the patio doors. The kitchen lay beyond. Spotless. No sign of whoever had cleared away the last meal, and no sign of anyone preparing the next meal yet.

She pulled the door open a little further then stepped inside. Cool air-conditioned air. Nice. Devereaux took a deep breath as she glanced around. She heard footsteps and giggling somewhere outside the room. Silently, she strode across the tiles on her toes and pulled up against the wall next to the arched doorway that led to a grand inner hall.

She could hear a TV now. Could hear Tanya talking. To herself and her toys, or to someone else?

Devereaux moved into the hall, one hand inside her jacket. She saw a flash of movement off to her left, beyond the next door. She went that way. A kid's playroom. A huge flat-screen TV on the wall was playing a kids' cartoon Devereaux didn't recognise but that was abundantly pink. Like a lot of other things in the playroom. Except Tanya was whizzing around with a green alien in one hand and a big plastic T-Rex in the other. A couple of growls and snarls later and it looked like the T-Rex had won out and was enjoying its dinner.

Cute. And not at all dainty. Devereaux realised she was smiling as she watched.

Then whipped around when she heard a shuffle behind her.

'You?' Mahmoud said.

His face was creased with suspicion. Just a few feet away Tanya carried on playing obliviously.

Devereaux grasped the door handle to the playroom and pulled the door shut. Then laughed. 'Oh my God, you're not going to believe this.'

One hand remained inside her jacket. Her fingers laced around the knife's handle. Her other gloved hand was down by her side.

'Tanya left her schoolbooks... and... well...'

She edged forward. The sultry look she knew men – and some women – loved so much snapped into position on her face. The confusion in Mahmoud's eyes was palpable. His eyes glanced down to her gloved hand.

'The truth is I really wanted to see you again.'

She reached forward. But he grabbed her hand and twisted her around and shoved her up against the wall. He pulled her wrist up into her back, pushed her shoulder to bursting point. He yanked her other hand out of her jacket. She left the knife there. For now. He pinned that hand to the wall.

'Who the hell are you?' he said, his face close to hers, his breath tickling her ear. His aftershave tickled her nose. It was nice. Not cheap. She vaguely recognised it.

Devereaux said nothing. She smiled.

He shoved her further into the wall, pushing so hard on her back it knocked the wind from her lungs.

'Who are you!'

'Please, you're hurting my arm!'

She sobbed. Let her arms go limp. Mahmoud's grip weakened a little as doubt likely wormed into his otherwise spot-on intuition.

His momentary lapse was enough. Devereaux snapped her arm free. Kicked back and dug her heel into Mahmoud's toe. She twisted and spun out of the hold and thundered a fist into his groin. He let go of her and stumbled back. She swiped at his legs as she launched forward and ended up on top of him on the floor, his arms pinned.

The knife was now in her hand.

'You silly boy,' she said. 'You thought I came for the girl?'

She tightened her grip on the knife and plunged it into the side of his neck.

'Her parents?'

She pushed harder and the blade sank several inches into his flesh. His eyes went wide in surprise and he gargled for breath. He bucked and writhed but there was nothing he could do.

'I came for you. Just you.' She shook her head. 'If only you'd realised that sooner...'

She pulled the knife free. Blood poured, and the panic and dismay in his eyes showed that he knew his life was over. Soon he was still.

Devereaux wiped the blade on his shirt to remove the blood, then sheathed the weapon once more. She looked behind her. The door remained closed. She could still hear the TV. Could still hear the girl playing.

She got up and moved to the door. Pushed her ear to the wood. Then used the butt of the knife grip to smash down onto the door handle. Three blows and the knob clanked to the floor.

Tanya's voice paused. She'd be panicking about the now locked door soon enough, but hopefully by the time someone opened it, the mess of Mahmoud would at least be covered up, if not cleaned up, and little Tanya wouldn't have to witness what had happened to her guardian.

Devereaux took out her phone, took a picture of the corpse by her feet, and sent it over to Paulo.

Job done. Time for her next country, and her next target.

14

COPENHAGEN, DENMARK

The upmarket bar-restaurant that Ryker found himself in could have been in virtually any big city in the world. A gleaming mirrored bar, a three-hundred-and-sixty-degree oval, sat centre stage in the space and included an over-the-top array of liquors and malts from all over the world, neatly arranged on glass shelves. Huge champagne bottles were dotted here and there. There were splashes of gold all over. The bartenders were smartly dressed in black and white and spent most of their time tossing chrome cocktail mixers about the place. Tables and booths surrounded the bar area, stretching out from it like an ocean around an island.

With a mix of drinkers and diners, the place was filled and bustling, though far from rowdy. The clientele here were mostly couples, a few groups of four or six. Everyone dressed to the nines for a Friday night out. Lawyers, accountants, corporate executives. And a healthy dusting of politicians given the bar's proximity to the Danish Parliament building all of two hundred yards away. There was money here, and lots of it.

Ryker sat back in his booth and sipped on his soda water,

keeping a close watch on the goings-on, but in particular on the couple seated directly across from him on two stools at the bar.

The man owned an apartment not far from here. Ryker had been lying in wait outside there for a couple of hours beforehand, and had followed the two of them on foot when they left the building. Looking around at the other customers, Ryker saw he wasn't exactly dressed for the occasion, in casual trousers and jumper, though at least everything he was wearing was dark which certainly helped him to blend, particularly sitting in the poorly lit corner as he was.

After a while the man excused himself from his female companion and wandered off toward the toilets.

Ryker got up from his seat and downed the rest of his drink as he headed across the floor to the bar. He grabbed a stool and moved it a couple of feet across so he was right next to the woman. He sat down and placed his empty glass on the bar though didn't bother to try to get the barman's attention straight away.

The woman paid him no attention at all. Ryker glanced at her. Smart red dress. Nails manicured and painted. Make-up understated but neat. She wore diamond stud earrings, a pearl necklace. A diamond bracelet.

'What the hell are you doing here?' she said without looking.

Ryker smiled. 'Good to see you, Penny.'

Ryker had walked away from his short-lived investigation into the circumstances of Grichenko's death. He saw little point in trailing around the Cotswolds when, for whatever reason, he had Kaspovich and whoever else on his back. So he'd moved his own goalposts. If he couldn't work from Grichenko's death, backward to the truth, he'd work from that night in Doha ten years ago, forward to the truth.

Aldern was dead. Did his death have anything to do with the botched assassination of Grichenko ten years ago? Ryker wouldn't rule that possibility out, but for now Aldern was a dead end. So Ryker would move on to each of the rest of the team from Qatar in turn; Kyle Elliott. Penny Diaz. Nadia Lange. Joey Weller. Ali Salman. He'd already realised some would be easier to track down than others.

Joey Weller had perhaps been the easiest. A classic tech geek, his whole career had been spent in offices and surveillance vans and even though he'd worked for the British intelligence services, he wasn't what anyone on the outside would typically think of as a spy. There were no secret identities, no aliases, no months or years on end spent working undercover. He had been the easiest to find, but also perhaps the least relevant to Ryker. He'd been in the van the whole time during that night. Along with Lange. Whatever had gone wrong in Qatar had gone wrong inside the palace, and so for now the two of them were bottom of Ryker's list.

Then there was Ali Salman. The ex-employee of the Qatari government. Ex-employee because that night in Doha he'd escaped with the rest of them on the boat to Oman, and he'd left behind his old life for good. He'd got a new life, a new identity, and one which Ryker had had no part in setting up, which meant extra effort on Ryker's part in order to find him now.

And so it came down to the final two. Kyle Elliott and Penny Diaz. He was aware both had remained working for MI6 after the Doha mission, though Ryker had never had any further operations with either. But their similarities to Ryker – their career choices, their outlooks on life – meant they were the easiest to track down. He thought like them. He lived like them.

From a purely logistical standpoint, it was Diaz who came

out on top. She was simply easier to get to. Ryker had been in England. He tracked Diaz's location to Copenhagen. A few hours on a ferry later and he was in the city, in a bar, sitting next to her.

'I asked you what are you doing here?'

Her tone was hard and cold. She still wasn't looking at him.

Ryker glanced around the room.

'You're working alone tonight?' he asked.

She set her gaze on him for the first time. Her look was hard. She was angry but trying her best to keep it bottled.

'I'm not working at all,' she said.

'Is that right? So who's your friend?'

She shook her head in disgust. 'Carl, I know you.'

'I'm not Carl anymore.'

Carl Logan had been his identity back then in Doha. Did she really not know he was now James Ryker, or was the drop of his old name a ploy?

'James Ryker,' he said. 'You know how it is.'

'My point was, I know you already know the answer to your previous question.'

'Fair point. Martin is a government minister here in Copenhagen. Defence, isn't it?'

'There you go. So why did you bother to ask?'

'So what's the play?'

She dug her nails into the bar top. She was not happy with this reunion in any way, shape, or form. 'He's my boyfriend. We've been together for months. There is no play.'

Ryker held his hands up. 'Fair enough. I was just interested, that's all.'

'No you weren't. So I'll ask again, why are you here?'

More exasperated now.

'Why do you think? Have you been watching the news?'

She sighed.

'I just want to ask you a few questions,' he said.

'Penny? Is everything okay?'

She nearly jumped out of her skin at her boyfriend's question. He put his hand on her shoulder. Of course, Ryker had seen him approaching, but wanted to gauge her reaction when she was caught off guard. Why? Because he knew spies and he knew every one of them played games, even when they were insistent that they didn't. He liked Penny. They'd worked well together. But that didn't mean he trusted her. Not then, not now.

'Martin? This is–'

'James,' Ryker said, holding his hand out. 'James Ryker. An old friend from–'

'Oxford,' Diaz butted in.

Interesting, that she'd chosen a real location from her past.

'You were at university together?' Martin asked.

'No,' Ryker said. 'I didn't go to university. We just shared mutual friends.'

'And you're here in Copenhagen?' Martin said, still on his feet, looking a little bemused, and perhaps a little wary now. 'What a coincidence.'

'Isn't it?' Ryker said.

'You're on your own?'

'Yeah.'

'Why don't you get us another drink,' Diaz said to Martin, giving his arm an affectionate squeeze at the same time. 'James, did you want one?'

She shook her head at him, ever so slightly.

'Yeah,' Ryker said, picking up his glass. 'Seems I'm all out. Gin and tonic, please.'

Martin turned back to the bar to try and get the attention of the barman who was busy smashing mint leaves in the bottom of a glass with a rolling pin. Diaz turned back to Ryker. Not happy.

'Please,' she mouthed.

Ryker shrugged.

'What are you doing?' she whispered.

Ryker didn't answer. Martin made the order and sat back down and Diaz shuffled back a little so they were in a narrow triangle.

'So, James, what brought you to Copenhagen?'

His English was smooth, the foreign accent noticeable but only just.

'Business,' Ryker said.

'Yeah? What business are you into?'

'Consulting.'

'Consulting? To whom?'

'Whoever needs it.'

Martin looked a little put out by the lacklustre responses, as though he didn't know where else to take the conversation. The barman delivered the drinks. Martin took a sip from his beer. Ryker took a sip from his G & T. Diaz hadn't touched whatever the colourful concoction was that she was having.

Ryker smiled. 'When you were in the toilet, I was asking Penny if she could remember when we last saw each other.'

'Oh, and?'

'Ten years ago,' Ryker said.

'In Oxford,' Penny interjected, as though worried that perhaps Ryker was about to say Doha.

'Oxford?' Martin said, a questioning look on his face. 'Ten years ago?'

She graduated from university nearly twenty years ago.

'It was a reunion,' Ryker said. 'Anyway, it was a big party. At this big old... basically a palace. Do you remember?'

'Kind of,' Penny said. 'Though it wasn't that big. Hardly a palace.'

'That's how I remembered it.'

'You were invited to a reunion party?' Martin said to Ryker, just a hint of suspicion now. 'Even though you weren't from the university?'

Ryker shrugged. 'We shared close friends. Like Pavel. You remember Pavel?'

Penny shook her head. 'Not really.'

Ryker frowned. 'Strange. I do. He was hosting the party that night. You really don't remember? Anyway, I always wondered what happened to Pavel that night.'

'How do you mean?' Martin said. He looked not just confused now, but a little annoyed, too, as he took a large drag of his beer. Perhaps because he could tell his girlfriend was becoming more and more uncomfortable, even if he had no idea why.

'It was just strange,' Ryker said. 'I barely saw Pavel that night. He just disappeared off somewhere. In fact...' Ryker scratched his head, '...I'm sure Penny was one of the last people to see him.'

'He disappeared?' Peter said. 'As in... vanished?'

Ryker shrugged. 'Who knows? We all left Oxford after the party, and I guess we've just lost touch.'

'Sounds like a strange party.'

'Very strange,' Ryker said. 'Thinking back on it now, at least. Though I did come across Pavel again recently.'

Ryker took another sip from his drink.

Diaz leaned over to Martin and put her hand on his leg. 'Do you think you could get me a glass of water.'

Martin frowned but was soon facing the bar again. Diaz glared at Ryker. She mouthed something to him. Something along the lines of 'fuck off'.

Ryker nodded. He downed his drink.

'Tomorrow,' he said.

He passed her a slip of paper across the bar. She whipped it out of sight and stuffed it into her clutch bag. A slick move. But when Ryker flicked his gaze to the bar he caught Martin's eye in the mirror. He was glaring. Had he seen?

Ryker got up from his stool. Both Martin and Diaz turned to him.

'It was nice to see you,' he said to Diaz – she beamed a smile now, though it was undoubtedly forced. 'And nice to meet you, Martin.'

'And you,' he said.

Ryker headed for the exit.

15

Frost covered the expanses of grass in Fælledparken the next morning when Ryker arrived at the prearranged spot. At a little before 9am he was more than half an hour early, but he didn't mind waiting in the cold. At least the sky was bright and cloudless. The bench he found was in the sun and the frost had already melted from the wooden slats. Ryker used a glove to wipe away the damp then took a seat and looked out across the park. A small lake was in the near distance, a thin layer of ice on top which children were in the process of breaking with sticks and stones. Dog walkers were out and about, people strolled, while others strode, taking a shortcut through the park on their way to work. It wasn't exactly bustling, but there were plenty of people about. Quiet enough for privacy, not so quiet as to put Ryker, or his guest, in any great danger.

By the time nine thirty came he was doing his best to keep his shivering at bay. By quarter to ten he wasn't just cold but agitated. He spotted a man and a woman a hundred yards away who were sauntering along. They were casually dressed, walking side by side, heads down, nothing particularly suspicious about them, except Ryker was sure he'd seen the same two twenty minutes or so ago in pretty much the same spot.

They took a bench. Ryker kept his eyes on them.

Ten o'clock slowly came and went. Ryker would give her until ten thirty. Then he'd set off on the warpath. There was only one reason for Diaz to not show up here today, and that was if she was hiding something.

Ryker ground his teeth as he continued to look around, his focus in particular on the nearby couple who remained on their backsides.

Footsteps behind him. Ryker turned.

'Sorry I'm late,' Diaz said.

She didn't sound it.

She sat down. Hands in the pockets of her long coat, her head huddled down into a scarf. She looked quite different today, make-up free and with her hair loose.

'Thanks for trying to ruin my night,' she said.

Ryker didn't say anything to that.

'That was really shitty of you, just turning up like that. Whether I'm working here or not.'

'So which is it?'

She didn't answer.

'Are those two with you?' Ryker asked, indicating with his head over to the other couple.

Diaz looked over.

'So what if they are.'

Not the answer Ryker had expected. A clever answer really. If they were with her, it blew away any facade that she was in Copenhagen for love, and it made clear to Ryker that he wasn't welcome here, that she didn't trust him, and that if he tried anything funny she had backup. Even if they were just two randoms, her response was enough to sow doubt in Ryker's mind – offer a little extra protection to her.

Of course, there was another possibility. That the two were spying, but that they didn't work with Diaz...

'What do you want from me?' Diaz asked.

'The truth.'

Silence.

'Let's get one thing clear,' Ryker said. 'I couldn't care less why you're in Denmark. Why your new boyfriend is a wealthy politician. What I do care about is what happened in Doha ten years ago.'

Diaz sighed. She was looking straight ahead to the water.

'Did you know Grichenko was still alive?' Ryker asked.

'No. And that's the truth.'

'Has anyone else contacted you about this?'

'No.'

'No one? Not even your bosses?'

She glared at him. 'James... that name suits you by the way, you know I'm not going to suddenly start opening up to you about my work. So don't ask me questions that you know you won't get a straight answer to. Ask me about the past, fine, but I can't and won't talk to you about my life now.'

'Okay, so have you talked to any of the rest of the crew from that night?'

'I wouldn't even know where to start.'

Ryker didn't believe that, but he let it go. He stared at her, could see she remained seriously uncomfortable.

She tutted. 'I'm the same as you here. I don't know what happened. I don't know why he was still alive, how he got a new life in England, who killed him there, or why. Come on, James, I honestly don't know what your role is these days, who you're working for, but I know you're experienced in this world.

Grichenko was an assignment. We carried out that assignment as we were asked to do, then we all moved on. That's how it worked then, and how it still works now. I know after all this time it looks like we didn't succeed in that operation after all, but you know what? I'm not sure I even care. My life is here, now, not in Qatar ten years ago with you.'

'I'm working alone,' Ryker said. 'As in, I don't work for anyone anymore.'

She looked a little taken aback by that. Had she not known? Had she not spent all night and early morning trying to figure out everything she could about where he'd been and what he'd done the last ten years?

'Then why on earth are you here?' she asked.

'Because we were duped, and I want to know why.'

She shook her head. 'Talk about opening a can of worms. What does it even matter?'

'Just tell me what happened that night. Walk me through what you saw, what you did.'

'You're asking me to debrief something we did ten years ago?'

'Well, we never really bothered at the time, did we? Instead, we all gave ourselves a pat on the back and moved on.'

'Because it didn't matter to us then. So why should it now? We completed the mission in our eyes, in our bosses' eyes, and we headed away. Until a few days ago I'm not even sure how many years it was since I last thought about that night.'

'I don't believe you. That night was a big deal to us all. Just talk to me. That's all I'm asking.'

She closed her eyes for a moment then sighed.

'Take it from when me and Elliott arrived,' Ryker said.

Everything up to that point had been on track.

'Me and Salman were inside,' she said. 'We had eyes on Alpha.'

'I remember. You were upstairs. Me and Elliott were on our way to join you.'

'Then Aldern came on to say something was wrong. Or something like that. I don't remember his exact words.'

Ryker did.

'You went to check on him,' she said.

'Leaving you, Salman and Elliott inside.'

'Then the comms went down.'

'Aldern's, then mine.'

She frowned. 'No, everyone's.'

'Everyone's?'

'Yeah. But not all at once. Aldern first, then yours when you went after him. Then Elliott. Then me and Salman.'

How had Ryker not known that before? Other than because he'd never asked the question specifically.

'Over how long?'

'Two, three minutes.'

'So Aldern's went down. Then I went outside to check on him–'

'And we lost you not long after that.'

'The last thing I heard was that Alpha was on the move.'

Diaz nodded. 'There was a group with him. All three of us followed as we didn't know if they'd split up, or even what they were up to.'

'You were all together?'

'No. Elliott was up front, on his own. Me and Salman were further behind.'

'And Elliott's comms went next?'

'Then mine and Salman's together.'

Ryker thought. 'So there was a signal blocker,' Ryker said. 'Aldern went dark in the northern part of the grounds. Then me when I went out there to find him. The three of you as you followed Alpha inside, but in the same direction, to the northern end of the palace.'

Diaz screwed her face like something he'd said made no sense. 'If someone had a signal blocker why was it only set up over part of the property?'

Fair point. 'To flummox us,' Ryker said. 'If we'd been dark from the get-go we would have known something was wrong. We would have aborted. Or we would have adapted sooner. We walked into a trap.'

Diaz's silence seemed like agreement.

'So what next?' Ryker said. 'You're following Alpha.'

'The group split up. Some went in the direction of the toilets. Elliott went with them. Others headed to the conference rooms and ended up in one of them. Sapphire, I think it was called.'

'How many?'

She thought about that for a moment. Necessary, or was she crafting a lie? 'Four of them, including Alpha. Salman and I stayed outside. That was when the first gunshot was fired.'

'From where?'

'From back near the toilets. We were all dark by that point so whether it was Elliott I don't know.'

'And you and Salman?'

'We stormed that room. But they were waiting for us. Seven, eight men. No Alpha. It was a firefight immediately. Salman lobbed a grenade. There was smoke everywhere. We backtracked before we were killed.'

'Back into the corridor?'

'Where Elliott raced up to us, saying he'd seen Alpha leaving. All three of us gave chase. We reached the fire exit stairwell. Me and Elliott headed down after him, but Salman said he'd go the other way to intercept at the bottom.'

'What other way?'

Diaz shrugged. 'I don't remember. Me and Elliott raced

down the stairs, we shot and killed two grunts on the way down. Then there was another explosion as we reached the bottom. We were both on the ground. Dust, grit, smoke everywhere. Elliott pulled me up and I was out of it, dazed. Once the fog had cleared we rushed outside, and that was when we literally ran into Salman and Aldern.'

'They were together?'

'Yeah.'

'How?'

'I've no idea. Salman said the job was done. Alpha was down. So we scarpered.'

'Salman said that?'

'Yeah.'

'Not Aldern?'

Diaz paused for a moment. 'Definitely Salman.'

'But neither said who'd actually killed Alpha?'

She shook her head. 'Why would I ask, in that moment?'

'We were betrayed, Penny,' Ryker said. 'Someone lied that night.'

'I've told you what I know. What I can remember.'

He chewed on that for a few moments. Did he believe her? Not fully. But he had her explanation. He'd see how it compared.

'Did you know Aldern is dead?' Ryker asked.

The shock on her face suggested no. That, or she was a good actor.

Hell, he knew that was true.

'When?' she asked.

'I don't know much about it.'

'But you think it's linked?'

He shrugged. 'If I were you, I'd watch my back.'

'I always do,' Diaz said.

Ryker got up from the bench. 'It was nice to see you,' he said. 'I mean that.'

'Please don't ever come to me again. Next time I won't be so amenable.'

Ryker nodded. She stayed in place as Ryker turned and headed off. Across the other side of the park, the young couple were arm in arm as they strolled away into the distance.

16

FRANKFURT, GERMANY

The clouds that hung above the skyscrapers of Frankfurt's financial district were thick and dark and cast the city below in bleakness. Though at least the temperature in Germany was a few degrees warmer than the frostiness of Copenhagen.

Ultimately, Ryker had come away from the Danish capital with little of solid use. He had a lengthy and memory-jogging account from Penny Diaz of the events in Doha years ago, but nothing that explained how and why Grichenko had escaped assassination back then, or why he was now dead. He wasn't sure he believed every aspect of the account she'd given him, and he'd be straight back to Copenhagen if he got a sniff that she'd tried to dupe him in any way.

For now, it was on to the next. Joey Weller may have been perhaps the least relevant, but he was by far the closest. The relatively short hop from Copenhagen to Frankfurt had taken Ryker only a few hours, but on arrival he had decided to rest up for a night in a basic hotel not far from the financial district. The downtime had given him plenty of opportunity for further research. He'd still been unable to get hold of full, official details of Grichenko's demise. The British press was reporting few concrete facts in relation to the cause of death and no specifics of persons of interest, but plenty of speculation about clandestine operations and rogue spies and the like. Very probably some truths were buried in those sensationalist accounts, whether the journalists knew it or not, but so far there was frustratingly little for Ryker to use.

Interestingly, though, there remained nothing in the press about himself being wanted in connection with the murders. Which again led Ryker to question if Kaspovich had simply been playing Ryker, or was there more to his deceit?

Ryker finished his coffee and threw the paper cup into a bin as he strode along. Businessmen and women in smart suits and coats strolled by, most with either phones or take-out cups in their hands. Germany's financial hub was a busy and supremely neat and clean area, even if it all felt just a little bit like most financial centres in most big cities across the continent and beyond.

He headed on through the revolving doors to 108 Neumarktplatz and over to the security booth where three suited guards were seated.

'*Guten Tag*,' Ryker said as he approached. 'I'm here to see Mr Weller at Anderson Associates,' he continued in German.

The guard he spoke to didn't say a word. His face remained stern and grumpy as he typed on his keyboard and stared at his screen.

'Your name?'

'James Ryker.'

A few moments later and Ryker was handed a lanyard with a visitor badge in a little plastic wallet.

'Through the gates,' the guard said. 'Reception is on the eighth floor.'

Ryker thanked him and moved over to the electronic glass

security gates. He glanced back to the guard who nodded. There was a click and the gates slid open. Ryker headed on through and to the elevator bank where a crowd of workers was steadily building and awaiting one of the six elevators.

Far from the most strict security Ryker had seen, though he guessed in a building that housed some fifteen different companies there wasn't much more they could do other than to provide basic control over who came into the building, and then rely on the companies themselves to keep their own spaces secure.

He eventually squeezed into a lift with six others. Floor eight was the second stop and Ryker squeezed back out and followed the arrows to a plush and modern reception area. Grey and black and white everywhere. Minimalist artwork, sculptures. A glass coffee table was covered with various financial journals.

He walked up to the reception desk. Two female receptionists there. Much more smiley than downstairs.

'I'm here to see Joey Weller,' Ryker said.

He explained who he was and the receptionist made a call and told Ryker to take a seat. He did. Behind and off to the side of the reception area was a security-locked door. A basic magnetic lock by the looks of it, simply needing a key card to open. There was another similar door off to his left. Two exits from the main office space and to the central elevator bank, the office likely wrapping around the central shaft like flesh on a bone.

After a few moments of waiting, the door behind the reception desk opened and a middle-aged lady in a navy skirt suit strode out and toward Ryker.

'Mr Ryker?'

He got to his feet.

'I'm Karin Scholtz, Mr Weller's assistant,' she said. She came to a stop next to him. 'I'm so sorry but Mr Weller isn't available right now. Perhaps I could help you?'

'Isn't available or isn't here?' Ryker said.

She looked a little put out by the question. 'Not here or available unfortunately,' she said. 'We could schedule a meeting for another time, if you like. And if you let me know what it's to do with?'

'I think if you could give him a quick call and give him my name, he might just make himself available now.'

She frowned. 'He's very busy. Perhaps I, or someone else on the team, could help you instead?'

'I really don't think so.'

Behind the reception desk the door opened again as a man and woman casually headed out.

'Are you sure he isn't in?' Ryker asked. 'I did see him come up earlier.'

She obviously didn't like the insinuation behind that at all, judging by the look she gave him.

'I already said–'

Ryker didn't listen to the rest. Instead, he brushed past her and strode to the door as another young man stepped through, and caught it just before it locked shut.

'Mr Ryker, you can't do that!'

He didn't heed the warning and carried on and found himself in an open-plan space. He paused a beat to look around. About fifty heads here. A few private offices were dotted around the outer edge of the floor, along with the entrance to a corridor in the far left corner.

'Please...'

Scholtz was right next to him.

'Where's his office?' Ryker said as he turned to her.

'If you don't come back this way I'm going to call security.'

No need. Ryker spotted the door. He could see the nameplate. Three offices along. Heads were turned his way as Ryker marched over there. He pushed open the door.

The office was empty. But the laptop on the desk hummed away. The sneak was here all right.

Ryker moved out. Went toward the corridor. Scholtz was no longer following. Most likely she was at reception asking them to call security. Ryker headed along the corridor, glancing into each of the meeting rooms he passed. No sign of Weller. He reached a stairwell and pushed open the door and moved to the stairs. He glanced over the railing and down. He couldn't see anyone on the bare concrete stairs, but he could hear someone. Hard soles on the hard stairs. Three or four storeys down.

Ryker set off at pace. He took the steps two at a time, moving fast, but also keeping his feet light. He first saw Weller when he was just past floor three. Had him in his sights less than a storey later.

'Weller!' Ryker shouted.

Weller didn't look around. Not until they were on the landing for the first floor, when Ryker was close enough to reach out and grab him by the scruff of his neck. He pushed him up against the wall.

'Please! Please!' Weller squealed as he cowered.

'What the hell is wrong with you!' Ryker said before he let go and Weller slumped a little.

A realisation seemed to spread across Weller's face. What had he thought? That Ryker was there to assassinate him?

Ryker put his hands on his hips and took a step back. Weller was panting, out of breath. His cheeks were red, though Ryker thought that might have been more from embarrassment than exertion.

'I'm sorry. I didn't know... I didn't know what to think.'

Ryker shook his head. 'If I wanted to hurt you I probably wouldn't just rock up to your workplace.'

'You would say that, wouldn't you? Except I'm well aware of your handiwork, don't forget.'

Ryker decided not to question that.

'Shall we go back up?' he said.

Just then the stairwell door banged open and two security guards burst into view. Ryker spun around.

'You!' the more grumpy of the two said. The same one who'd given Ryker his badge minutes before.

Ryker got ready for the inevitable. He hadn't expected this morning to go like this, but so be it. He'd tackle the two guards, then drag Weller out of there and somewhere quiet.

Ryker clenched his fists. Took a half step forward...

Weller jumped in front of him.

'It's okay. It's okay,' he said, waving his arms at the guards. 'Just a mistake. He's with me. It's fine.'

The guards paused. As did Ryker. They looked dubious. Perhaps they'd quite fancied a ruckus to brighten up their day.

'He's with me,' Weller said again. 'It was just a misunderstanding, okay? We'll go back up to my office.'

The guards exchanged a look then one of them said something into his handheld radio that Ryker couldn't quite hear.

Seconds later they turned away and grumbled to each other as they headed back to their positions.

Weller turned to Ryker. He still looked like he might piss his pants any second. Was he really that scared of Ryker? Why?

'Why don't we start again?' Ryker said.

Weller nodded. 'Yeah. Perhaps we should.'

'It's good to see you, Joey.'

He didn't get a response to that.

'You lead the way,' Ryker said. 'Office, or we could go–'

'Come up to my office,' Weller said. 'The more people I know are around us, the better, as far as I'm concerned.'

Ryker smiled. 'After you.'

17

'Well, look at you,' Ryker said as he sat back in the comfy leather chair in front of Weller's clutter-free desk in an office that was modern and shiny. 'You're doing all right for yourself.' He glanced beyond Weller's shoulder. 'Not a bad view either.'

'What did you expect? That I'd still be stuck in a comms van in some shithole country?'

'You're doing yourself a disservice.'

'Not anymore I'm not.'

There was a knock on the door and Scholtz came in, tray in hand, a cafetière and two dainty mugs on top. Her face was screwed with suspicion still.

'Thank you,' both Weller and Ryker said as she put it down on the desk.

'What do you want me to do about–'

'Just tell them I'll be late,' Weller said, waving her away.

She left the room without another word.

'Am I interrupting something?' Ryker said.

'You know damn well you are.'

Ryker said nothing to that. He poured himself and Weller a coffee. Added a couple of sugars to his. He sat back and stared across to his old colleague. Weller had been a young man in Doha. Early twenties. Clever but naive. He'd aged and rounded out a lot over the last ten years. The few flecks of grey in his designer stubble suggested he probably dyed the thinning but uniformly dark hair he had on top. He also wore glasses. Neat, designer. A fashion statement, Ryker felt. Together with his nice suit he looked like he'd been born in a corporate office. A far cry from the scruffy jeans and colourful T-shirts Ryker had been more used to seeing him in.

'What do you want from me?' Weller asked.

'So when did you stop working for your country?' Ryker said. Weller's annoyance at Ryker ignoring his question was obvious. 'Or are you–'

'No, I'm not still *spying* for anyone. I left that life more than eight years ago. I left it for good and I've never looked back since. Not until you showed up today.'

Ryker looked around the sleek office. There were two photo frames on the bookshelf off to his right. One showed Weller with a striking lady of South East Asian origin, the other showed two cute young kids. Weller was a family man now. This was certainly a more sensible job for such a man.

'So how did you end up here?' Ryker asked.

Weller sighed before he spoke. 'The easiest way to explain it, is that back in the day I was always seen as the tech guy. An add-on. Essential, yes, but not the main ingredient. But tech wasn't really my forte, it was just what they needed.'

'So what is your forte?'

'I started life as a programmer, but my real passion, then and now, has always been numbers and data. I...' He paused and then sighed again. Ryker wasn't sure why. 'I spotted a gap in the market for big data exploration. Techniques that could be used to help all sorts of financial institutions, from investment companies deciding which stocks to buy, to insurance companies trying to work out premiums, to banks trying to determine which businesses and people to loan money to and under what terms. I... Sorry, what?'

'Nothing. But you lost me after about the fifth word. So you sell data analysis products for big bucks, right?'

'We create products, license them, sometimes sell them. We develop software, we analyse data for others. And yes, for big bucks.'

'Which explains the nice office. And probably a salary quite a few times higher than tech guy.'

'A *lot* higher, yes.'

Ryker rolled his eyes. He took a sip of the sweet and thick coffee. Pretty good.

'What?' Weller said. For the first time he was looking more confident and up for a fight. A little bit riled by Ryker's tone. That was better than him being in his shell.

'Sorry?'

'The look on your face,' Weller said. 'Like I've done something wrong in getting here. You think I sold out, is that it?'

Ryker shrugged. 'Not my place to judge.'

'Damn right it isn't. I gave years to the cause. More than most people in this world ever will.'

'The cause?'

'You know what I mean. The things we used to do. The people we hurt and were killed because of us. Families torn apart. And for what? Us versus them? Good versus evil?'

Ryker held his tongue.

'No? You have nothing to say about that? How many people have *you* killed?'

Still nothing.

'You don't know? It's that high? Or you just can't bring yourself to say it out loud. Or is it that you don't even care?'

'I know.'

'And you're happy with that? You're happy about the things you've done in your life? Those families who lost a father, mother, brother, sister, whatever? All because someone behind a desk somewhere decided they were bad. No trial. No judge or jury. Just a bullet in the head, or a syringe in the arm or a rope around their neck. You feel justified?'

Ryker clenched his teeth.

'That's it, isn't it? You decided in your own mind that everyone you killed was bad. They deserved it somehow. That's fine. You're a moral crusader. You didn't set out to hurt people randomly, you feel justified because someone gave you the order. That makes it okay to you. Well, it didn't make it okay to me. *That's* why I left. Not because I wanted more cash and a nicer car.'

'I left too,' Ryker said.

That seemed to throw Weller a little.

'I don't work for anyone anymore. And I won't ever again. I'm here on my own, for myself.'

Weller sat back in his seat and sighed. 'You know what? That just makes it all the more sad. Even after leaving them behind, you won't, or can't move on.'

'You heard about Grichenko?' Ryker said. He wanted to change the subject. Weller's attack had riled him more than he cared to admit.

'I saw it on the news,' Weller replied, shuffling a little uncomfortably, though Ryker hoped the moment of confidence and one-upmanship from Weller would at least make him more open now.

'Who else has spoken to you already?' Ryker asked.

Weller pinched his eyes. 'No one has. Why would you think that?'

'Oh, I don't know. Perhaps because of the way you tried to run out of here when I showed up to talk to you about it. Like you were prepped, or like you couldn't be seen to go against–'

'That's got nothing–'

'Somebody threaten you?'

'No!'

'Somebody tell you not to talk to–'

'Ryker, you're barking up the wrong tree.'

'You're sure about that?'

'Yes!'

'If you lie to me...'

'I'm not that stupid. I'm not like you. I just want to mind my own business.'

Ryker took a few moments to finish off his coffee as he thought. Did he believe Weller? The man was a different prospect to Diaz, that was for sure. He certainly wouldn't trust him one hundred per cent – it wouldn't have needed much pressure from another party to get him to lie about everything now.

'I want you to talk me through what happened in Doha,' Ryker said.

Weller scoffed and shook his head. 'Why? Why do you even care?'

'I just do. Then I'll be gone. And if you tell me the truth, everything you know and can remember, you won't see me again.'

Weller nodded. 'I think that would be best for both of us. But what do you want to know? You do realise I never left the van that night?'

'I know. So walk me through what happened. As you saw it.'

He sighed. 'I imagine this could be a short story.'

'That depends. You were in the van. Listening to the audio. Watching Lange's drone feed, and watching our markers on the map. Take it from when me and Elliott reached the palace. Everything was working as expected up to then, right?'

'Right. At that point I could see each of your markers, I could hear you all too.'

'And where were we?'

He looked a little confused. 'How do you mean?'

'Explain where we were, according to what you could see.'

'I don't have a photographic memory.'

'I'm surprised.'

'Very funny.'

'Just try.'

A pause, then, 'You and Elliott were moving inward, toward Salman and Diaz. Aldern was out with the cars.'

'Then?'

'Then Aldern began to move. He said... I don't remember his words, but he was going to check on something.'

'He was already moving when he said that? Or did he say that then begin to move?'

Weller scrunched his face. 'Does it matter which?'

'It might do.'

'I honestly can't remember. Both happened within seconds. He headed off... north it would have been. There was a cluster of trees there, in the gardens.'

'Which is where I went. Looking for him.'

Weller nodded. 'Aldern's comms went down. His marker too. Though... definitely his comms first.'

'You're sure?'

Weller looked up to the corner of the room as though searching there for the answer. 'Pretty sure, yeah. Comms first. By that point he was in the trees, I think. Then his marker went.'

'Was that the same for me?'

Weller scratched his head. 'I really don't know. Me and Lange were fighting to figure out what was going on. Starting and restarting everything we had, checking and double-checking, but it was like a cascade. Comms, markers, Aldern, you, then...' He trailed off.

'Then what?'

'I can't remember exactly about the other three. Whether they were at the same time or not.'

'Were they still together when they went dark?'

He shook his head. 'I'm sorry, I just don't know.'

'The black spot was in the north of the grounds,' Ryker said. 'I'm pretty sure we all went down because of our positioning. What kind of jammer could do that? Where would it have been located physically?'

Weller sighed. 'You're talking about tech from ten years ago, operated by a party we haven't identified. Even if I gave you some options it would be meaningless unless you had more information.'

'Give me some options anyway. Was it someone on site? Could it have been remote? Another man in a van? A team hundreds of miles away?'

'Most likely on site.' He held his hands up. 'But I'm just telling you most likely. The others options you said are *possible*. Of course, you could have a drone nearby operated by a crew miles away. It's theoretically possible to use satellites to block radio and other signals, but why would someone have gone to all that trouble? A simple physical jammer on sight is the most obvious explanation.'

'Why didn't our equipment pick it up?' Ryker said. He realised after he'd spoken that his words were a little accusatory. 'What I mean is, didn't the gizmos you and Lange were using sweep for countermeasures?'

'Yes, and no. We tried. We didn't see anything untoward, but clearly we were wrong.'

'Wrong, or lying.'

'I'm not lying to you!'

'No, but someone is. And you can be damn sure I'll find out who.'

Weller practically quivered at Ryker's words.

18

Ryker didn't stay in Weller's office much longer, and after leaving the building he set off on the half-mile walk back to his hotel. Nothing Weller had said contradicted Diaz's version of events, but then Weller hadn't really given much. He'd been on the outside, looking in, and had a pretty decent excuse for not knowing what had gone wrong, and now claiming ignorance to the whole thing.

Yes, it was all a little too convenient that he was relying on his remote role, the confusion of the moment, and the ten years since to not be able to recall the sequence of events clearly. Weller was certainly intelligent, but did he have the gall to lie to Ryker's face?

The trip to Frankfurt wasn't a waste exactly, but it had been frustrating so far. A short rest, then on to the next.

He ducked into a coffee shop and joined the short queue inside. He looked to the street outside as he waited his turn. A woman moving past the windows caught his eye. He wasn't sure why at first. She was shortish and wearing a long thick coat, grey scarf, black bobble hat. He could barely see any of her face, and her smart and dark winter gear matched a huge chunk of the people around him in the financial district, and yet...

'Can I help you?' the young barista asked.

Ryker turned and ordered a cold drink. He'd had enough coffee this morning already and wanted to quench his thirst. He took a pastry, too, then headed outside. He looked right. The direction the woman had gone in. No sign of her now. At least no obvious sign of her among everyone else.

He carried on his way, his eyes working a little more keenly now than before.

After a couple of turns he was sure he spotted her again. Behind him now. About twenty yards away. Hands in pockets, head down, trying to blend.

Ryker slowed his pace as he walked along to the next junction. Then when he was five yards away he suddenly sped up, not far from a jog, and took a sharp right onto the next street. Once around the corner he abruptly came to a stop and pulled up against the wall. If this woman was intent on following him, she'd most likely be hurrying now, too, to get to the corner before Ryker turned again.

He waited. And waited.

No sign of her. He edged right up to the corner. Passers-by eyed him oddly. He peeked around.

There she was. Rushing forward. Straight into him. He reached out and grabbed her and pushed her up against the wall. Her hat fell off her head, revealing wavy, dyed-red hair that framed a face he knew but hadn't seen in an age. She squirmed for a second until their eyes met and Ryker let go.

'Hello, Nadia,' he said.

~

Ryker's hotel room was cramped for one, it was even pokier with two of them. Ryker was propped on the edge of the single bed. Nadia Lange was in the chair by the window next to which was the tiniest of tables. They were all of three feet apart.

Ryker still wasn't sure he'd made the right choice inviting her back here rather than staying somewhere outside and neutral.

'I'm guessing you came here for the same reason I did,' Ryker said.

'Weller?'

He nodded.

'That's how I found you,' she said. 'I was outside his office waiting. I was going to approach him when he came out.'

'I decided not to wait.'

'I noticed.'

Had he initially passed her when he'd entered the office building? If so, she hadn't registered at all at that point. He was disappointed in himself for that. He should have been more on guard.

'So you followed me instead?' he asked.

'There was nothing sinister about it.'

'You weren't very good at it.'

She laughed. 'Perhaps you could teach me some tricks.'

'You came here to speak to Weller? About Grichenko?'

'Yeah. Though I'm kind of glad I found you instead.'

She smiled at him now. He held her stare for a moment. The dark make-up around her eyes added a devilish intensity to her look. In a good way.

'You're still working for The Man?' Ryker asked.

She nodded.

'You're working right now?'

'I'm not going to pretend otherwise,' she said, looking down.

'What are your orders?'

'To find out who killed Grichenko and why. Which I'm thinking is what you're doing too.'

'It is. Except I'm doing it for me.'

'I figured. I knew you'd left. I heard about your new identity, all that.'

All that? How much did she know? And how had she heard exactly?

'So you'll be reporting this conversation?' Ryker asked.

She caught his eye again. 'That depends.'

'On what?'

'On what I get out of it.'

Ryker humphed. 'Have you spoken to any of the others?'

'Weller was first on my list. Given his new far from clandestine life, he was the easiest to track down.'

Ryker nodded. He'd thought the same, though had gone to Diaz first purely because he felt she'd have more to say. Which turned out to be quite accurate really.

He wouldn't tell Lange about his visit to Copenhagen. Not yet.

'What did he tell you?' she asked.

'Not a lot.'

She laughed. 'He never was too chatty. Imagine being stuck in a van with him for hours on end.'

'What about you?' Ryker said. 'What do you remember from that night?'

'I remember quite a lot from that operation actually,' she said with a look of cheekiness now.

Of course, he knew why she gave him that look. The planning for the Doha op had seen the seven of them cooped up together for several weeks. Hours on end every day spent with each other in a safe house with a single communal area. Ryker and Lange had gotten close. Very close. But it had never been a serious thing. Just a bit of fun to pass the time while they planned and waited. Still, Ryker felt a little awkward now, looking back, though he wasn't sure why.

'The thing is,' he said, 'that night has always bugged me. I hated that it wasn't a clean op. We should have been in and out of there without a hitch. The only reason I never dug into what went wrong before was because as far as I knew Grichenko was dead.'

'That, and the fact that rule number one is to follow orders and never question.'

Ryker humphed again. He wasn't sure if she was mocking or not. 'The point is, something did go wrong that night. Someone in our team lied to me. Lied to you. I want to find out who and why so we can figure out who betrayed us. For all you know, it could be someone you're still working with.'

She fidgeted a little at that. The thought had surely crossed her mind already. Lange was still an operative, even if Ryker didn't know the full details of who her bosses were. Someone on the Doha crew had lied, but there would have been someone else in the shadows directing that. A boss somewhere, who could still be in position, still calling shots.

Maybe it was even Lange herself who'd betrayed them in Doha and was still working for the same boss. Ryker couldn't rule it out.

'Tell me then, James, what do *you* remember of that night?'

No point in keeping it to himself. He gave her every detail he could think of – from his own recollection at least. He didn't add the details he'd learned from Diaz. He took her through the sequence; Aldern saying he was moving to check something out. His comms going down. Ryker following and getting into a fight with two men whom he still didn't know the identities of. The firefight and explosions inside which Ryker could hear but had no part in, and finally the chase back to the van where he was told Grichenko was dead.

'The two men in the trees, they targeted you,' Lange said. 'It wasn't random.'

'No, it wasn't.'

Salman and Diaz were ambushed too, by the conference room. And according to Diaz the first shots were fired where Elliott was, suggesting maybe someone had tried to take him out. Before all that Aldern had disappeared. Every one of them had come under attack.

Except for Lange and Weller.

Ryker had never thought of it like that. If someone had put in place a plan to save Grichenko, and to attack every single one of the crew inside the palace, why hadn't they also attacked the van?

'What about you?' Ryker asked.

Lange went on to give her version of events. To start with her story was unsurprisingly similar to Weller's.

'There is one thing that's helped me a bit though,' she said.

'What's that?'

'I've the benefit of a little bit of a memory jog.'

Ryker raised an eyebrow. 'How so?'

She fished in her backpack and took out a laptop computer, then spent a few seconds firing it up. They sat in silence as she did so. Her eyes fixed on the screen, Ryker's on her. He was trying hard to get a read on her, her reasons for being in Frankfurt, for following Ryker like she had, for now being so apparently open with him.

But he also couldn't escape comparing how she looked now to ten years ago. Not ten years older, that was for sure. Her face was a little fuller, her skin a little more tanned. Her hair was redder and her make-up was darker. All in all she looked–

She glanced up and caught his eye and both of them smirked. She'd sussed him, and wasn't bothered by it in the slightest.

'Take a look,' she said. She turned the screen to him and he shuffled along the bed a little closer. A map. Five little red dots. She turned the sound up and voices filled the room. Seven voices, Ryker included. His mind took him back ten years with a startling clarity.

'Everything was recorded?' he said, not sounding as shocked as he was. 'Surely that's not protocol?'

Plausible deniability had been a cornerstone of black ops as long as black ops had existed. The less evidence that was kept of an operation the better. Yet here Lange was with a full record of the surveillance and comms from that night.

'Definitely not protocol,' she said. 'This is my own personal insurance.'

He held her eye a few seconds. Did he believe her? It was a reasonable enough explanation, even if it was an incredibly risky move. Lange was sitting there openly admitting that she'd broken very clear rules. On the off-chance she'd need some evidence to save her own back one day? She'd put her own career in jeopardy, and was laying it all out in the open for Ryker, a man she hadn't seen for ten years and had no real clue who his allegiances were now to.

The only alternative was that their bosses had wanted this record all along, but why on earth would the government have wanted anything at all recorded from that night?

'Why are you showing me this?' he said, his suspicion clear in his tone.

'I know you. I know what motivates you. The truth. Rules don't bother you. I trust you.'

She held his eye the whole time. He didn't have a response. Because, unfortunately, he couldn't say the same thing to her. He'd been burned too many times in the past. Plus, he wasn't sure he even believed her, as much as a large part of him wanted to.

'So this is when you all started to go dark,' she said as she pointed to the screen. 'Here's Aldern, by the trees.' She flicked forward. 'Aldern went down. You followed him outside. A couple of minutes later you go dark too. Elliott, Salman and Diaz were still live at that point.'

And steadily moving northwards, Elliott at the front.

'Then Elliott stops here,' Lange said. 'That spot is right outside the toilets. Salman and Diaz carried on to outside this conference room, further north, but all are still live.'

Ryker's eyes were firmly fixed on the screen now, his ears tuned to the voices of his crew members. A conversation he'd never before heard because his comms had already gone down by this point.

One of the red dots flicked off.

'Wait,' Ryker said. 'Pause it.'

Lange clicked a button and the voices stopped.

'What is it?'

'Elliott went down next.'

Lange nodded. 'And the gunfire started seconds later.'

'That doesn't make any sense.'

'What doesn't?'

'That Elliott went dark first.'

'What do you mean?'

'The dark spot was in this northern section,' Ryker said. 'Right? But Salman and Diaz were already further ahead than Elliott. Further north. So why did his go down first?'

Lange looked a little flummoxed by the question. Not because she didn't get his point, he thought, but more likely because she didn't have an explanation.

'If there was a signal blocker,' Ryker said, 'which I think we can agree on, its jamming capabilities spread outward, right? A circle?'

'Yeah?'

'So going by the timings of when we went dark, and where we were at that time, we should be able to pinpoint the location of the blocker?'

'In theory.'

'Go on then.'

Lange hesitated for a second, as though concerned about something Ryker had said. But then she got to work. It took several minutes, but the answer was pretty much what Ryker had thought it would be from his own mental map of the layout and what he now knew from that night.

'The most likely location was around here,' Lange said, pointing to the spot on the map.

Outside the palace. About halfway between the building and where Ryker had got into a fight with those two men.

'Do you think that's what Aldern had seen?' Lange asked. 'He'd spotted whoever was lurking there? Or their equipment at least?'

'Possibly.'

'And the two men who attacked you?'

'It's consistent. It's all consistent. Except for one thing.'

'What's that?'

'It still doesn't explain why Elliott went offline after me. It should have been Salman and Diaz.'

'What are you saying?'

He thought about that for a few moments. 'I'm saying it's time to go and speak to the man himself.'

Lange looked at him a little dubiously.

'You? We?'

Good question. The truth was he'd rather work alone. Others weren't put at risk that way. Experience had taught him that over and over. It was one of the biggest reasons why he'd left his old life behind. Why he was now a loner. He'd cut ties with the few people he was closest to in order to protect them, from him.

'I get it,' Lange said. 'I really do. But let me put it this way. You go out there on your own, chasing down Elliott and Diaz and Salman, and we'll just be stepping on each other's toes, because I'm going to be doing the exact same thing.'

Interesting that she'd included Diaz in that. So did she really not know that Ryker had already seen her? And also no mention of Aldern. So she did know he was dead?

'I won't tell anyone,' Lange said. 'You know me, James. That's not what I'm about. No one will know you were helping me. I've nothing to gain from it. Hell, my boss would be horrified if I told her. Probably more horrified than knowing I have this recording.'

Her. Ryker wondered who Lange's boss could be. Not that he knew every honcho in the UK's intelligence services.

'Please?' Lange said.

'You already know where Elliott is?'

She dug in her pocket and took out her phone. She tapped away then turned the screen to him to show a map. Ryker stared for a couple of seconds. She was certainly well prepared.

'Looks like Switzerland is our next stop then,' he said.

19

'This was your solution?'

The woman, her voice a hiss, barely more audible than a whisper to Leia. Neither she nor the man were in the room, though they were close judging by the sound of their voices. Next to her, Leia's father remained tied, his hood in place still. She nestled into his side.

'We needed leverage,' the man said. 'We'll still get through this. Remi'll understand. We'll still get our money.'

Moments later they were both back in the room.

'No. You won't,' Leia's father said, even as his body remained slumped, unmoving. His voice was strong and stern and sent vibrations through Leia. 'You won't get your money. They'll kill you both.'

Silence. Leia could imagine the worried faces behind their balaclavas.

'The people who made you do this. I know them better than you do. I know what they're capable of.'

'Keep your mouth shut,' the man said.

'Or what? You can't touch us. You need us. Your only hope of getting out of this alive, of getting your money, is if we're okay. Any other outcome... and you're dead.'

~

Frankfurt was dark and blisteringly cold when Devereaux arrived. Just how she liked it. There was a biting easterly wind coming all the way from Siberia and bringing with it the howls of wolves and bears. At least that was what Devereaux imagined the noises were as the freezing air whistled through the skyscrapers of Frankfurt's financial district. It was 9pm and the streets were quiet with only a few stragglers from the working day still remaining. The bars here were steadily emptying as those not bothered about a hangover in the office tomorrow morning headed off to more trendy and lively nocturnal areas of the city.

Nocturnal. Devereaux liked that word. It evoked thoughts of night-time predators, prowling in the dark, stalking unseen.

Exactly what she was now doing.

She'd only been in Germany a few hours, but the information she'd been provided from Paulo meant she was happy enough to swoop immediately. No need to wait another day. Not when she had other places to be, other people to see.

She checked her watch. About half an hour to go, if the target kept to his usual schedule. She carried on walking, heading out of the financial area, and it wasn't long before her surroundings became all the more dark and seedy. Still few people about, even despite the tempting offerings writhing in the red-lit display windows that lined this street.

Perhaps it was the weather keeping the punters away tonight. Or perhaps the punters were all inside already, enjoying themselves.

This was Devereaux's first visit to the Bahnhofsviertel district of Frankfurt. So far, she liked what she saw. She'd read up about the area on the journey here from the Middle East. A fascinating story, she felt. The red-light district in Frankfurt had grown hugely in the aftermath of World War II. The area had been lightly hit by the Allies' bombing raids, which meant after the war plenty of hotels were still operational in Bahnhofsviertel, many of which were used to house military personnel from the US occupation forces. Naturally, the large groups of young men needed some downtime and titillation, and up sprouted the brothels to fill their needs as if delivered from Mother Nature herself.

She spotted Coco's in the near distance. One of the smaller establishments on this street. Some of the buildings were six, seven storeys high, but Coco's took up a narrow two-storey one toward the far end of the district. A tall, wide and gruff-looking bouncer was stationed outside the closed door. Devereaux caught his eye as she sauntered along. He didn't react. Cold, hard, purposeful. She kept going. Headed around the next street and circled around until she was on an alleyway behind the brothels. Pitch black, damp, frozen. The alley stank with industrial bins piled high with waste, and dripping who knew what.

Devereaux came to the back exit for Coco's. The metal door had no handle on the outside, but it did have a lock. She took out the torsion wrench and picks and quickly worked the lock until each of the pins was released. The door inched open and Devereaux slipped inside then carefully pulled the door back shut again.

She was in a dark room. Just a sliver of light coming into the space from the partially open door at the far side. A storage room by the looks of it, with racking on both sides of her, boxes filled with... she had no clue.

Devereaux edged forward, up to the doorway. She looked out into the garishly-lit corridor. Several doors off it, all closed. Soft music was playing somewhere. She could hear voices too. Rocking. Murmurs of pleasure.

She looked at her watch. Shouldn't be long.

Only a few minutes passed until she heard a buzz further along the corridor by the front. A moment later and she heard a thunk as the front door opened. Then footsteps and voices. She pulled herself back a little, further into the darkness of the room.

A man and woman came into view. The man wore a long overcoat, dressed for the winter. The woman teetered on five-inch heels and wore nothing but strands of lace. Devereaux took out her phone and carefully snapped a picture as they came her way. They reached the final door on her left, just a few yards from where she was standing. A knock. The door opened from the inside and the man headed on in.

'Enjoy yourself,' the woman said in accented English.

'I always do,' the man said.

The door was closed again. The receptionist – if you could call her that – glanced in Devereaux's direction for a second. Devereaux didn't move. Just stared. The woman shivered slightly, but then simply turned and sauntered, hips swaying, back to the front of the building.

Devereaux sent the picture and waited. Shouldn't be long this time. Paulo knew where she was. She certainly wasn't convinced by this method of operation, but she wasn't calling the shots so what did it matter?

From all her years of experience she knew there were many different ways to eliminate a target. Broadly, the methods fell into three camps: Clandestine – poison, overdoses, induced heart attacks and the like – was in many ways Devereaux's preferred approach. Much less heat on her that way. Accidents – car crashes, falls down stairs, etc – could be hard to organise and get right but were interesting to plan. Then there was sending a message. That was what Paulo and Kyri wanted from Devereaux, in Dubai, here, and for each of the other targets she'd been given. Sending a message meant violence. Often extreme. Sending a message meant blood. Witnesses too, if possible. Much more risky for Devereaux, but then that was why Paulo wasn't carrying out his own dirty work, she assumed.

Still, she'd be lying if she said it wasn't a whole lot of fun this way.

Her phone screen lit up when the message silently came through. Green light in the red light. Devereaux smiled to herself.

She put her phone away and stepped into the corridor and quickly moved up to the door. She pulled the handle down and darted inside and pushed the door closed with her heel.

The man was just finishing getting undressed, pulling his underwear off his ankles. The woman – bra and knickers still on – was to Devereaux's left, filling a tumbler with whisky or brandy. Devereaux whipped the syringe from her pocket and lunged for the woman first. She stabbed her in the neck with the needle.

'What the hell!' the man shouted.

Devereaux tossed the woman to the floor. She smacked her head on the corner of the massage table as she went. At least that rendered her unconscious a little more quickly.

'You stupid...'

The man was coming for her. Starkers. His flabby belly jostled, his manhood swung freely. Devereaux almost burst out laughing.

Instead, she shimmied and grabbed his arm and twisted it around and then hammered down her fist onto the elbow joint.

Snap.

She let go and grabbed his face, hand over his mouth, to muffle his scream. She kicked out his legs and shoved him onto the bed.

She took the second syringe from her other pocket and

jabbed it into his neck. A smaller dose for him. Enough to keep him quiet, not enough to numb his pain or to send him to sleep.

With him docile and murmuring like a drunkard, she rolled him onto his back. His broken arm flopped uselessly by his side. Better safe than sorry, she secured him to the bed with two pieces of rope. One around his belly to pin his arms, the other around his legs. She shoved his whities into his mouth then looked over him. Her eyes fell on his groin. She pushed her hand into her inside coat pocket and pulled out the hunting knife.

She cackled, her eyes fixed. 'Do you think I could slice it off in one swipe?'

She grabbed his flaccid penis and pulled it up straight. He moaned and writhed a little. As much as he could.

'Let's see.'

She swooshed the blade in a narrow arc. The man bucked and jostled and tried his hardest to scream. His lack of fight was almost disappointing. Almost.

'Nearly,' Devereaux said, laughing. She swiped again then tossed the dripping appendage onto his chest. She shrugged. 'You won't be needing that anymore.'

She lifted the knife high and stabbed it down into his gut, just below his sternum. The blade sank into the thick flesh there. His body jolted again, his eyes squeezed nearly shut. She clutched the handle of the knife with both hands and yanked and tugged to use the blade's teeth to tear a gouge down to his waist. His abdomen opened up like a flower blooming. Well, except this flower was filled on the inside with blood and ropey intestines which spewed outward.

The man quivered a few seconds more, his panicked eyes fixed on the ceiling the whole time. Whether or not he was religious, he was surely pleading, begging, praying for this to be over with.

It soon was.

Devereaux took the underwear from his mouth. Wiped her knife on them then sheathed the blade. She took out her phone and snapped the photo and sent it to Paulo.

She crouched down to the woman who remained motionless on the floor. Still breathing. She'd be fine. Although a little shocked when she woke to find her client inside out. Perhaps it was time she found a new job.

Devereaux moved for the door.

20

'You want some more water?' the woman said.

Leia nodded. It hadn't escaped Leia's attention that, unlike her father, she remained unbound. Was that because they didn't see her as a threat? Certainly if there'd been a weapon to hand – a gun, a knife – then Leia would have swooped for it.

No, that wasn't right. Because there was a gun. Two, in fact. Both the man and woman had one. Always either on them or on the table in the far corner where they lurked. Leia could make a move for one of the weapons, if only she were braver. Her father certainly would do if he had the chance.

The woman moved over, cautious, as she had been ever since Leia's father had been brought here. The whole dynamic was different now.

'How much were they paying you?' Leia's father asked. His voice was quiet and considered. A genuine question of interest.

The woman didn't answer.

'How much? Because I can tell you two are new to this. Always the same with those people. They pay the worst. But you know what? Pay the worst, get the worst.'

Still no answer. The woman pushed the bottle's top onto Leia's lips and she drank deeply, guzzling, trying not to spill the liquid.

'Fifty thousand? A hundred?'

'That's enough,' the woman said, calm, too, but she was talking to Leia, ignoring everything her father said.

'They offered you pennies. You're working for the wrong people.'

The man burst into the room. 'Why don't you shut the fuck up for once!'

Leia hadn't heard him approaching. How long had he been there on the outside? He bounded over. Swung his fist back and clattered it into Leia's father's head.

'No!' Leia screamed.

Another fist, then he lifted his boot and drove it down onto Leia's father's leg. He shouted in pain.

'You don't talk to us,' the man said through gritted teeth. 'Got it?'

Another thump to his head.

'Leave him alone!'

Leia jumped over to the man and lashed out. She hit him, her fists balled as she pounded his sides. He barely even registered the blows. He wasn't the biggest guy, but she was too small and weak for her efforts to be meaningful. He pulled back his hand and slapped her hard across the face, swatting her away like a fly.

She fell back down to the concrete floor with a thud. The man moved back over to the opposite corner as tears rolled down Leia's cheeks.

The dive bar Devereaux settled on was in an area that couldn't have been more different to the glitzy financial district she'd been to earlier in the evening. Downtrodden was perhaps a kind way to describe it. But it was exactly what she wanted tonight.

One night in Frankfurt. That's all she would have, then she'd be on the move again. Tonight she would enjoy some downtime. Tonight she would drink.

It was already late when she arrived. The dark, wood-panelled space had a dozen or so tables and booths, and a long strip of a bar with several stools. A sole barman was in position behind the bar. He was tall and beefy with a thick beard and tattoos visible underneath his smart but tight-fitting shirt. The look was more hipster than biker. All in all, the punters here were something of a mishmash. Young, old, rough, smart. Mostly men. A few women, but none who weren't in the company of members of the opposite sex.

Devereaux took a stool at the bar and was only halfway through her first whisky – the second most expensive they had, which wasn't saying much – when the inevitable happened.

'I've not seen you in here before,' the man said in his native German. A local, Devereaux thought from the accent, though she was no expert.

She didn't turn to him. She could see his reflection in the grubby mirror behind the bar as he propped himself up on the wood next to her. He was a little younger than she was, and had a clean-shaven face and deep-set eyes that in the mirror looked like two pools of black.

'Maybe because I'm not an alcoholic and don't drink in bars every night.'

She downed her whisky and signalled the bartender for another.

The man was looking at her curiously. She still didn't turn around to him and after a few moments he caught her eye in the mirror.

'You're not from Germany,' he said. 'I can tell from your accent.'

She didn't say anything.

'So where are you from?'

The barman sloshed another measure into her glass.

'He's paying,' she said, indicating the man next to her with her head.

The man mumbled something but was soon digging in his pocket. He bought himself a large beer and went to take the stool next to her.

'I didn't say you could join me,' Devereaux said.

He paused. She turned to properly look at him for the first time. His face was much kinder in the flesh than in the mirror, and she felt ever so slightly sorry for him when she saw the hurt puppy-dog look in his eyes. Hazel. Not as dark as she'd thought. Nice actually.

'But thanks for the drink.'

She chinked his glass. He straightened up but didn't move from the spot.

'Get back to your friends now. Maybe you can buy me another drink later.'

She turned to his group – three other men – who were doing a bad job of not staring. All looked a little unsure as to whether their chum was winning or not.

The man hesitated for another couple of seconds but by then Devereaux was facing back to the mirror. The conversation was over. For now.

He skulked away. Devereaux took a sip of her free drink. How many more could she milk from the crowd in here? An almost too simple game, but an easy way to pass the time while she decided what else to get up to tonight.

'You shouldn't play with them like that.'

A gravelly voice to her right. Devereaux turned to the shrivelled old man, three stools away from her, who was smirking as his beer glass jostled in the shaky grip of a withered hand.

'It's not fair on them,' he said. 'Poor things.' He took a sip from his beer then carefully put his glass back down. 'We don't get many like you around here.'

'Many what?'

But he was already facing away from her and didn't answer.

'Is this seat taken?'

A smooth voice behind Devereaux. She rolled her eyes. Too soon. Free drinks were one thing but she wanted time to think too.

She turned around to the man, ready to unleash, but then paused when she saw him. She didn't answer his question. Just turned back to the bar and took another sip from her whisky, then set her eyes on him in the mirror. He took the stool next to her regardless.

'What are you drinking?' he asked. English this time.

'I'm good for now,' she said.

She stared at him in the mirror, a strange feeling rattling through her stomach. What was that?

'Whatever she's having,' he said to the barman. 'And get her another too.'

Devereaux didn't protest. He gave a sickly smile as he fixed his gaze on her in the mirror. She didn't look away. Just took him in. He was casually dressed. A leather jacket. Jeans. His dark hair was slicked back. He had a couple of days' stubble which suited him well.

'Of all the bars, in all–'

'Why don't you fuck off,' she said.

He laughed.

'How's your hand?'

She flicked her eyes down. Her injured hand was on her lap. She'd been able to reduce the dressing somewhat over the last day or so and the bandages were far less obvious now. Far less obvious to most people.

'Tell you what,' she said, facing him now. 'Let me return the favour, then we can compare notes.'

He smiled. A broad smile that lifted his cheeks and made his eyes squint and showed off his nice white teeth.

'Why are you here, Paulo?'

'Just checking in on you.'

'I don't need you checking in.'

'I didn't say you needed it.'

She knocked back the rest of her second drink. Grabbed the third which the bartender had poured into a fresh glass as though he couldn't bring himself to pour so much neat spirit into just one.

'You enjoying yourself yet?' Paulo asked.

She held his eye for a few seconds. She wanted to hate this man so much...

'In this bar?'

'No. Working for me. I think you are. I said to Kyri, you really couldn't have been more perfect for this job.'

They went silent for a few moments. Paulo was staring at her still. She was busy thinking through her movements of the last few days. Spain. Cyprus. Dubai. Here.

'Let me guess,' she said. There was only one conclusion. 'My phone? My new phone, that is, given you still have my old one. Along with my money.'

He nodded. 'Easiest way to track someone these days.'

It made sense. She certainly hadn't seen him or anyone else following her around. That still didn't explain why he felt the need to be here now, rather than keeping tabs on her from afar though.

'I don't need a babysitter,' she said, more disgruntled now. 'If you don't trust me to do this–'

'Then what?'

She didn't say anything.

'And of course I don't trust you,' Paulo said. 'Who would trust someone like you?'

She grit her teeth at that. She didn't like the way he'd said those last words, as though she were beneath him.

'But that's not the reason I'm here,' he added.

'Then what?'

He shrugged and gave her a knowing smile. She ground her teeth even harder, but it wasn't because she was angered but more because she was trying her damnedest not to smile back at him now.

'What do you want to talk about then?' she asked after a few moments. 'You must already know everything about me.'

'Not everything,' he said. 'Only what I could find from others. Like how you came to do what you do.'

Teeth clenched again. That part of her life was something she really didn't want to talk about.

She took another sip of whisky and swirled the liquid around her gums until the alcohol burned.

'It seems unfair to me,' she said. 'I'm at such a disadvantage. You know so much about me. But you?'

'You're telling me you didn't look into me?'

'Of course I did. But there wasn't much to find.'

He shrugged. 'My past isn't as interesting as yours.'

'Maybe that. Maybe something else.'

He laughed, then drained his glass dry and ordered another two drinks. Devereaux felt compelled to finish her drinks too.

'May as well just get the bottle,' she said to him.

'You want to know something about me?' Paulo said.

'Yeah.'

He nodded but didn't say anything for a while, as though building up to something. The barman looked strangely unimpressed as he poured them new measures. Paulo waited until he'd skulked off before he began.

'When I was a boy, my best friend lived next door to me.'

'Where was this? I don't even know where you're from.'

'Not important. But we were typical boys, if that means anything to you at all. We played together all the time. Climbed trees. Played football. Cycled. Caught frogs, insects, rodents, whatever. Did kid things. Boy things. We'd go to the park, and in the summer we'd stay out all day and into the evening. We'd sit by the pond throwing sticks and stones into the water. We'd take fishing rods down there and not move for hours, hoping to catch something big enough to take home to eat.'

'And did you?'

He laughed. 'Never caught a thing. It didn't matter. We still did it. You see, as long as we were out of the house, as long as he was away from his dad, everything was okay.'

Paulo sank half of his drink.

'His father beat him?'

Paulo shook his head.

'Not that. I mean, yeah, he was a violent man, but it wasn't the beatings that terrified Joe. Or me.'

Devereaux felt she knew what that meant.

'The worst thing was, everyone knew what he did. But nobody did a thing to stop it. My mother told me never to go into that house. And I could tell she was seriously worried about it. The whole building had this aura of darkness around it. The look on Joe's face every night when he had to head back into there... it broke my heart as much as it terrified me.'

Devereaux clenched her fists at the thought. She'd rarely seen herself as a warrior of justice, but that didn't mean she didn't have morals, and she certainly was happy to dole out retribution on despicable people.

'What did you do?' she asked.

Paulo smiled again. 'I knew that would be your instinct. Violence. It's so natural to you. It's admirable, in a way. That's why I wanted to tell you this. The thing is, I wasn't supposed to go in that house. But I did. Quite often. When we were sure he was out, we'd play in there sometimes. In the winter, or if it was raining. Plus, he had a better games console than me. Some old thing. A Spectrum something or other.'

'You don't strike me as a gamer.'

He shrugged.

'I always felt so awkward in there. Not just because I was defying my mother but because...'

'The aura.'

'It was like that house was haunted. But then one day, Joe's dad came home earlier than expected. He went into a rage when he saw me there. I don't know why. I don't know what tipped him over that time. Perhaps he was just scared that I was getting too close to Joe. He must have known Joe confided in me about the things he did.'

Devereaux found herself shaking her head in disgust at the thought.

'Anyway, I knew Joe would suffer that night. I had to do something to stop it all. It was the middle of the night. I snuck downstairs. Grabbed the biggest knife I could find in the kitchen. Headed out. I clambered up the drainpipe to their bathroom window. I knew the frame was loose. I got inside, walked across the landing to the parents' bedroom, moving in absolute silence. I felt so powerful. Like a freaking ninja. They were both fast asleep in there. I crept over. Joe's dad was flat on his back, snoring like a hippo. I pulled the knife up against the skin on his neck.'

Paulo paused. He sighed and finished off his drink. Devereaux expected him to carry on but he didn't.

'And?' she asked. He smirked. He had her. She cursed inwardly but she genuinely wanted to know the end of the story.

'And what?' he said.

'What did you do to him?'

'I did nothing to him. I went home and I went to bed.'

'You didn't kill him?'

'Of course not.'

Silence. What the hell was this?

Devereaux frowned.

'I never saw Joe again,' Paulo said. 'We moved a few weeks later.'

She stared at him. He wouldn't make eye contact with her.

'Is any of that true?' she said.

He returned her gaze now and smiled again. 'Maybe.' Then he laughed. 'Would you like it to be true? Would it make me weak in your eyes that I didn't cut him open?'

Devereaux said nothing.

'Would you prefer if I'd told you a story of how at nine years old I sliced a man's neck open as he lay peacefully sleeping next to his wife? With his child in the house? What does that say about you?'

He took her glass now and finished that drink off too. Devereaux's body was tense with anger. She didn't know what to say.

'My past really doesn't matter,' he said. 'Neither does yours.' He paused again as he stared at her. 'I see the way you look at me. I know what you're thinking. *That's* why I came here.'

'Asshole.'

She shot up from the stool and strode across the bar to the toilets. Several heads turned in her direction as if the other customers could sense her agitation.

She stormed into the grotty ladies' room. A pokey space with nothing but a sink and two cubicles.

She knew he was right there behind her...

She spun around but he grabbed her wrists before she could even think about attacking. She drove forward and pushed him up against the door which slammed shut. She fought against him, trying to release her wrists.

She couldn't.

Then she leaned forward and planted her lips on his.

It only took a few seconds before both their mouths were open, their tongues dancing, their hands roaming. She pressed up against him. He was aroused all right. His hand slid up under her dress and he grabbed her backside and squeezed hard.

She pulled back an inch and laced her fingers into his belt to unlock the clasp. She slipped her hand down into his boxers and he murmured with pleasure. With a deft flick she popped his fly open and he shimmied behind her. She pressed her hands out on the door. He lifted her dress higher, pulled her knickers aside then thrust himself forward into her.

They moved in unison, hips swaying back and forth. His breaths, deeper by the second, were loud in her ear. He moaned. She purred. Both were soon steadily heading to a climax as he moved faster and faster, and harder. She reached the top first. Her jolting and heightened moans spurred him on until he exploded and Devereaux let out a deep, satisfied sigh as he pulled away.

She took her hands from the door, her whole body relaxed as endorphins surged.

'So that was why you came here,' she said, her breathing heavy.

'It wasn't just me who came.'

She was still facing the door so he didn't see the look she gave to that. She turned to face him. He finished doing up his fly then headed over to the basin. Devereaux adjusted her knickers and pulled down her dress.

As she did so her hand brushed against the handle of the knife strapped to her thigh. She stared over at Paulo, head down as he splashed cold water onto his face.

She closed her eyes for a second.

Then reached for the knife as she darted forward.

She pulled the blade from its sheath. Held it aloft, ready to drive down into Paulo's back. He remained hunched down, his face in his hands as the cold water cascaded.

She was only inches away when he suddenly burst into action. He sidestepped, spun around as he straightened up. Grabbed her flying wrist and drove her forward, snarling. He slammed her against the mirror. Grabbed her other wrist and pulled her away from the basin and back up against the door as he held both her arms aloft.

The knife remained in her hand. She fought against him. Tried to pull the knife down. It inched closer and closer to his neck. She grimaced with effort. His face was creased with rage.

He leaned forward and pushed his lips onto hers. She pinned hers shut. But only for a second. Then with a roar he slammed her wrist against the wall. Slammed it again. Again, until the knife came free and clattered to the floor. He relaxed his grip just a little as he moved further forward. She closed her eyes and this time didn't hesitate when his lips touched hers.

A few seconds later he released her and stepped back.

'Try that again...'

'And what?' she said. 'You'll fuck me?'

She gave him a twisted smile and couldn't quite read the more stoic look she received in return.

He came toward her once more, but as he reached his hand forward she realised it was only because he was going for the door handle.

She stepped aside and he pulled the door open.

'Perhaps next time I see you it'll be third time lucky,' she said.

He caught her eye and smiled. 'See you around.'

A moment later he was gone.

21

Ryker and Lange rented a car for the long drive from Frankfurt, to deep into the mountains of Switzerland. Setting off the next morning, the weather was sunny but chilly. They both took turns driving. For the most part the cabin was filled with an awkward silence, as if neither was quite sure what they were doing on this mission together. Or perhaps it was mostly because Ryker remained deep in thought about what he'd learned so far from his discussions with Lange, Diaz and Weller, and how much he still didn't know about what was happening around him.

He also remained curious as to what Lange knew that he didn't. She'd been perfectly clear that she remained a government agent, so there was almost certainly information she was privy to that she hadn't yet shared with Ryker, and that she wouldn't share with him. Not deceit exactly, though he would remain wary of her.

With Lange now driving, Ryker had even more time to think as he stared out of his window at the endless white. The dual carriageway they were on had been cleared of snow, and was heavily gritted, though due to recent heavy snowfall only one lane on each side of the central divider was open, and for the past half hour they'd been chugging along at fifty miles an hour behind an articulated lorry, no way for them to get past.

Ryker spotted a sign indicating a service stop in ten kilometres. Probably the last chance they'd get to stop and rest before they turned off this road and headed deeper into the mountains. His belly grumbled at the thought of a hot drink and some food.

'What do you know about Grichenko's murder?' Ryker said as he looked to Lange.

Even though her eyes remained on the road ahead, the out-of-the-blue question seemed to knock her a little. Ryker kept his gaze on her as he awaited a response. He was well aware he was unlikely to get the whole truth, but it would be remiss if he didn't at least try.

'I haven't been personally involved in the investigation,' Lange said.

'So who is involved? Outside of the police I mean.'

'MI5, obviously–'

'No, I'm asking for names. Who?'

'I can't tell you that.'

Ryker humphed. 'There must be something you can tell me. How did Grichenko come to be in England in the first place? Who helped him set up his new life and who's been protecting him for the last decade? Why? How were he and his wife murdered? What forensic evidence was left by the killer? What leads are there on the murderer? Were they acting alone or did someone hire them?'

'That's a lot of questions.'

'And I know you know the answers to at least some of them.'

There was a long pause. Ryker stared at her the whole time and he knew she was becoming increasingly uncomfortable.

'They were poisoned,' she said.

Lange glanced at him briefly, then back to the road ahead. Ryker processed the information. Really it was basic, but it was still something. More than had been reported in the press, that was for sure.

'Poisoned with what?' he said. 'I was at the scene. There was nothing which suggested hazmat gear was being used, nothing to suggest contamination was a risk. So I'm ruling out anything radioactive, and anything biological that could spread.'

She glanced at him again but said nothing. Interesting, because he'd very deliberately dropped the fact that he'd been to the crime scene. She didn't question that. Did that mean she already knew? Was she in contact with Kaspovich? Ryker didn't like the idea of that at all.

'So?' he said. 'What were they poisoned with? How?'

'Potassium cyanide,' Lange said. 'As simple as that.'

'Old school.'

'Old school and hard to trace the origins of. Nothing unique, nothing to indicate a possible source. And it's quick-acting. Most likely they ingested it in the house where they were found.'

'And it was quickly ruled a murder, rather than suicide. Why?'

A pause before, 'I'm not sure I can tell you that.'

Ryker shook his head. 'Cyanide. An interesting choice of poison. Normally quite easy to detect, so the murderer wasn't trying to cover up how they died. We both know the reasons for using more sophisticated poisons; Novichok and the likes. They're designed to be used covertly, to avoid detection. Deaths are recorded as heart attacks or stroke unless there's a particular reason to suspect foul play.'

'Grichenko was living under an assumed identity. Whoever his handlers were, his death would have raised suspicions.'

'So you're saying he had handlers?'

She didn't answer that. Had it been a slip? It did add a

slightly different context to the situation. Had Grichenko been protected by the British government the whole time? But then it was the British government who'd originally wanted him dead.

'So what do you think the choice of poison tells us?' Ryker asked.

'What do you mean?' she said, sounding confused. Playing dumb?

'Want to know what I think?' Ryker said, more irked by the moment now it was clear that Lange wasn't being straight with him.

'I'd love to,' she said. Her sarcasm was obvious.

'The killer was a hired gun.'

Her frozen reaction suggested she was trying too hard to show nothing. Which suggested he was spot on. 'This wasn't personal for the killer, and I'm betting there were clues left as to who the killer is. Forensic evidence at the scene. Perhaps you've identified a car they travelled in to that village using ANPR. Perhaps you've already got CCTV captures of them at service stations or in an airport. But the real question is who paid them?'

'That's a good theory.'

'Tell me I'm wrong.'

'About which part?'

'Come on, Nadia. What do you know about the killer? About who set them up. Tell me.'

'There's a rest stop coming up,' she said, indicating out the window. 'I could do with a break.'

And just like that she shut the conversation down.

That was fine by Ryker. She'd given him a little. Cyanide. More than he knew before. The murders weren't personal. There'd been no violent rampage. The deaths were cold, calculated. Performed by someone detached from the victims. Someone professional. That narrowed the field down a lot, though it did leave Ryker wondering one thing; was the killer working in an official capacity? A state-sponsored assassination? Did Lange have direct evidence of that?

Or perhaps he was going off at a tangent.

Lange sighed as she pulled off the carriageway, out from behind the lorry. 'Finally,' she said. 'Hopefully we never see that thing again.'

They carried on up the slip road for the service stop which consisted of a small petrol station with a café diner next to it. There was only one other car in the car park.

'You fill up,' Lange said. 'I'll grab some food.'

'No. Why don't we have a proper break. Get something in the café.'

She looked at him dubiously but then turned away from the petrol station and pulled into the café car park.

Ryker stepped out first. His skin prickled as the icy air hit him. Lange came around to his side and pulled her backpack from the footwell where Ryker had been sitting. Ryker showed no reaction, though he was glad she was bringing that with her. The inanimate object had been sat between his legs for the last two hours like a siren calling to him. With Lange's laptop inside, he knew that bag contained all the answers that Lange had but which she wasn't willing to give him. He'd get access somehow. If she ever left the damn thing out of her sight.

They headed on into the café. A rustic affair that wouldn't have looked out of place on a desert highway in 1950s America. Except for all the snow outside, that is.

There was only one other customer inside. Lange and Ryker took seats in the opposite corner from him. They each ordered coffee and a filled baguette then sat in awkward silence for a few moments.

'What's on your mind?' Ryker asked.

'I heard about what happened to you.'

The way she was staring at him made Ryker think of a shrink diagnosing a patient.

'Heard what?' he said.

'About what happened last year. Why you left.'

'I left the JIA long before last year.'

The doubt on Lange's face suggested she wasn't sure what he meant by that.

Ryker had worked for the JIA for nearly twenty years. An organisation which had now been disbanded entirely, and in large part due to Ryker's actions on his last assignment for them.

'I was helping out an old friend, that's all,' he said.

'Moreno?'

How much did she know?

'No. Peter Winter. You know of him?'

'I know the name. But I've never met him.'

'Moreno only became involved because of my own mistakes.'

'I thought it was all to do with her past?'

Ryker didn't say anything to that. He held Lange's eye until she looked down when the waitress brought over the food and drink. They both tucked in silently.

'Sorry,' she said. 'I didn't mean to pry. I was just interested, that's all. Of course, I read about some of it in the papers, but we both know they spin the truth however it fits. And they only spin what they're given in the first place, which in cases like that is rarely more than a glimpse of everything.'

'What happened, happened,' Ryker said.

'But weren't you and Moreno together?'

Is that why Lange was asking? Or was that just a smokescreen to her digging?

'We were never together like that,' Ryker said. 'But she was very important to me. She still is. Which is why I'll never see her again.'

Lange frowned. 'That makes no sense to me.'

'It doesn't have to.'

Because it did make perfect sense to Ryker. Sam Moreno had been a breath of fresh air in his life. Ryker had long operated alone, but that didn't mean he didn't need companionship, and Moreno had been so very similar to him in that respect. Herself an intelligence agent, they'd first met during an op in Africa. An op which she'd come home from severely injured. He'd helped her through her long period of rehabilitation, but last year his association with her had very nearly gotten her killed. He'd only agreed to help his old boss, Peter Winter, as a favour. Then the investigation had ended up focused on a prominent businessman named Bastian Fischer, and that had drawn out Moreno's own chequered past and set old enemies after her.

Between the two of them they'd seen off each and every one of those enemies, but Ryker knew from experience that there were plenty of skeletons left in both of their closets still. It was only a matter of time before the next one escaped. As it had done for him when Pavel Grichenko had been murdered.

However much Moreno meant to him, however much he missed her company, the further away from her he was, the better for both of them.

'Maybe I'm just a bit jealous,' Lange said with a shy laugh.

'How do you mean?'

'You met Moreno on an op, right?'

'Yeah.'

'Same as me and you. Yet after Doha we never saw each other again. We never spoke to each other again. With Moreno... you literally killed for her.'

And he'd do it again.

'Another way to look at it,' Ryker said, 'is that you've survived the last ten years. Perhaps that's in part because you've had nothing to do with me. Perhaps you've been better off without me.'

He didn't quite know what the look of disappointment he saw in her eyes meant.

Neither said anything more on the subject and they continued to eat and drink in silence.

'Shall we get back to it?' Ryker said after wiping his mouth with his napkin.

'I just need to use the toilet first,' Lange said.

'I'll wait here for you.'

She paused for a moment before getting to her feet.

Leave the bag, he willed.

She did.

She headed off. Ryker already had his hand in his pocket, his fingers grasped on the thumb drive. As soon as she moved through the door, he whipped the device out. A quick glance to the waitress, who was minding her own business, then he ducked down. He unzipped the top of the bag. The laptop was right there, its ports facing him. He pushed the thumb drive in and a little green light on it blinked twice. It was working. But it would take time. The imaging software he'd preloaded would take a full copy – an exact replica – of the laptop's hard drive. Most likely he'd have to battle through encryption to access her files, but he'd worry about that later.

He zipped the bag up again, thumb drive still in place. As he straightened up he realised the waitress was now staring over at him. But what did she care? It was Lange's bag but for all the waitress knew they were husband and wife and both of their things were in there.

Ryker indicated for the bill and Lange came out of the toilets moments later. Ryker got to his feet as she reached the table.

'We set?' he said.

'You don't need the toilet?'

'I'm good.'

She picked the bag up. It looked like she was about to open it up but then the waitress came over with the bill and, to Ryker's relief, Lange pulled the bag over her shoulders. He dropped a couple of notes onto the table and they headed out.

'You want to drive?' Lange said.

'Do you mind doing the honours again?' Ryker asked. Perhaps a little unfair on her, but he couldn't risk her taking out her laptop now. 'This cold is playing havoc with my knee.'

She looked at him dubiously. 'The indestructible James Ryker, eh?'

'Something like that,' he said with a laugh.

22

Did Ryker feel even a little bit bad for his deceit? No. Not at all. Yes, he and Lange were allies right now, but that didn't mean he owed her anything, and he sure as hell knew she hadn't been entirely forthcoming with him so far. They each had their own agendas, their own lives, their own secrets. They were together out of convenience for them both; it didn't mean anything more than that.

The backpack sitting heavy between his legs, Ryker kept his focus on the outside as they carried on their journey. Only a few miles after the café they turned off the main carriageway and more than an hour later they were on a narrow road that snaked around the edge of a mountain that rose off to the right. To their left was a basic metal barrier, beyond that a several hundred feet drop into the valley below. The piney, rocky landscape was covered in snow as far as the eye could see. With the sun shining in the sky the white powder dazzled.

The road they were on hadn't been gritted or cleared properly and the snow that had fallen most recently was still fresh and fluffy and sitting atop a hardened layer of compacted ice. Treacherous. Though with a four-by-four and snow chains they were making steady progress nonetheless.

'The turning should be coming up soon,' Ryker said, after checking the GPS on his phone. 'About half a mile.'

'A far cry from Frankfurt,' Lange said.

'Elliott's not the only one of us who's worked hard to get away from it all.'

Lange glanced at him. A little longer than she should have done.

'Look out!'

A rabbit bounded out from a snowy bush and into the middle of the road. Lange slammed the brake pedal. The car jolted and the tyres roared in a battle to keep traction. Lange wrestled with the wheel but couldn't stop the back end of the car from fishtailing. The rabbit hopped out of sight as the car crashed side-on into the verge and the bush the critter had jumped from.

A mound of snow thumped down onto the car from above and Lange jumped in shock.

Ryker looked over at her and laughed. Soon she was smiling too. Relief, more than anything.

'At least you didn't swerve the other way,' Ryker said. 'Or we'd still be in free fall.'

'And you were saying earlier about how safe I'd been not coming near you these past ten years.'

'We all make mistakes,' Ryker said.

She opened her door and stepped out. Ryker instantly went for the bag's zip. Opened it only a couple of inches. Bingo. The thumb drive's light was solid green. Copy done. He pulled it out. Closed the zip.

'It doesn't look too bad,' Lange said, ducking her head back in. Ryker flinched at the sound of her voice, straightening up in an instant, but he'd already pulled the device out of view. She glanced down to the bag, then back to Ryker but said nothing.

'Let me see,' he said.

He pushed open his door which was wedged against the thick bush. He shoved harder and another mound of snow dropped down from above. He grimaced when some of it slid down his neck.

He pulled himself out to inspect the damage. None really, other than a few scratches to the paint and a few minor dents, though there was a good foot of snow on top of the car now, largely over the windscreen. Too thick for the wipers to get rid of it.

'We good?' Lange said.

'Help me clear this snow off. Then we're good.'

It didn't take long. Ryker's hands were ice cold, his gloves sopping when they were done, but it could have been worse.

'Maybe it's your turn to drive,' Lange said. 'And if you see another rabbit, it's them or us.'

Ryker smiled, but said nothing.

'If your knee can take it?'

'Yeah. We're not far now anyway.'

He moved around to the driver's side.

Luckily, none of the tyres were stuck and with a few heavy revs and a few wheelspins they were soon on the road again. Ryker took a right turn and they were heading down into a valley, forest all around them now. The track was barely wide enough for a car and the snow here was thicker and softer than on the mountain pass, no visible indentations at all, suggesting no vehicles had been down here at least for a few days.

'Is it wrong that I'm thinking of *The Shining* right now,' Lange said.

'I'm not sure we're going to find a grand old hotel out here.'

'I meant more because of Elliott than the building. Aren't you even a little bit wary about what we're going to find?'

'I'm always wary.'

Silence for a few moments. 'You and Elliott seemed close back then.'

Ryker thought about that for a moment. 'We were very similar. In some ways. Do you know why he left?'

'I know he came out here three years ago. But that's all I know. Haven't a clue what happened in the seven years before that. Wasn't able to find out either.'

Ryker raised an eyebrow at that. The conversation died down as they carried on along the twisting descent.

'The next turn should be on your right,' Lange said. 'Then it's just a half mile more.'

Ryker took the turn. A near identical-looking track. A few hundred yards later and the road forked. Ryker slowed to a stop.

'Which one?' he asked.

Lange was staring at the phone screen as though she couldn't quite figure it out. Ryker looked over each of the tracks. Both were covered in pristine snow.

'I think the one on the left,' she said. 'This split isn't visible on the map I'm looking at. Maybe this is just a drive or something.'

Ryker didn't say anything as he released his foot from the brake and let the car roll forward.

'The snow here is too thick,' he said. 'I'm not sure we'll make it down there.'

'Yeah,' Lange said with a sigh. 'At least tuck in a bit before we get out.'

Ryker did, though he wasn't sure if that was more to allow other traffic to pass, or to try and hide their vehicle from view if someone passed by.

They set off adjacent to the narrow trail, within the treeline to avoid the thickest areas of snow. Still, in places it was well over a foot deep. With jeans and basic boots on, Ryker's legs and feet were soggy and cold by the time they came out of the woods into a clearing.

The cabin was all of twenty steps ahead of them. They came to a stop as they looked over. A single-storey building. Weathered wooden slats. A wrap-around porch that was just high enough, and just covered enough from the roof above, to keep it clear of snow. Smoke gently wafted out of the single chimney pot in the centre of the roof.

'Someone's home,' Lange said.

'Let's be careful here,' Ryker said.

Lange nodded. 'You know, for Weller and the others I'd contemplated calling in advance. I decided against it to make sure they didn't try to evade me. But for Elliott, there simply wasn't an option. No registered landline or mobile phone. I don't even think this place has electric.'

'Come on, follow me,' Ryker said as he set off with caution.

The snow around to the left of the hut was trodden down, ever so slightly, though to the right it remained untouched except for the tiny indents of birds' feet.

'This way,' Ryker said as he veered off to the right.

'Great. More wading.'

And the snow was even thicker and harder going than before, but there was a reason for his decision.

'Stop,' he said.

'What?'

Both of them were talking at little more than a whisper.

Ryker's gaze ran along the snow to a point at the edge of the hut where a couple of inches of wire were just visible above the fallen powder.

'Tripwire,' Lange said.

Ryker nodded. It was why he'd chosen the least trodden route. The trodden route was surely the way Elliott wanted people to go. Why was that?

'How are we even going to see wire like that with the snowfall?'

'We're not. So be extra careful.'

Ryker was soon moving forward again. Treading with even more care now than before. He reached the set of steps that led up to the porch. Three steps visible, at least a couple more buried beneath the snow.

He moved up, his eyes working overtime, looking left, right, up and down, for any indication of booby traps of any kind. A window was coming up on his left. He turned back to look at Lange who was a few steps behind him. He mouthed to her to duck and each of them stooped down as they passed under the glass.

Ryker spotted another tripwire as he neared the corner, only an inch from the wooden walkway and virtually impossible to see against the grain of the wood. He indicated it to Lange who nodded. Both lifted their feet silently over the top. Ryker's heart gently drummed in his chest.

There was the door.

He took another step forward.

BOOM.

An explosion behind him.

Shit. Lange. Ryker spun around. A cloud of white filled the air. There was a cascade of splats as snow, ice, whatever else clattered back down.

The wispy fog cleared...

Lange, in one piece, was hunched down. She was fine. The explosion had been several feet further behind her, out in the snowdrift by the corner of the house. He and Lange hadn't set it off.

Which meant...

'Don't you fucking move.'

Ryker froze as the barrel of a shotgun was pressed against his skull.

23

'Elliott, put the weapon down,' Ryker said as he slowly raised his empty hands in the air. His eyes were fixed on Lange a couple of steps in front of him. She looked shocked. Just because of the gun to Ryker's head, or something else? 'You know us. We're not here to hurt you.'

Elliott didn't say a word. He was breathing heavily.

'We're only here to talk about–'

Ryker didn't finish the sentence. Elliott swiped the shotgun against the back of his head and he plummeted to the deck.

'No!' Lange screamed as she rushed forward.

A boot to the head and Ryker was seeing stars. There was a clatter. A booming gunshot sent Ryker's head spinning even more. A thud. Another gunshot. A groan of pain. Elliott, not Lange.

Then muffled shuffling. And finally, 'Come on, get up.'

Lange. She was holding her hand out to Ryker. He shook his head as the fog slowly cleared. He took her hand and used her to pull himself to his feet.

Elliott was down. Sprawled and writhing. Lange had the shotgun in her hand. She pointed it down to Elliott. Luckily both shots had been wayward, Ryker saw, as neither of them was bleeding.

'Way to go, hero,' Lange said to him with a cheeky twinkle in her eye. 'You really showed him.'

'You've got some moves for a tech.'

'Who said that's all I am? And anyway, have you seen the state of him? It was hardly a challenge.'

Ryker looked down at his old colleague. Lange's words were an understatement. Elliott looked a mess. Tatty clothes, unkempt hair and beard, bloodshot eyes. His skin was mottled and saggy he was so skinny, and he looked a good decade older than he really was, his features as withered as they were weathered. Ryker had to look carefully to make sure it really was the man they'd come to see.

'I can smell the alcohol from here,' Lange said.

'Which was the exact reason I didn't tackle him straight away.'

'Yeah, right.'

'It would only have taken a flinch of a drunken finger on that trigger to turn my head inside out.'

Lange smiled. 'You keep telling yourself that, macho man. Thing is, you owe me now.'

A position Ryker never liked to be in.

'Come on, let's get him inside.'

The inside of the cabin was as dishevelled as its owner. Who knew when it had been built, or why really. There were only three rooms in the pokey space; bedroom, bathroom and everything else. Each of the rooms was grotty and grimy and cluttered. Bottles lay everywhere. Elliott had sank into a hole of alcohol oblivion.

They were in the open-plan living space. Elliott secured to a basic wooden chair with rope. Ryker and Lange were sitting opposite him on what passed as a sofa but was more like a rotting clump of sponge, as stained as it was worn.

In his years working as a field agent, Ryker had heard plenty of stories of burnouts. Had seen first-hand when colleagues and others had fallen off the rails and never returned. Suicides in his line of work were among the highest of any profession. Given his own experiences it wasn't hard to understand why.

Whatever the reasons for Elliott shunning the outside world for this life of miserable solitude, there was no doubt Ryker felt for him.

'Elliott, I'm sorry we had to do this,' Ryker said. 'The ropes I mean.'

He was awake, though his head was slumped. He didn't answer Ryker.

'We're not here to hurt you. I promise. We just need to talk.'

'Then talk.' His voice was brash and he sounded alert enough.

Ryker looked to Lange who nodded as if to tell him to carry on.

'Good work with the tripwires,' Ryker said. 'A nice little alarm system. Good distraction, too. I thought when the explosion went off you'd snared Lange. You were too quick for me.'

Elliott lifted his head now. He seemed more lucid all of a sudden. 'It wasn't supposed to be a distraction. It was supposed to tear you into pieces. I'll have to rearrange the explosives.'

Ryker smiled. 'I pity the postman.'

Elliott said nothing to that.

'Let me be honest with you–'

Elliott laughed sarcastically. 'Honest? Don't take me for a fool, however much you think that of me.'

Ryker paused for a second. 'I don't take you for a fool. And I really don't care what happened to you. I don't care why you ended up here. Why you're wasted, why you look like shit. What I do care about is Doha.'

Elliott looked a little surprised now. A little perturbed too.

'You remember Doha, right?'

Elliott nodded. 'That was a long time ago.'

'A different life for us all.'

Well, perhaps not so much for Lange, but Ryker felt the point was valid.

Elliott took a long, slow inhale, then took even longer with the exhale.

'Okay,' he said. 'But first I need some coffee.'

He looked over his shoulder to what passed as a kitchen.

'I'll do it,' Lange said, getting to her feet.

She headed off and grabbed the rusting kettle and took it over to the creaky taps.

Elliott was staring at Ryker. 'You look older.'

'I am,' Ryker said.

'Rougher.'

'I think we both know why.'

'I often wondered what had happened to you.'

'Same. To you, I mean.'

'Yeah. Except I heard a lot about you. You've seen some shit all right.'

'I suppose I have.'

'That's why I was sure when I saw you, that you were here to kill me. I know how it works.'

'I've no reason to kill you.'

'Haven't you?'

The kettle finished boiling. As Ryker looked over, Lange slipped her phone back into her pocket. She quickly made the coffees and was soon coming back over with three mugs.

'No milk or sugar,' she said.

'I'm lactose intolerant,' Elliott said. 'And sugar spikes my heart too much.'

Obviously alcohol and caffeine was the answer then.

Ryker took one of the mugs from Lange. She placed Elliott's on the floor by his feet.

'What am I supposed to do with that?' he snapped.

He pulled on his arms – pinned to his sides by the rope – as if to emphasise the point.

'First something from you,' Lange said.

Elliott tutted. 'Fucking tease. Same as always.'

He spoke the words with genuine venom and Lange looked a little taken aback. What was the story there? She looked over to Ryker as if seeking his help. He didn't say anything and Lange took a moment to compose herself. If Ryker could have offered her advice it would have been simple; don't let Elliott rile you so easily.

'There's no phone signal here,' Lange said, pulling her mobile from her pocket. She remained on her feet.

Elliott cackled. Deliberately mocking. 'Are you fucking kidding me? Have you seen where we are?'

'Yes,' she said. 'I have. And I know there's a ski resort twelve miles north of here. There's another village three miles east of that. To the south of here there's another resort and–'

'What's your point?' Ryker asked.

'My point is that I know exactly where the towers are to provide signal for those areas. I checked all this out before we came here to make sure we'd be contactable. Where we are now is in perfectly good range of the towers. And I was checking my phone on the last part of the drive here. We were fine even when we got out of the car. So why the black spot right here?'

Elliott was glaring at her now. Ryker understood the answer to her question.

'You've got a jammer?' Ryker said.

Elliott didn't say anything.

'Where? Why?'

'It must be in here,' Lange said. 'Let's see if we can find it, shall we?'

She set her cup down onto the floor next to Elliott's then began rummaging. Ryker kept his eyes focused on Elliott the whole time. Elliott kept his mostly on Lange, his teeth gritted. He really didn't like her much. Ryker hadn't realised that before. Was that just from Doha or something else?

Elliott finally looked back to Ryker when Lange disappeared into the bedroom, out of sight of them both.

'Come here,' Elliott said, his voice low.

Ryker hesitated for a second.

'Come on,' Elliott said.

Ryker slowly got up from the sofa. He took half steps over, hands at the ready by his sides as if a sudden attack was a realistic prospect.

'Down,' Elliott said.

Ryker crouched.

'You trust her?' Elliott asked in a whisper.

Ryker didn't answer.

'You shouldn't. I know her better than you think. Better than you do, even if you did fuck her. Don't believe a word that comes out of her mouth.'

Ryker held Elliott's eye a few seconds. He opened his mouth to speak but then heard Lange's footsteps and looked over to see her coming back into the room.

'What did I tell you?' she said, holding the small box up in her hand.

Ryker glanced to Elliott who was smirking at him knowingly.

'Why do you have that?' Ryker asked.

'Why do you think?'

'You know a thing or two about these?' Lange said. Both she and Ryker retook their seats.

'Probably not as much as you do, dear.'

Ryker took a sip from his mug. The coffee was rancid. He set the mug back down.

'Doha, ten years ago,' Ryker said. 'Pavel Grichenko. We were supposed to kill him. Except our plans were interrupted. And we failed.'

Elliott's smirk fell. 'Failed?'

'He survived.'

Ryker let that hang, trying to gauge Elliott's silent reaction. He could read nothing. 'We didn't kill Grichenko that night. In fact, he's been living a new secret life in England of all places. Up until last week when he was murdered, that is.'

Elliott remained silent. His face neutral.

'You didn't know?' Lange said.

Elliott didn't answer.

'At least one of our crew was in on the deception,' Ryker said. 'I need to know who, and why. The people working against us that night, they used a jammer to disrupt us.'

Ryker looked down to the device on the floor by Lange's untouched coffee.

'Probably a device very similar to this one,' Lange said. 'Portable. Covers a broad range of frequencies over a short distance.'

Elliott shook his head. He looked pissed off. 'Pathetic.'

'What is?'

'Just because I have one now, ten years later, doesn't mean a thing.'

'Doesn't it?' Lange said.

'Maybe it doesn't,' Ryker said. 'That's for you to convince us.'

'I don't have to convince you of anything.'

'It'd help get us out of your home if you did,' Ryker said. 'Take me through what happened that night. Your perspective.'

'My perspective would be a lot clearer with some caffeine in me.'

'No,' Ryker said. 'I'm not playing. You tell me or we find another way.'

Elliott held Ryker's hard glare a few seconds. Then burst out laughing.

'Oh, priceless. What? You're going to torture me if I don't play? Have you any idea what I've been through to get me here?'

Ryker hadn't.

'No. Of course not. Your friend, however...'

He set his eyes on Lange.

'Fine,' she said, jumping to her feet. She strode over, picked up his coffee from the floor and grabbed the hair on his neck to yank his head back. 'Open wide.'

'Lange,' Ryker said.

It didn't make a difference. She poured. To start with Elliott looked like he was going to try and drink the hot liquid as it fell, but after only a couple of seconds he pursed his lips and dipped his head and growled in anger as the steaming liquid sloshed down over him.

The cup was soon empty. Lange flung it to the floor and returned to her seat.

'Now you've had your coffee,' she said.

Ryker glared at her. She didn't seem to take too kindly to that.

'What? It wasn't even that hot.'

He looked back to Elliott who slowly lifted his head as the dark liquid dripped from his face, his hair, onto his already dirtied shirt. Steam rose all around him.

'You fucking–'

'Enough,' Ryker said, looking from Lange to Elliott. 'Just

start talking. Tell me exactly what happened when you were inside the palace. After I left you to go after Aldern.'

Elliott huffed. 'Now there was a prick.'

Ryker didn't say anything to that. He expected Elliott to carry on. He didn't.

'What happened when Alpha went on the move,' Ryker said.

'I followed.'

'And? What about Salman and Diaz? They were inside with you, too, right?'

'They were behind me. Alpha had... I don't know. Five, six, seven others with him. Then they split up. Some headed one way, some another. Salman and Diaz stayed on Alpha.'

'Why? You were in front. You could have taken Alpha.'

'Two of them, one of me. Diaz called it.'

Ryker looked to Lange. 'No, that's not right,' she said.

'What?'

'You called it. Not Diaz.'

'Not how I remember it.'

Except Ryker and Lange had both heard the recording. Elliott had definitely called it. Or, at least, he'd suggested it, and Diaz had confirmed it.

Everyone was silent for a few moments.

'Diaz called it,' Elliott said.

'Okay,' Ryker said. It was simply a point of difference he'd have to keep in mind. 'What next?'

'The ones I followed headed off to the toilets. I was bloody fuming. There I was following these three into the fucking gents for a piss. Then my comms went down.'

'Before or after Salman's and Diaz's?'

'I've no idea.'

'You don't remember?'

'I've no clue. What difference does it make?'

'Try to think,' Lange said.

'Oh fuck off.'

Then silence as both Ryker and Lange stared at him, but he didn't amend or add to his answer.

'Keep going,' Ryker said.

'It was dark. I was in the toilet block with three guys. Standing at a urinal trying to squeeze some piss out. It was fucking bizarre. I mean, I knew, and they knew. We all knew. It was only a matter of time. One of them moved first. End of story.'

'Went for a gun?' Ryker said.

'That's what I assumed. But I was quicker. I took him out. Then... all hell broke loose.'

'You fired the first shot?' Ryker said.

'Yeah. So what? But pretty soon there was shooting everywhere. It was carnage.'

'Just in the toilet?'

'Everywhere. No one else came in there, but I heard shooting, shouting all around.'

'And then?'

'Once they were all down I scarpered. I headed after the others. I spotted Alpha, being escorted away. I had to make a decision. I was going to go after him on my own but then I saw Salman and Diaz.'

'By the stairwell?' Ryker said.

Elliott shrugged. 'Kind of. I told Salman to head around the west exit to try and intercept.'

'You told him that?'

'Yeah.'

Diaz had said Salman suggested he do that himself. Was that another important contradiction?

'Me and Diaz chased down the stairs. Diaz nearly got wiped out by an explosion. Still don't know what. Grenade. RPG. Booby trap. Whatever it was we were both floored, but she was closer and took a bigger hit than me. I dragged her out of there. I wasn't even sure if she was breathing or in one piece at first. I just knew I had to get us out.'

'She didn't run out with you?' Ryker said.

'Run? She could barely even put her legs down. We were nearing the gates when Salman and Aldern caught up with us. They helped me with her.'

'Aldern and Salman were together?'

'Yeah.'

Same as Diaz had said.

'Did they say how they'd found each other?'

'Not that I remember. I just remember Aldern said it was job done. Alpha was down.'

'Are you sure?'

'About what?'

'That it was Aldern who said that?'

'Aldern said it. And the way I saw it, Aldern had done it.'

Except Diaz had claimed it was Salman who'd confirmed the kill. And actually in the van, when they were escaping, it was Elliott who'd confirmed the kill to Ryker. So was one of Elliott or Diaz simply mistaken in their recollection of what Aldern and Salman had said, or were they inadvertently giving two different accounts of a lie the two of them had concocted?

Lange's phone buzzed. Elliott laughed. 'See, this is why I have that jammer. How fucking annoying is that?'

Lange ignored him as she dug her phone out and headed over into the kitchen area. She had her back turned to Ryker as she answered the phone and began a muted conversation.

'What did I tell you,' Elliott said, whispering again. 'Who do you think she's on the phone to? They'll be storming this place any second. I'll be dead. You? Collateral damage maybe. Take it from me, she's a snake.'

Lange was off the phone already and heading back.

'You should listen to me,' Elliott said.

'Listen to you about what?' Lange said, not hiding her suspicion.

Neither Ryker nor Elliott said a word about it.

'Who was that?' Ryker asked.

She looked to Elliott first then moved over to Ryker. She crouched down. Her eyes met his.

'We have a problem,' she said. Then even more quietly, 'Joey Weller's dead.'

24

Ryker drove the whole way back to Frankfurt. Darkness had fallen before they'd even left Switzerland, and Lange spent a good deal of the drive on her phone, either in hushed, and very one-sided conversations, or tapping away emails and messages to whomever. She'd not told him anything in Elliott's cabin other than that Weller was dead, though Ryker truly believed her lack of information at that point was because the sketchy details were still so new, and she really didn't know anything else.

Still, Ryker became more and more irked as they moved north, well aware that Lange, through all her conversations, was finding out more and more, but being ever so careful not to let anything slip that she didn't want Ryker knowing.

She finally put her phone down and then tutted and shook her head as she looked out of her window.

'What?' Ryker said.

'I can't believe this. We were there, in Frankfurt. Only yesterday. I didn't even get a chance to speak to him.'

That's what she was bothered about? That Weller had been murdered before she'd gotten from him what she needed?

'What happened?' Ryker asked. 'What do you know?'

She glanced over to him. He knew by now what the look meant. The 'what can I tell him' look.

'He was gutted,' she said, looking fearful as the words passed her lips. 'Literally gutted. Sliced open like a pig in a butcher's shop.'

Ryker clenched the steering wheel a little harder.

'At a brothel of all places.'

'Do you know who did it?'

'No. I don't know if there's any suspect even. The investigation is in the hands of the local police for now, so we're only getting snippets. I'll be the first on the scene from UK intelligence. If my boss can get me clearance in time. Otherwise we're just going to be playing catch-up.'

To Ryker it felt like they already were.

'This isn't a coincidence,' Ryker said. 'Grichenko is murdered, then a few days later Weller, right after we both go to Frankfurt to speak to him.'

'I know what you mean, but it makes no sense.'

And she seemed to really mean that. Was there any likelihood at all that Lange, or the people she worked for, were responsible? Ryker couldn't rule it out, as ludicrous as it seemed.

'Grichenko and his new wife were killed quietly, discreetly,' Ryker said. 'Poison. But what you've told me about Weller suggests something else altogether.'

Lange didn't say anything.

'This could be a revenge attack,' Ryker said.

'Revenge for what? Weller's a bloody accountant or whatever now. And I know he had nothing to do with what happened to Grichenko.'

'You *know* that?'

She tutted. 'You know what I mean.'

Did he?

'So what do you think then?' he said.

Again Lange was silent.

'I know you feel conflicted, but I really can help,' Ryker said. 'If you tell me everything you know, it's not going to do you any harm. It could help us both.'

'That's not it at all.'

'What's not?'

She sighed and turned away.

'Then maybe Weller was into something else,' Ryker said. 'Drugs or whatever. He's been taken out in a revenge attack by a gangbanger. Or an angry pimp because he beat up a prost–'

'No,' Lange said. 'It's not any of that. It is connected. I just don't understand how. Or why.'

'So you are at least confirming his death is connected?'

No answer now. Perhaps she'd not meant to say that.

'Which means, for whatever reason, we could all be targets,' Ryker said. 'Me, you, Diaz, Salman, Elliott. Do the others know what's happened?'

'Well obviously Elliott doesn't,' Lange said. 'I don't even know where Salman is. We've been working on tracking him, but he's kept himself so clean. Diaz...'

'Diaz what?'

'I know she still works for... she still works in intelligence, but it's not that easy.'

'What's not easy?'

Ryker hadn't found it that difficult to track her down. Lange didn't say anything.

'If you're saying what I think you're saying, then any one of us could be next,' Ryker said. 'Come on, Nadia, talk to me properly. Drop the battle lines. I thought we were working together here. Don't make me operate with one hand tied. You're only hurting yourself if you do.'

But he got no response. Lange didn't even seem to be

listening. Moments later she was on the phone again. She barely said a word through the conversation before the phone was put down.

She looked over at Ryker. She was shaken.

'Diaz is fine,' she said.

'That's good,' Ryker said, though her apparently positive words didn't explain why she was now so rattled. 'Was that it?'

'You can't come with me. I need to do this the right way.'

Ryker gripped the steering wheel a little more tightly.

'There's a town coming up in a few miles,' she said. 'If you drop me off there, someone's going to pick me up and take me the rest of the way to Frankfurt.'

'So this is it. We're done?'

'There isn't another way.'

'Yes there is. Instead, you're cutting me out, even though you know the danger.'

'No. I don't know the danger. Maybe there is *no* danger for me, or for you. But I don't have a choice but to leave you. There's more happening here than you realise, Ryker.'

'I'm well aware of that. It's just a shame you won't tell me what.'

She didn't say anything to that.

'And you must realise I'm not going to just slink off,' he added.

'I know. I wish there was another way.'

But her words felt meaningless to Ryker, and the conversation ended there. Minutes later they'd turned off the Autobahn, and Lange gave Ryker directions to the car park of an out-of-town shopping centre. The centre included not just shops but restaurants and a cinema, and despite the late hour the car park was still heaving. He parked up on the far edge, furthest away from the shops. As he shut down the engine the heavens opened. Sleety rain pelted down.

Lange had her phone pressed to her ear again.

'Okay, I'm here already,' she said before putting the phone down. She turned to Ryker. 'They're five minutes away.'

She grabbed the straps of her backpack.

'Thanks for everything,' she said. 'And... I'm sorry it happened like this.'

'You don't want to wait in the car? It's pissing it down.'

'No. It'd be better if you're not here when they arrive.'

With that she opened her door and stepped out.

'See you around,' she said.

She closed the door and headed off into the rain, toward the shops. Ryker watched her for a few moments. She looked back twice as she walked, as if checking if he'd gone yet. Seconds later she moved between two parked vans and was out of sight.

Ryker stayed where he was for a few moments, contemplating. He could follow her. Head back to Frankfurt, or wherever else she was going. Watch her, and her investigation, from a distance and slowly figure out what she knew, and what she didn't. Or he could run and hide. Lay low in case he really was the target of someone now.

There was another option, of course. He could continue his original plan. He'd already been to see Diaz once. Lange said she was fine, and the earlier conversation had all but confirmed that Diaz remained an agent. She was not only well enough protected, but was perhaps too protected for Ryker to talk to her again.

What of Ali Salman? Ryker still hadn't figured out where he was. He would try to. Tracking down Salman now was perhaps more important than ever, given the discrepancy in Diaz and Elliott's accounts.

Elliott. For all his faults, despite whatever had gone wrong in his life to turn him into a washed-up recluse, and putting aside the fact he could have been lying through his teeth to Ryker earlier, could Elliott still be a capable ally if they were all on someone's hit list now?

Plus it was also still weighing heavily on Ryker's mind that Elliott seemed to know a lot more about Lange than Ryker did... What was the story there?

He turned the engine back on. Then headed out the way he'd come. Without hiccups, he'd be back in Switzerland by dawn.

25

'You still haven't told me how much,' Leia's father said. *They were alone with the woman again. Where did her partner keep going? To beg with the man who should have been paying them? Was it telling that he wouldn't make calls in here anymore? Perhaps he had a bad signal, which could give some clue as to where this place was. Or was it that he didn't want anyone overhearing the conversations he was having – not even his partner?*

Was he plotting something?

'Are you sure you can trust him?'

No answer.

'Who's he even speaking to right now. I bet you don't know, do you?'

Silence.

'I know you two are together. I might have this sack covering my eyes, but I can tell by the way you talk to each other. Like Bonnie and Clyde.' *He chuckled. Still his words got no response.* 'But everyone has their price. We all know that.'

Leia never took her eyes off the woman as her father spoke. Her bodily reactions gave everything away. Even with her father bound and his head covered, he was in charge in this room in moments like these.

'You ask me, he's out there now trying to do a deal. You messed up. My wife is dead. There's too much heat on you. They won't pay up now. Believe me. They won't pay. Yet your lover is out there begging for a cut-price deal. It's pathetic. And it'll get you both killed.'

Still she said nothing.

'But there is another way. So why don't you listen very carefully to what I've got to offer. A proposal for you. A way out of this for all of us.'

Outside the confines of the car, the night was pitch-black and ominous. For miles now Devereaux had been on a twisting mountainous pass. No street lights here, just the beams from her rented car's headlamps that bounced through darkness as the car snaked left and right. Every now and then she got a glimpse of what lay either side. The soaring mountain one way, a fall into the abyss the other.

She couldn't explain why but more than once she imagined what it would be like to take the car right over the edge. How it would feel to fly through the air, to plummet down into the depths. She could imagine the breathlessness of the plunge, the deep thud of her heart in anticipation of certain doom.

What would the impact be like? A sudden, horrific and final smash? A rolling, bouncing calamity where her bones and organs were slowly battered and pulverised? Would there even be an explosion? A fireball that engulfed her and melted the skin and flesh off of her...

All it would take was one slip of the tyres. One moment of hesitation in the turn. One moment of distraction.

It never came. The rubber remained stuck to the icy surface like it was glue, and before long, with a strange feeling of a lack of fulfilment, of disappointment, she was off the treacherous, mountainous track and heading down into a valley.

The headlamp beams were more steady now, though the light struggled to penetrate the blackness of the forests that surrounded her. She carried on, following the GPS until she was less than half a mile from her destination. There'd been no fresh snow through the night so far, and for the last few miles she'd been keeping to the tracks in the fallen snow from previous traffic. But up ahead those tracks came to an end. Devereaux slowed the car and came to a stop. Someone had been here recently. More than that, they'd pulled over here. Turned around here.

This was far enough.

She turned the engine off and stepped out. Took her backpack from the boot. With a flashlight in her hand, she moved into the woods. She'd walked for only a hundred yards before she turned the light off. The torch was there if she really needed it, but she wanted to complete her approach with stealth. She was confident of her bearings, and she'd feel her way through the darkness.

The night was cold and crisp as she edged forward. The woods were silent, with not even the sounds of night-time predators. Perhaps because they were such adept hunters, sneaking through the black without sound, like her. Or perhaps because there was simply no life out here in the void.

She kept going, each footstep tentative. Up ahead she could see the end to the treeline. With her eyes by now adjusted to the darkness, she could make out the rim of a clearing in the thinner-than-thin moonlight.

This was it.

She reached the last tree. Stopped. Stared straight ahead to the outline of the cabin. No lights were on. Wispy smoke trailed up from a chimney, the swirls almost invisible, their presence like an illusion against the night sky.

Devereaux reached around and took her backpack off her shoulders. She put the torch away. She didn't need that now. She put the bag back in place then took a step forward.

Click.

Bright white light burst into her eyes. She squinted and cowered down and brought her arm up to her face. Spotlights. Five, six, seven, dotted around the clearing. Some of the lights were on the cabin itself, others rigged into the trees.

She back-stepped toward the woods, past the first tree, then another, then another. She crouched down and waited. Her eyes never left the cabin.

No lights came on inside. No sounds drifted over. There was no indication that whoever was home had been alerted.

She carefully peeled her backpack off her shoulders again. Took out her binoculars. Held them to her face and scanned. She spotted a motion sensor on the corner of the eaves directly in front of her. There was another to her left, not attached to the cabin, but in the trees near one of the lights. A third the other side. No obvious black spots that she could see.

This place had no mains electricity. Not out here. So how were the lights powered? A generator? Batteries? Solar?

A minute passed. The lights remained on. If anything this could prove useful. Devereaux used the time to make a mental map of the layout of the grounds. To the left of the cabin the snow was well trodden. To the right not so, with just two sets of neat prints, though the snow by the cabin there was ruffled and dirt-strewn like something had turned over both the white powder and the ground beneath it recently.

Devereaux thought she knew what that was. With the lights on she could see the trail of wire. This place was one big, rigged booby trap.

She smiled to herself. This could be fun.

The lights clicked off. Darkness once more. Devereaux didn't move a muscle. She waited, and waited, as her eyes slowly accustomed. Then she moved off to her left, keeping in the treeline, snaking around the edge of the cabin, aiming for the tree where she'd spotted the motion sensor. If she took a wide approach and came upon that tree from the back, she'd be able to disable the sensor without triggering the lights again. Then she'd have a clear run to the cabin.

She moved even more slowly, even more cautiously than before. Her eyes darted. She strained her ears. She tensed the muscles in her body so that each step was measured to the minutest of details.

Her foot was three inches from the shallow snow on the forest floor when she felt pressure on the leather of her boot, pushing against her big toe.

She froze, then ever so slowly pulled her foot back, and placed it down to the ground. She carefully crouched down and reached out.

Wire again.

So it wasn't just the cabin that was rigged. The forest was too.

Who the hell was this guy? No wonder there were no sounds of any animals out here. This bastard and his explosives had likely killed every last critter.

She rose up and went to step over the wire.

Click.

The lights burst back on again. Devereaux's heart thudded in her chest.

Impossible. She wasn't in view of the sensors.

Unless…

She heard him before she saw him. A soft crunch. Rubber on snow.

She ducked and whipped around.

The lights clicked off. How?

Her eyes pulsed, already unused to the darkness once more. Silence again. Except for the pounding of her heart.

She went to take a step, then that crunch of snow again. Behind her now. Several footsteps. Getting closer.

She spun.

Click.

The lights blared again, dazzling her. She squinted as she drew the hunting knife from its sheath. She spun on the spot. Looking this way and that. There was nothing there.

He was playing with her.

Click.

Darkness. She heard him. A different direction again. Closer than before. She spun and swooshed the knife, slicing through the ice-cold air. No contact.

But the next moment she felt a rush of air next to her and her legs were whipped from underneath. She fell flat on her back, sending up a plume of snow. Now she saw him. The outline of him at least. Right above her. Before she could move he dropped down onto her, his hefty weight like a battering ram that knocked the wind from her lungs. Her arms were pinned at her sides. The knife dropped from her grasp. She flailed for it as a fist smashed into her face. Blood surged in her mouth. Another fist and the darkness around her was spinning. Her hand searched but the knife was nowhere.

He leaned in. His foul breath reeked of cheap alcohol.

'Who are you?' he sneered.

She didn't answer. Both his hands wrapped around her neck and he squeezed, crushing her windpipe. Her eyes bulged and she rasped for breath. Still she flailed for the knife. It wasn't there. Just snow and frozen leaves. She tried to reach for the hands on her neck, but with her arms pinned it was impossible.

'Who are you!' he shouted, anger and venom and what sounded like distress in his voice.

She drifted. This really could be the end, she knew. Her mind strangely took her back to the drive here. To those thoughts of hurtling over the edge of the mountain. Of plunging to her death. There'd been a certain satisfaction to those thoughts. A certain peacefulness and acceptance of her life ending like that.

But this. No, she couldn't die like this.

Wherever her knife had fallen, it was out of reach. But the other side of her...

She grasped the wire, squeezed her hand around it, and pulled.

The explosion lit up the forest in a strobe of light. Snow and dirt and debris and shrapnel flew into the air, smacked into Devereaux. A blast wave, heat. Then nothing.

Her head was in a spin. A piercing ringing consumed her, all she could see was a wall of flickering white.

The white slowly dissipated. The ringing faded to a gentle hiss. The forest took shape around her. She was alive. She wasn't even that badly hurt. Perhaps the rigged explosives weren't designed to be fatal. Or perhaps she'd just got lucky.

The security lights were blaring once more. She was on her side. The man lay right in front of her. His face was mucky and bloody. As she imagined hers was too. A pair of night-vision goggles rested haphazardly on his head.

She achingly pulled herself to her knees. Her movement

seemed to give him focus. As if she'd awoken a beast, he suddenly shot up and reached out and grabbed her and they fell back onto the ground. But the blast had taken a toll on him, and the fight was more evenly matched this time. Both took blows in the melee. Fists, elbows, knees, all at close quarters as they frantically grappled.

That was when Devereaux saw it. The glint of metal under the white beam of the security lights. Not her knife... something else.

She was on top of him. He was trying to twist out from underneath her, trying to regain prime position. Rather than fight it, she decided to go with it.

She dropped her weight to the side. He took the bait and went to roll them around so he was on top. She let him. But then used their momentum so that when she was on the bottom again, they simply kept on going. She held him close, pulling him with her, aiming to get him onto his back once more...

Crack.

Devereaux flinched. Both at the gory sound, and the even more gory sight as the trap snapped shut around the man's head, gripping his skull in its jagged teeth like a shark with its prey. Devereaux looked down at him, panting as her heart raced from exertion. His head, his whole body quivered as blood leaked all over.

After a few moments his body went still, even as his bulging eyes remained open and staring up at her.

She sighed in relief and hung her head for a few seconds as she regained her composure. Then she slid off him and looked around. Her backpack was all of three feet away. Her knife right next to it. So close. It didn't matter now.

She stood up and looked over the man, his mangled head. Then she took out her phone. No signal, but the message would get through soon enough. She snapped the picture and sent if off along with a brief note.

Someone's feeling a little trapped.

She didn't know why. It just seemed apt. She smiled to herself, then picked up her bag and her knife, and walked away.

26

Ryker could tell another vehicle had been on the road to Elliott's place since he and Lange left yesterday because of the additional tyre grooves in the snow. Not only had someone been, but they'd parked and turned in the same spot as Ryker had. He already had an ominous feeling as he stepped out of the car into the drizzly morning. At least the deeply overcast skies had brought with them above freezing temperatures for the first time in days, though the grim-looking morning carried a melancholy mood with it.

He headed on foot along the path toward the cabin. He had a flash of a thought that perhaps the vehicle that had created those tracks had simply taken a wrong turn somewhere and the driver had turned on the track to head back to the main road.

Wishful thinking.

By the time the cabin was in view, that positive thought was dead. The cabin looked lifeless. No smoke swirling up from the chimney, like there had been yesterday. No one in sight – but signs that someone had been here. He could see footprints in the snow. Multiple sets which hadn't been there before. One set snaked from the right of the cabin into the woods at that side.

Another set came out of the woods off to his left, heading toward the cabin. A final set left the cabin and entered the woods just to Ryker's left. Two sets coming out, only one set going in. Ryker knew what that meant.

He was too late.

He didn't head for the cabin. Instead, he beared left and into the woods. He zigzagged through the trees. The smells hit him first. Explosives. Charred wood and leaves. Similar smells as had filled his nostrils yesterday when Elliott's mine had exploded a few feet from Ryker.

The next smell that hit him was more metallic. Blood.

He passed by a hulking trunk and then paused. He held his breath. Even his heart froze for a moment as he stared down at the ghastly remains. Elliott's body was sprawled on the ground. All around him the thin snow under the canopy of the pine trees was swept among dirt and leaves. There hadn't just been an explosion here, but a violent and desperate scuffle. One which had ended horrifically and tragically for Elliott, with his head clamped tight in the jagged jaws of an animal trap.

Ryker moved forward to his old colleague and crouched down. He didn't need to check his vital signs. Even if the damage done by the trap's jaws had somehow not proved fatal, then the hours he'd been out here in the cold certainly would have finished him off. Despite the early morning drizzle, Ryker could tell from the shimmer of the blood covering Elliott's head and the ground around him that it was frozen over.

Ryker sucked in his disgust. Not just at the gory sight, but at the thought of the person who'd done this. A person who'd killed Elliott in such a gruesome manner, and who he was sure had also gutted Weller in Frankfurt.

Whoever the killer was, these murders were personal. These murders were meant to send a message.

Ryker had received the message loud and clear.

He took out his phone to call Lange. She didn't want to jeopardise her career by teaming up with him, but perhaps she'd think twice now.

No signal.

The jammer.

Ryker rose up then looked to the cabin. He moved over there, treading carefully as he went. Elliott was lying dead in a pool of his own blood, but as far as Ryker knew his booby traps remained in operation. At least those that hadn't already exploded.

He stepped over two tripwires before he made it to the front door. Then he paused. Was the door itself somehow wired up? Ryker slowly reached out for the handle. Then he put paid to caution for a flash of a second as he grasped the metal. Nothing. He twisted the handle and pushed open the door a fraction of an inch at a time, looking and listening for any telltale signs. Still nothing.

When the door was a foot ajar he slipped inside.

The interior stank of stale woodsmoke – a combination of the damp morning and the lack of attention to the fire that had been burning at some point in the night. Other than that the pokey space looked and felt exactly as it had the day before. The footprints in the snow suggested the killer had been in here, but from what Ryker could see there was no evidence of their presence inside. The cabin certainly hadn't been turned over.

Ryker continued in, still moving with caution, just in case. The jammer that Lange had found was nowhere to be seen now. She'd found it in the bedroom, at least what passed as a bedroom, so Ryker headed in there.

The camp bed was scruffy and falling apart. The only other furniture in the room was a tatty wardrobe. Ryker moved to it and opened the doors. The jammer was right there at the bottom. He picked it up and turned it off then took out his phone again as he straightened up and turned around.

He paused. Stared over into the corner of the room. Frowned. Something didn't make sense. He moved back out into the main living area and looked over to the kitchenette.

Just as he thought. The far wall here was two or three feet further in than the bedroom wall. He walked up to it and placed his ear right up against the wooden slats. He could hear the faint hum of machinery beyond. The relaxed whir of a fan nearly at rest.

Ryker moved back into the bedroom. Into the far corner. He knocked on the wall, banging with his fist all across it. He found the weak spot. Knocked a little harder and the false panel came away. He put the panel aside and stared inside the cramped space.

'Elliott, you sneak.'

Computer equipment hummed away. Wires trailed all over. Atop a small and rickety desk sat two ageing monitors. Battery packs littered the floor. No sign how Elliott got the power to recharge them, but somehow he had.

Ryker stepped to the desktop tower and powered it on. The screens flickered to life.

Locked. A thumbprint was needed.

Ryker hung his head and closed his eyes. But really, he knew he had no choice.

Ten minutes later and Elliott's computer was unlocked and Ryker was searching through as his old colleague's body rested on the bed in the room next door. He had his own laptop next to him, and was steadily transferring everything that Elliott had. While he waited he was doing his own cherry-picking, sifting at speed through Elliott's files for anything of interest. Most of the large files contained nothing more than routine CCTV captures of the outside of the cabin and its grounds, and judging by what Ryker could see the files were only kept for seven days at a time.

He scanned through the files for the last twenty-four hours and it didn't take long to find the captures from the night. The cameras even had a night-vision setting. Good equipment.

When the shadowy figure appeared on the screen he hit pause. Even with the bright security lights on there was little he could tell of their features. He pressed play, reduced the speed to 0.5 and watched in slow motion as the killer emerged from the woods. Black boots, long black coat, hood over their head, which was facing down so that nothing could be seen of the face. But the shape of the person, the way they walked... Ryker was sure it was a woman.

She entered the house. There were no cameras inside and he fast-forwarded. She spent less than three minutes inside before she was on her way.

When she was out of sight of the cameras, Ryker sat back and sighed as his brain rumbled.

A female assassin. He'd known plenty in his past. Most were now dead. But not all. Was this someone he knew?

The download progress was only thirty per cent. He had a bit of a wait on his hands.

He dug into his pocket and took out the thumb drive that contained Lange's hard-drive data. He plugged the device into his laptop and opened up the directory. The data was password protected, but it only took his decryption software three minutes to break through. Ryker set up a basic keyword search. Female. Suspect. Assassin. Grichenko. There were only a small number of files that contained all four of those words and Ryker rifled through at speed.

Found it. He shook his head. Disgust? Annoyance? He wasn't

quite sure what emotion washed over him as he stared at the report. Lange had already known. MI5's and MI6's number one suspect in Grichenko's death was a female. They didn't have a name, but what they did have was a grainy image of her at the Port of Dover. And another in Spain.

Spain? What did that have to do with anything?

Ryker set up a new search and minutes later was reading through a crime-scene report of a bloodbath at an abandoned meat factory in Andalusia just a few days ago. The same nameless woman was the number one suspect.

Who the hell was she?

Ryker was midway through typing another search when he froze, mid-keystroke.

A sound. Not in the cabin, but somewhere outside it. He didn't move a muscle as he listened. No, it wasn't a sound, exactly. It was more a feeling. Vibration.

He remained rooted for several more seconds as he tried to place it.

A motor. Not far off.

Helicopter.

That was no coincidence. Ryker scooped up his laptop. Paused a second as he stared at the progress bar. Not even fifty per cent of Elliott's files had transferred. So be it. Ryker disconnected the wires. Put his equipment back into his bag. He moved out of the room and placed the false wall back into place.

He took one last look over to Elliott.

'Sorry, buddy.'

Then he headed for the door. By the time he was outside the whir and din from the rotors filled his ears. He couldn't yet see the craft over the tops of the trees, but it wasn't far off. He made a beeline for the track that would take him back to his car. But the helicopter was coming in from that direction and seconds later Ryker realised exactly where it was.

They'd found his car. They were hovering right above it.

Ryker slunk into the trees, crouched and waited. Moments later the helicopter passed by overhead. He watched as it came down into the clearing next to the cabin. No military or other obvious markings on the helicopter. The whir of the rotors was deafening, and even at distance the force of the air displaced by their rotation blasted into Ryker.

Four men jumped off, each of them bulked up in winter outdoor gear. Hats on, sunglasses, he couldn't quite make out enough of their faces to determine if he knew them or not.

'You two, go to the car!' he was sure he heard someone call from inside the helicopter. 'You two take the cabin. Find him!'

The men rushed off.

Then another two figures jumped down into the snow.

Ryker stared at the man and woman. The woman was Lange. A brief thought flickered in Ryker's mind that maybe this was a positive turn. That she'd come out here because she'd had second thoughts about ditching him. But no. Because Ryker's gaze soon fixed on the man she was with, and at that point he knew all bets were off.

Kaspovich.

27

Ryker clenched his fists in anger. At Kaspovich, at himself, at Lange. Had she lied to him the whole time? Tried to play him for her own benefit? Well, he'd kind of always suspected that, but he hadn't suspected it was because she was in cahoots with Kaspovich, the sneaky prick.

But for what end?

Ryker couldn't exactly say he hadn't been warned. Elliott had told Ryker not to trust a word Lange said. What had Elliott known?

Ryker knew one thing for sure. He wasn't going out to them. So only two options remained. Go to his car and fight those men off and drive away. Or run.

The helicopter's rotors were slowly coming to a stop, the noise from them and the engine dying down by the second as Lange and Kaspovich remained standing, staring around them.

There was a call from inside the cabin. Both of them turned and headed in. No doubt they'd just found Elliott's body.

Would Kaspovich try to pin that on Ryker too? Was that the game here? From the outside Ryker certainly looked to be in the shit. He'd been at Grichenko's murder scene. He'd been with Weller hours before he'd been killed. He was here now, had even moved Elliott's body and no doubt left forensic traces of his presence in the process. He was linked to four murders.

Yet what he'd seen in Lange's files suggested they knew who the real culprit was. The female assassin. Surely they didn't really believe him responsible. So were they trying to set him up, or was there an alternative answer?

Perhaps they were simply trying to figure out Ryker's own agenda.

Seconds later a hissing noise penetrated through the quietening roar of the rotors, coming from Ryker's right. One, two, three, four bursts.

The tyres of his car being slashed.

So that was one of his options taken away. But Ryker still remained rooted as he thought through his next move.

Kaspovich, Lange and two of the men emerged from the cabin. They spread out and stared across into the woods.

'Ryker!' Lange shouted. She was looking at a single spot in the woods as she called, but not where Ryker was crouching. 'Ryker! Please come out. We're here to help you. We know what's happening now. Don't make this harder for yourself. For us all.'

Ryker grit his teeth in anger. Did she even believe the words that spewed from her mouth?

Ryker had seen enough here. Any moment they'd be coming into the woods after him. He turned and carefully, silently, edged away, further into the trees. He'd moved all of ten steps before he heard shouts behind him.

'Ryker!' Kaspovich now. His voice boomed through the trees. 'I know you're out there. This is your last chance.'

'Don't be stupid, James,' Lange shouted. 'You can't do this on your own. Elliott's dead. Weller's dead. Salman too. We just found that out. He was in Dubai. Living a quiet life as a security guard. We're all targets. There's only three of us left. We need to help each other.'

Ryker ignored her and kept on moving. Soon the helicopter's rotors were starting up once again. He hoped that was simply because they'd had enough and were leaving already, but seconds later when Ryker heard rustling behind him, he knew that wasn't the case. They were on his tail. Boots on the ground as well as an eye in the sky.

He picked up his pace. Turned off to the north-west, where he knew if he continued to head down he'd eventually get to a village, even if it was some ten or twelve miles trekking over mountainous, snowy and icy terrain.

He looked behind him every few steps. He was sure he could see the flash of one of the men's coats, about twenty yards back. Were they gaining on him?

Ryker opted against caution now and moved more quickly, though the gradient of the sloping ground was becoming steeper, making it harder and harder to keep his footing.

'I see him!'

No. It was no good. He couldn't lose them like this. His only option was to lure them in and attack.

He looked over his shoulder as he continued forward. But he could see nothing of them, which made him feel all the more vulnerable. Were they already circling around him somehow?

Then the helicopter whooshed overhead. Ryker instinctively glanced upward, even though the craft remained unseen somewhere above the trees.

Big mistake. Ryker went to put his foot down, but with him staring up he misjudged. His foot slipped. He tumbled forward. He tried to place his other foot out to balance himself but that was already swinging wayward as he toppled.

Before he knew it he was on his side, sliding down a steep, icy verge. He smacked into a tree trunk but rather than stop him it simply spun him around and he was on his back sliding head first and down. Down, down.

He scrabbled with his hands, trying to gain a grip on something, anything other than snow.

No use. He slid out over a rocky ledge and was in free fall.

Ryker plummeted. Cold air whistled. He tried to adjust his body. Tried to see how far the ground was below him.

Too late.

Smack.

Cold. That was the first sensation he was aware of after he crashed down with a jolt. Wet. That was the next sensation as the blood dribbled from a gash at the side of his head.

Black. That was the final thing he could grasp as he drifted to unconsciousness.

28

Ryker didn't think he was out for long. The main reason being that he could still hear the helicopter swirling somewhere above him when he groggily opened his heavy eyelids. He stared up at the grey clouds. His body was crumpled and twisted and sunken into thick powdery snow.

He lifted his torso up, propping himself on his elbow as he scanned around him. The ledge he'd fallen from was fifty feet above, but he'd been lucky. The groove in the rock where he'd fallen was by far the shortest way down as the rocky outcrop rose up to both the left and right. The only way for the chasing pack to get to him was to jump down after him, or to move further afield to find an alternate route.

Was the latter what they were trying to do?

Ryker groaned as he got to his feet. Everything ached, though nothing was broken. A small gash on the side of his head left a trail of blood in the white snow. He'd have to take a closer look later to determine if he needed stitches.

His backpack was still strapped to his shoulders.

Crap. His backpack.

He slid it off, opened up and took out his laptop. Mangled.

The metal and plastic was all twisted. The screen was cracked and blistered. Ryker growled in frustration. Perhaps the hard drive was salvageable but he'd need a whole load of new equipment to even try to recover the data.

He took out his phone. Similarly, the screen was cracked, but it was still powered on. He wiped the dribbling blood off his face with his sleeve as he stared at the screen. The device suddenly burst into life and vibrated in his hand. He could make out just enough to see who was calling him. Lange.

The helicopter swooped by overhead and Ryker crouched and shuffled sideways so he was under the cover of the dense pine trees. The call went unanswered, but Ryker only had one option. For all he knew they were already in the process of tracking the precise location of the phone.

Ryker cracked the back off the handset and pulled out the battery. He snapped it in two then took out the SIM which similarly ended up in the snow in pieces. Next, he ripped the hard drive from the battered casing of the laptop. He replaced the drive in the backpack, put the bag over his shoulders, then took one final look around before he got moving.

There was no sign of Lange or Kaspovich or the other men chasing him on foot now. Perhaps they'd already regrouped, or were all in the helicopter. For the next ten minutes, as he limped along on battered legs, he continued to hear the chopper hanging overhead, passing right by over the top of him more than once. They couldn't see him beneath the trees, but did they have thermal imaging or suchlike to keep track of him?

After that initial ten minutes of traipsing through the forest, though, the sound of the helicopter finally faded to nothing, and Ryker was left in an uneasy silence.

The helicopter had gone. Why? Had they landed somewhere to set a trap, or had they cut their losses and left Ryker to it?

He'd have to be ready either way.

The trek through the frozen woodland was strenuous and blisteringly cold, particularly with Ryker's clothes sopping wet. More than once he considered whether he should stop and set up a fire to help warm up and dry out, but he had to believe that delay could end up causing him even greater problems.

The strenuous trek reminded him of one of his most torturous experiences, back when he'd been in training for his life as a clandestine field agent. He'd been up in the wilds of the Scottish Highlands on an escape, an evasion training exercise with a band of soldiers who he'd fallen sorely out of favour with. Following a violent confrontation which had long been coming, the relatively inexperienced Ryker had suffered a broken fibula. With no method of contacting their base camp, his supposed 'team' had left him to die. Ryker had literally clawed and dragged his body toward safety before being rescued by a search party. He'd spent weeks in hospital overcoming severe hypothermia, never mind the broken leg.

As he walked now that leg ached all the more, as if in response to the morose memories. He only hoped this episode would have a better ending.

More than five hours later and Ryker passed through the treeline and could see the village below him. He was shivering violently and he knew his energy, his resolve, his will was all at rock bottom.

He also knew he was a state. Dirty, clothes scruffy and torn and wet. Dried blood caked on his face. But he was hardly going to be able to do much about that right away. What he needed was a means of transport.

The village consisted of little more than fifty buildings, mostly chalet-style homes with a collection of basic shops. As he approached he remained on the lookout. He wouldn't have put it past Lange to be here already, lying in wait, even though Ryker had seen or heard nothing of her or the others or the helicopter for some time now.

Ryker, head down, moved on into the centre of the cluster of buildings and stopped by a tree across the road from a run of three shops.

He stood in wait thinking through his next step.

He didn't have to wait too long. Perhaps he was due a bit of good fortune after all.

A black Range Rover pulled up into one of the roadside parking spaces. A man and a woman got out. Both were smartly dressed, both forties or perhaps early fifties. The man had a deep scowl on his face as he blasted down his phone to someone. The woman looked embarrassed by his ranting but he didn't notice at all.

Ryker moved across the street, walking at pace to intercept them as they walked toward the café a couple of buildings along. Ryker could hear the conversation more clearly now. In French, the man was berating some poor sod because of the fall in the stock price of something or other. With every hurled expletive the woman next to him flinched a little. Ryker made a beeline for them. The woman saw him at the last second. The man – momentarily staring up to the sky, exasperated, as he moved – didn't see him at all. Ryker barged into him, and ended up taking a tumble onto the grit-covered ground.

'What are you doing!' the man screamed to Ryker in his native tongue, glowering down at him like he was a piece of dog muck. Then he glanced to his companion whose expression was only a little more friendly.

'Sorry,' Ryker said, groaning as he spoke. 'I'm really sorry. Please... help me up.'

Ryker held out his hand and the man looked seriously put out by the suggestion.

'Please,' Ryker said again as he shuffled to try to get to his feet.

'And now we even have these homeless bums infecting the alps. What next?' the man said as he glared from Ryker to the woman. The woman grumbled her agreement and shook her head in disgust before the two of them walked away leaving Ryker on the ground.

He got to his feet as he watched them heading into the café.

Then, the key fob clutched in his hand, he turned and strode for their ride.

Next stop, sunny Spain.

29

The woman was sitting on the table, twiddling the gun in her hands. Leia's eyes were only half open. She didn't want to sleep but her weary body craved it. Next to her, her father shuffled position, rousing her.

'You should take my offer,' he said to the woman. 'You'll never get a better one. Two million dollars. I know that's way more than you were supposed to get.'

The woman didn't register his words at all.

Leia groaned. Her head was pounding. Tiredness, hunger, distress. How long had they been here for now, in this room? Twelve hours? Twenty-four? It felt like days. The man was gone again. How long had it been? To get food, he'd said. Leia and her father had only been given scraps so far, as well as the paltry water. They'd not been out of this room at all, not even for the toilet. Instead, they'd been provided with a bucket in the corner. Leia's father had robustly objected to that. To a fourteen-year-old girl being subjected to such humiliation. Yet they'd both had no choice but to use it.

'So?'

'I said no,' the woman replied. 'Now please shut up.'

Leia's father chuckled. 'I know I'm asking a lot of you. A betrayal.

But two million dollars, and you walk away. Weigh it up. Two million and you live. Or you get nothing and, most likely, you'll die.'

The woman said nothing now. Yet Leia knew that slowly her father's words were wearing her down. Something about the way she sat so solemnly when he talked. The sighs and the deep breathing.

'Even with this sack on my head, I can tell you love him. He loves you too. But let me put it another way. How much for him to betray you instead?'

The journey to Copenhagen gave Devereaux plenty of thinking time. She didn't just think of her past. More recent events dominated her mind. Two people in particular. From all the digging she'd carried out, Paulo's life remained something of a closed book to her. Information on Kyri's past was a little more readily available, even if it was far too bland to be the whole story.

At the age of thirty-nine, Kyri, a Cypriot national, had inherited a real estate portfolio from his father, which he'd steadily built over the last three decades. Developments he'd had involvement in included several prominent apartment blocks and hotels along some of the Mediterranean's most exclusive and idyllic spots. But most of the properties had other partners, and Kyri was wealthy, but far from super-rich. There was nothing in his public profile which suggested a relationship with Pavel Grichenko, either in the past or up until she'd killed the Russian in England last week.

So what was the real story there, and what else was Kyri involved in that Devereaux didn't yet know?

Questions about Kyri's past aside, it was Paulo she thought of most, and she was still thinking about him even as she stalked her new prey through the frozen streets of Copenhagen. She wondered with interest when she'd next 'bump' into him. There'd been no sign of him in Switzerland, but would he be here in Copenhagen? Or was he done with her now? Was it down to her to find *him*?

One thing she was sure of, she wasn't done with him yet.

The woman turned off the street and into the park. Devereaux looked around then headed that way too. They'd been walking for more than a mile already. It was gone 8pm, not exactly late, but it was dark and cold out and the streets were quiet. This park was deserted and had no lights on at all.

Devereaux had been on the tail of this woman since she'd arrived in the Danish capital earlier in the morning. She'd had a pretty bland day, all in all. A visit to a gym. A visit to a library. Lunch with her handsome and extremely smartly dressed boyfriend. The rest of the afternoon and early evening she'd spent at his apartment. Devereaux had waited outside there for several hours. He'd come home a little after 6pm. Had left again a little after seven. Black tie, chauffeur to pick him up and everything. Devereaux was half tempted to follow him to see what the shindig was. Why hadn't he taken his lady with him? Instead, Devereaux had remained in wait, contemplating how long she'd stay in place before she simply went up there to finish the job quickly.

Then the woman had emerged. Alone.

Interesting.

A secret lover's rendezvous, perhaps? That would make this a whole lot more exciting, though it was seeming increasingly unlikely now that the woman had come into this dark, cold and isolated park, where she was walking alone.

Odd, to say the least.

The woman was fifty yards ahead, walking quickly in trainers, and with a long and thick coat that went down to her knees. She had jeans underneath. No. This wasn't a lover's rendezvous. She wasn't dressed for it. The woman headed along a twisting path, only barely lit by the lights from the nearby streets and buildings. She moved down a dip, underneath a stone-arched bridge. When she was halfway through the tunnel she slowed momentarily. She didn't look over her shoulder, or anything like that, but a moment later she picked up her pace.

Then abruptly turned off to the left when she'd exited the tunnel.

Devereaux glanced around her. What the hell?

She moved a little more quickly, still not making a sound. Through the tunnel. She came out the other side then stopped.

Where was she? No sign of the woman now. Devereaux held her breath, strained her senses. Could hear and see nothing.

At least not until there was a flicker of movement in the patch of black in front of her. In among trees?

Devereaux moved forward, a little more cautiously now. A sliver of moonlight escaped through a gap in the clouds allowing her to more easily make out the scene. A copse of trees. Thick bushes beyond.

Then there was movement to her right. The snap of a twig to her left.

Breathing right behind her.

The woman wasn't alone. Devereaux had been tricked.

She ducked and spun and crashed her elbow into the figure behind her. Solid contact. Side of head, she thought. She heard the second person racing toward her on the other side. She sidestepped and tried to right herself, was ready for the attack.

She wasn't ready for the gunshots.

Bang. Bang.

The first bullet thudded into the frozen grass next to her. The second sank into her thigh. Devereaux grimaced in pain. Adrenaline surged as anger bubbled and she drove forward, grabbed the hand holding the gun. She twisted the arm to adjust the aim then forced her finger onto the trigger. A single pull. A single bullet. A splat as blood and bone and brain erupted – some of it spattering onto Devereaux's face and clothes. She let go and the body crumpled to the ground.

She had hold of the gun now. She crouched down. Looked closely at the person she'd killed. The face was unrecognisable but she could see it was a man. The second person was shuffling on the ground next to her. Conscious but dazed.

Devereaux stood up and drove her heel down onto their torso. *Crack*. A scream. Female. Her target? She took out her phone and shone it onto the face. No. Not her target. Devereaux didn't know her at all.

'Please,' the woman said.

Devereaux glared at her, pointed the gun to her face.

'Please. You don't have to kill me.'

English. An English accent.

'The police are coming. Don't make this worse for yourself.'

That was true. Devereaux could already hear the siren.

'Where is she?' Devereaux asked.

No response.

'Tell me where she is!'

A slight shake of the head.

Devereaux fired again. The bullet blasted through the woman's eye. She dropped the gun and turned on her phone's flash and snapped a picture of each of the corpses. She looked all around. No sign of her target now.

Her insides boiled with rage. Blood slid down her leg which throbbed with pain.

As best as she could with the bullet in her thigh, she turned and ran. She retraced her steps. Through the tunnel, along the path. Her eyes busy as she went. No sign of the woman still. She'd scarpered, no doubt.

In the near distance Devereaux could see strobes of blue

beyond the wispy tree branches. She reached the road. Turned in the opposite direction of the blue lights and moved as quickly and as calmly as she could until she was deep within the city's streets.

She stopped in a dark and secluded alleyway, then pulled down her trousers to inspect the wound. The bullet wasn't too deep. She'd dig it out herself. Later. For now she'd have to settle. She used her knife to cut a swathe of fabric from her jumper which she tied around her leg to at least stem the flow of blood, and to soak up what she lost to halt the blood trail. She could do nothing now about her blood, her DNA that was already at the crime scene.

With anger and embarrassment still bubbling way, she took out her phone and sent the two pictures to Paulo, along with a message.

I was ambushed. Target escaped. Who are they?

Her brain whirred with unwelcome thoughts as she waited. Would she hear back from Paulo at all? Would he want her dead now?

Two minutes later a reply came through.

Don't leave town.

She clenched her teeth. She'd been wondering all day when she would see Paulo again. What would happen next time she did. Would they have sex again? Would she try to kill him again?

Perhaps neither. Perhaps it was he who'd try to kill her. Perhaps not even him, but simply her replacement.

Her brain fired. She could run. Hide. Recover. Take stock, then action.

No. That wasn't her style. Paulo, or whoever he sent, was coming. She'd be here to take on whatever came her way next.

She'd wait. She'd be ready. And sooner or later she'd get her revenge for tonight having turned to shit. When she found her, Devereaux would make Penny Diaz suffer like she'd never made anyone suffer before.

30

'How much for him to betray you instead?'

That was her father's killer line. The full meaning and repercussions behind his words were huge, and even with the balaclava on, Leia thought she could see the resolve slipping from the woman's face. Because through the course of their captivity, there were times when they'd been left alone with the man too. And each time Leia's father had worked the same way, playing to his emotions. Playing in turn to their fear, their paranoia and their greed. In a strange way, Leia had never admired her father so much, even despite the fact that she was in pieces about her mother's death, and in abject fear that she'd never leave this place alive.

The question still hung in the air when the man strode back into the room, two brown paper bags in his hand. He slapped the food down onto the table and looked to his accomplice – his lover – then over to Leia and her father. He paused, his agitation clear in his body language.

'What were you talking about?' he said to the woman.

'Nothing.'

The man looked over to Leia and her father.

'That's not quite true, is it?' her father said.

'What's he talking about?' The man faced the woman, who stood straight now. One hand only inches from the gun in the waist of her jeans. The man was the same.

'Don't listen to him,' the woman said. 'He's trying to cause problems. As always.'

'No, that's not it,' Leia's father said. 'Not problems. Solutions. It's in your hands now.'

Leia could hardly breathe. The tension was choking.

'Did you reach Remi?' the woman asked.

The man didn't answer straight away. That said a lot.

'Yeah,' he said. 'I did.'

'And?'

'And he's coming in half an hour. We're going to get our money. And we're going to get out of here.'

He spoke with conviction, but Leia somehow knew his words were an absolute lie.

Devereaux did exactly what she was told. After receiving the text message from Paulo she headed straight back to her hotel room. In the closet bathroom there she used a pair of tweezers to pull the slug from her thigh and stitched the wound with a needle and thread and nothing to kill the pain but a pack of paracetamol and a bottle of cheap brandy she'd bought from a nearby convenience store.

Still, her whole leg remained on fire, her body ached. She wanted nothing more than to sleep for hours, perhaps days, until she felt better. Instead, she sat up, thinking.

She'd been working for Kyri and Paulo for only a few days. In that time she'd lost a finger and been shot in the thigh. And she was getting paid nothing for any of this. How much more would she put up with?

She'd tried her hardest to find out more about both Paulo and Kyri. After all, sooner or later – hopefully sooner – she'd be turning the tables on them and she'd have to know who she was dealing with. Despite her efforts she'd found relatively little about the duo. It wasn't just Kyri and Paulo that Devereaux wanted to find out more about though. Thus far she'd kept a relatively closed mind to the lives of the targets she'd been given. It didn't matter to Devereaux who they were, or why Kyri wanted them dead. She'd long ago learned to live and work that way. Emotion and reason didn't come into what she did. But the failed attempt on Penny Diaz had given her pause for thought, because she very much did not like how close she'd come to being shot dead by the two ambushers.

Who were they? And why had they been protecting Diaz?

The more she thought about it, the more she seriously contemplated cutting her losses and skipping town and figuring a way to end all this by ending Kyri and Paulo.

Despite her reservations, she remained in her hotel room, and a little after 11pm, her phone pinged.

Her heart thudded a little harder as she picked up the phone and scanned over the message.

Svensson's bar. Half an hour. Dress smart.

The walk to the bar was painful. It'd been hard enough heading back to the hotel earlier, before she'd pulled the bullet out and stitched and dressed the wound, but in two-inch heels the pain that shot up through her leg each time she put her foot down made her head pound, even with a cocktail of painkillers and alcohol inside her. Still, she made it to the bar in twenty-five minutes.

She wore the same skin-tight black dress she'd had on in the bar in Frankfurt, smartening the look up just a little through the addition of classy-looking though cheap jewellery, and by putting on her short, blonde, ready-styled wig that she knew always drew attention. She was trying her best not to think about how tonight might end, given the calamity in the park, though at least Paulo had asked to meet in a public place. That was a good start. And if he did turn on her, she'd be ready.

She was pleasantly surprised when she stepped inside the bar to see it was quite a different affair to Frankfurt. No wood panelling in sight. The place wasn't exactly ultra-high-end, but one look around the customers showed it attracted people with more than a few pennies to spare.

She took a seat at a table in a corner, no drink. Paulo could do the honours. She waited for fifteen minutes. With each one that passed, her anxiety levels rose a little. Finally she spotted him. But then she clenched her fists and dug her nails into her palms when she saw he wasn't alone.

Kyri was there too.

They headed on over. Devereaux tried her best to show no reaction. Paulo's face was impassive, though Kyri beamed her a smile and leaned in for a kiss on each cheek before he sat down opposite her. Paulo sat next to Devereaux as if to block her in.

Under the table she slid her left hand down her leg so her fingers were right next to the handle of the knife once again strapped to her inner thigh.

'Blonde? I think I prefer you natural,' Kyri said with a nonchalant shrug. 'Care for a drink?'

'Vodka,' Devereaux said.

Kyri nodded and beckoned a young waitress over and ordered vodka, a red wine and a glass of sparkling water.

'Paulo's driving,' Kyri said when he turned back. 'I don't want him getting wasted like last time.'

Devereaux clenched her teeth. She could tell by the sly twinkle in Kyri's eye that he knew what had happened between

Paulo and her in that bar in Frankfurt. The question was why the hell would Paulo have told him? She didn't feel betrayed. More embarrassed.

'Sounded to me like you two had quite an evening.'

'It certainly wasn't a whole evening,' Devereaux said. 'Barely a few minutes.'

Kyri laughed, a little too heartily, but after a few moments his face went neutral and then sour.

'Wig aside, you look like crap,' he said.

'I've had a rough night.'

'You and me both,' he said. 'I've had the shakes all the way here. My vitamin D levels are dying just in anticipation of the cold here.' He held up his quivering hand as if to prove his point. 'I don't like having to leave the sunshine to sort out other people's mess.'

Devereaux said nothing. The waitress brought the drinks over and Kyri paid with a far too large bill and told her to keep the change.

'Who were they?' Devereaux asked. 'The people in the park?'

'A problem. For you. But the best thing to do right now is to stick to the plan.'

'They were police? Spies? What?'

'You don't need to know.'

Devereaux's eyes narrowed. 'You came all this way to tell me this?'

'No. I came all this way to try and solve this crap. To try to keep people off your back. I think you know what I'm getting at, don't you?'

'Not really.'

'Shame. Because I thought you were intelligent and I don't want to have to spell it out to you. I can't undo the mess you created, but I can help to make it go away. You stick to the plan. We have an address for you.'

'This isn't how I work.'

'You'll work how I tell you to. I think I explained that last time.'

Devereaux paused. She didn't really have a response to that. At least not one that Kyri would want to hear. 'What–'

'You'll get this done tonight. Then you'll leave Denmark. Okay?'

Devereaux said nothing.

'Do you understand?'

'Yes,' she murmured.

Paulo grabbed her hand – her injured one – and pulled it off her lap and pushed it down onto the table. She only resisted a little. She didn't want to make a scene right here.

'Are you sure?' Paulo hissed. 'Or perhaps we need to take another finger first.'

He mimicked slicing off another of her digits using his hand as a pretend knife. Devereaux did now whip her hand away as she glared daggers at him.

'That's enough, both of you,' Kyri said. 'She gets the point. I know she does. And I'm glad to see your hand is getting better already.'

Paulo was smirking now. Devereaux wanted nothing more than to slice his face into pieces so he'd never be able to look at anyone like that again.

'But please, no more mistakes,' Kyri said.

Devereaux said nothing, just nodded.

Kyri took a big sip of his wine. There was still more than half left as he stood up.

'I can leave you two here alone, if you like?' he said with a cocky look on his face.

'No, it's fine,' Paulo replied, getting to his feet too. 'I'm done with her.'

'Shame,' Kyri said. 'She got all dressed up for you too.'

He cackled and then turned and headed off toward the exit. Paulo remained hanging over her. She held his eye for a few moments though she really didn't have anything to say. Eventually he shook his head, as if disappointed, before moving off after his boss, leaving Devereaux trying her best to keep her rage from bursting out.

Under the table she slowly slid the knife back into its sheath, then let out a long exhale as she tried to calm down.

Next time. Next time she'd get them both. No matter the consequences.

31

The thirty minutes took an age, at least for Leia. The nervousness in the room heightened with each second that passed. The man and the woman were both on edge, agitated, practically climbing up the walls like they'd both had pure caffeine injected directly into their bloodstreams. There was relief, resentment, distrust, annoyance, perhaps even some happiness, all rolled into one. To Leia it was like a pressure cooker of emotion and she knew there'd be an explosion sooner or later, she just didn't know what that explosion would entail. Either for the captors, or for her and her father.

'Okay, it's time,' the man said, checking his watch.

'They're here?' the woman replied, looking around her as though questioning his revelation. Leia certainly hadn't heard a car or anything like that, and the few times either of these two had taken their vehicle out, the engine's vibrations had only weakly reached up into this room.

'They will be,' the man said. 'I'm not waiting around in this place another second. Let's get them outside.' He looked over at Leia. 'Get the hood back on her.'

Leia looked over at her father who'd been strangely quiet through *this. Why? She'd thought his words, his offer to these two, had broken through. That one would turn on the other and she'd soon be free. Had she got it all wrong? Was this the moment she'd be taken to her fate? Certain death, and probably a horrible one, if they were handed over to her father's enemies.*

The woman came over, sack in hand. She bent down toward Leia who cowered back into the corner. She quivered with fright as the sack was brought toward her.

'I'm sorry,' the woman whispered.

'This is your last chance,' Leia's father said.

Leia flicked her gaze from the woman and to the man behind her. He was reaching for his gun.

'Look out!' Leia screamed.

Why did she say that?

The woman burst up as she pulled the gun from her waistband. By the time she was facing the man they both had their weapons trained. On each other.

'I should have known,' the woman said.

The gun trembled in her grip. The man shook his head in disgust.

'What choice did you leave me?' he said. 'I knew you'd cave.'

'Except I didn't. You did. Remi's not coming, is he?'

He shook his head again.

'So what now?'

BANG. BANG.

Two shots. One from each gun. They both collapsed to the floor.

There was something satisfying about the chance of such a quick redemption, even if Devereaux remained wary. Was this really her opportunity for revenge, or was it merely a trap set by Kyri and Paulo?

No, she wouldn't believe that. It was time to make amends.

Earlier in the evening it had been cold and frosty. Now snow was pouring from the sky in thick flakes. Devereaux had her hood up and kept her head down as she walked, but the snow still peppered her face and covered the front of her in glistening flakes from head to toe.

Her leg continued to throb with pain, but with adrenaline now surging in anticipation of what was to come, she was managing to block it out. She rounded a corner, out of the chilling breeze and dusted herself down with her leather gloves. The cobbled alley she was in lay between two hulking brick buildings – inner city factories built at some time during the industrial revolution. Relics now. Devereaux had no clue what purpose the buildings had originally served. She had little clue what purpose they now served. Well, except for the building beyond the plain-looking wooden door thirty yards down. Completely innocuous. Certainly no insignia to show a business was based here. Not even a number to show this was an entrance.

Devereaux carried on down toward it. She was unfamiliar with this part of the city. Relatively gentrified, from what she could gather, the area of once heavy industry was now fashionable with young professionals and the like, judging by the trendy cafés and shops, though the streets around here were quiet and unexciting at this time of night.

The alley was less than quiet, it was lifeless.

Except for Devereaux creeping along as the snow continued to fall down on her.

By the time she reached the door she'd already spotted two cameras. One was hidden away underneath the stone sill of the window on the storey above the door. Another had been close to the alley entrance, similarly well hidden. Though not hidden enough. She wondered if the occupants were already eyeballing their screens as they pondered Devereaux's approach.

She reached out and pressed the buzzer. At least she expected it was a buzzer, though she could hear no sound at all from beyond the door.

She realised as she stared that the peephole in the door contained yet another camera lens. She could tell by the way the circle twisted – ever so slightly – to focus, and by the almost imperceptible mechanical whir that accompanied the movement. Or perhaps it *was* imperceptible, and her mind was just imagining the noise.

Either way, she kept her head down as she waited, so as to not have her face caught clearly in view.

'Yes? Can I help you?' came a crackly male voice through the intercom speaker.

His Danish was about as good as hers. Definitely not native. She decided to go straight to English.

'I'm here for Diaz.'

A pause. 'Who are you?'

'Nadia Lange.'

'We weren't expecting you.'

She wondered if there was supposed to be some sort of secret exchange, like she'd seen in movies.

The weather is nice at this time of year.

Yes, but not as nice as it is in Timbuktu.

'Just let Penny know I'm here.'

Another pause. 'Let me see your face.'

Devereaux lifted her head now. She stared into the peephole and couldn't resist but break out into a smile.

Then she turned and walked away.

She moved slowly, in the opposite direction to which she'd arrived, just far enough so that she was out of view of the cameras by the door.

She pulled into the arched doorway of the building opposite and melted into the shadows.

What would their response be, she wondered? Clearly they would know she wasn't Lange. Would they simply sit tight now? Call for backup? Or would they send someone – more than one person – to check the street?

Devereaux's eyes swept across the building's fascia as she waited. In the gloomy alley, beyond the snow that was still falling, she could make out nothing behind the blackened windows. Were they actually blacked out or were there just no lights on up there?

She heard something. A rumble and click. The door across the other side of the alley being unlocked. She didn't move from the spot as she watched the door swing open. A man stepped out, pistol in his double-handed grip, the barrel of the weapon pointing to the ground in front of him as he crouched low. A second man, identical pose, followed him out.

Devereaux waited. The first man, the one closest to her, was scanning around. His eyes fell upon the footprints in the snow. Devereaux's footprints. Leading away from the building and right to...

She smiled. Then burst forward.

The knife was already in her hand as the man looked up in shock. She flung it through the air as he lifted the gun. Devereaux darted right a split second before he opened fire. The bullet whizzed through the air, missing her by a good few inches. A rushed shot. But his aim wasn't helped by the fact that he was himself attempting to duck to avoid the flight of the knife.

He couldn't avoid it, but he got lucky when the handle of the knife only smacked into his shoulder, and the weapon landed with a soft *whoomph* in the snow.

He didn't get a chance to fire again. Devereaux was already on him. The other knife in her hand now. She bent down and thrust the knife up and the blade plunged deep into his neck, under his chin, heading upward to the back of his throat. There was so much power and venom and momentum in the blow that his whole body lifted from his crouched position. If she'd been even stronger he'd have been off his feet, dangling from the wedged knife like a sprat on the end of a fishhook.

The whole move had taken no more than a couple of seconds. Enough time for the second man to have figured out what was going on. He was turned in her direction. Aiming his gun, ready to pull the trigger. Except he had no clear target.

Devereaux ducked down, used the dead man's body as a shield. She grabbed his wrist, twisted the gun around and put her finger over his to pull the trigger.

One shot. That was all she needed. His companion had been so close to making a difference, but his indecision had cost him his life. The bullet splatted into his face, just below his left eye, and he crumpled to a heap on the ground.

Devereaux pulled the gun free from the impaled man's grip then yanked out the knife and he slid into a heap on the ground next to his fallen friend.

She put the gun in her pocket, picked up her first knife, then rushed for the open door.

Stairs. She climbed them two at a time as she sheathed one of the knives and grabbed a grenade from her pocket. She rounded the corner. Saw the partially open door across the landing.

'Shit,' said the woman who was waiting there.

Not Diaz. The woman went to close the door but Devereaux was too quick. She flung the grenade. Perfect shot. Right through the diminishing gap. There was a startled yelp a second before the explosion erupted. Smoke and grit and debris filled the air but Devereaux continued forward, through the open doorway. She used her hearing now as much as her sight to feel her way through the dark and smoke-filled space.

Off to her left. Footsteps. She darted that way. Saw the man. She spun in an arc and swooshed the knife out. The blade sliced through his neck and he collapsed to the floor gargling his last breaths.

Another figure to her right. Devereaux didn't even have time to look to see if it was a man or a woman. It didn't matter. She spun again as a bullet whisked past her face. Closer this time, but not close enough. She thrust the knife out and it squelched as it slid through skin and flesh. She drove forward and slammed the figure up against a wall.

A man, as it turned out. She twisted the knife once. Pulled it out and thrust it into his belly again. The blade sank even further this time. A further twist and she let go and he collapsed, clutching his abdomen as if doing so would stop his guts from spilling onto the floor.

Shuffling behind her. Not someone coming for her. Someone trying to move quietly.

Devereaux turned. She looked to the crouched heap on the floor. Penny Diaz. The woman looked petrified. Her skin and clothes were streaked with blood and she had a piece of shrapnel several inches long wedged in her arm. No weapon in sight. Only a couple of yards from her was a cupboard which had been pulled from against the wall. In the wall was a metal sliding door, only four feet high. It was partially shut, a gap of about a foot for it to be fully closed.

A panic room lay beyond, perhaps. Or an escape route. The woman had been so close to safety.

Had the grenade crippled the mechanism? Or was it just incredible bad luck?

Devereaux broke out into a smile as she looked down to her quarry.

'Please,' Diaz begged.

'You made me look stupid,' Devereaux said, the smile now gone.

'Please,' was all Diaz could muster once more as she cowered back further against the wall.

'I don't like to be made to look stupid,' Devereaux said. 'All of this.' She waved the bloody knife around in the air. A few drops of red dropped to the floor as she did so. 'All of this was because of you. They all died because of *you*.'

'I'm... sorry.'

As if that mattered. Devereaux shook her head. 'No. But you will be.'

She lunged forward, the blood-dripping knife held aloft.

32

The dashboard thermometer slowly crept up as Ryker headed further and further south. What had started as a more than chilly minus eight when he'd taken the Range Rover in the Alps, ended up as a positively balmy sixteen Celsius by the time he was driving through the mountains of Andalusia. High up in the peaks there was just a dusting of snow, a gentle reminder that even the Mediterranean experienced winters, though thousands of feet below, on the winding mountain passes, it was a warm and sunny and calm day.

On taking the car in Switzerland, Ryker had headed straight for the border. Of course, he expected the couple he'd stolen the vehicle from would have reported the theft to the police as soon as they'd realised, but a simple car theft was unlikely to see an immediate cross-border search operation initiated, so Ryker was content to remain in the stolen car for the whole of his journey to southern Spain. Now, after an overnight rest in the inland Cuenca province, where he'd also been able to tend to his scrapes and cuts and obtain some more appropriate clothing, he was only half an hour from his destination near Marbella.

Marbella. Ryker had been before. It was an area so full of

contrast. Beautiful coastal scenery, exclusive hotels, expensive restaurants, millionaires' villas, a port which regularly displayed some of the flashiest yachts in the world. It was also a hotbed of criminality, from low-level drugs and violence and other crimes that went hand in glove with the rowdy nightlife in the area, through to large-scale organised gangs, many of them headed by foreign nationals, and the majority of them at least in part focused on the import into the country of illegal drugs from Africa and the Middle East.

It was that criminal element that had once more drawn Ryker here. He'd had little chance to properly research the sparse lead he'd got in Switzerland. Largely because he'd had no means by which to retrieve the data on the hard drive from his now discarded laptop. He was simply working off what he could remember from Elliott's cabin, together with the little extra he'd gleaned from basic internet searches on a newly purchased smartphone. He had a good enough place to start at least. A name, a place.

According to Lange's files, Mohammed Khaled was one of the dead men from the abattoir killings. Khaled was a dual Spanish and Moroccan national who had been something of a local criminal boss. Not a kingpin exactly, but someone who'd made himself wealthy through criminality. Now he was dead, killed by the same female assassin who was stalking Ryker and his colleagues from the botched operation in Doha a decade ago.

But what the hell did Khaled have to do with that?

Ryker left the Range Rover a couple of hundred yards from the villa entrance. Here, high up in the sierra, there were gigantic villas dotted about the rocky rise, though most of them were well secluded behind trees, thick shrubs, and high walls. The home belonging to the deceased Mohammed Khaled, and his wife, Yasmin, was no different, and as Ryker approached the closed entrance gate, flanked either side by a handsome stone wall, he still hadn't had even a glimpse of the villa that lay beyond.

He walked up to the intercom by the gates and pressed the buzzer.

'*Qué?*' a male voice answered a few seconds later.

Ryker noticed that the intercom also contained a discreet camera. He looked directly into the lens, trying his best to look... normal.

'I'm here to speak to Mrs Khaled,' Ryker said in plain old English, even though he could get by just fine in Spanish if he wanted.

'She's not here,' the man replied.

'When will she be back?'

'She won't be. You should go.'

'You haven't even asked who I am. Why I'm here.'

There was a click and then silence. Ryker waited for a few seconds, as if there was an outside chance the gates would suddenly start to slide open.

They didn't.

He pressed on the intercom again.

'I told you–'

'Please tell Mrs Khaled I'm here to talk about her husband's murder.'

Silence.

'Tell her I know who did it. That she killed my friends too.'

Click. Then silence again. Ryker remained rooted. Calm.

Success this time. Seconds later he heard footsteps crunching across gravel. Two sets. With a mechanical whir the gate slowly slid open, disappearing behind the wall.

Ryker was left standing face to face with two men. One was tall and brutish, a snarl on his face. Muscles rippled under his T-shirt. He was grasping a pistol in his right hand.

The other man was shorter, plainer, a little more smartly dressed in linen trousers and a partly buttoned-up shirt. He had no weapon in his hand, but he was the one Ryker focused on.

'Are you armed?' the shorter man said.

'No,' Ryker replied.

He did have a knife, though he'd left it in the Range Rover. He had nothing on him at all here. No phone, no wallet. Just his clothes and the key fob for the car.

The shorter man stepped forward and patted Ryker up and down while his friend with the gun stood watch.

'My name's James Ryker. What's yours?'

No answer to the question.

'You work for Mrs Khaled?'

Nothing.

'Okay, come this way,' the guy said when he'd finished what he was doing.

Ryker headed off behind him. The man with the gun waited a couple of seconds then moved in tow. He pressed the barrel of the gun into Ryker's back. Ryker rolled his eyes. Perhaps these two thought they were doing a decent job of security here. They weren't. It might put off an everyday Joe, but it would take seconds for Ryker to put them both on the ground if he wanted.

The most interesting thing was that they were here at all.

Ryker took in the gorgeous villa as they approached. The Khaleds certainly weren't shy of a few euros. The two men escorted Ryker into the home, through an airy hallway, into a back room and out through the wide-open bifold doors onto a patio. Beyond the patio was a sprawling lawn with a glistening pool at the far end. To his right was an outdoor dining table and six chairs. One of the chairs was taken by a woman.

The shell of a woman at least. Dressed in a pink velvety tracksuit, she was sunken into the chair. Her features were similarly sunken, her eyes bloodshot, her cheeks droopy, her light, dyed hair mussy. Her skin was ashen.

She fixed a weary gaze on Ryker.

'What do you want?'

Her English was good. Better than the guy's was.

'To talk to you about the woman who killed your husband.'

Yasmin Khaled glared at Ryker for a few seconds. 'You know who she is?'

The way she said it suggested she didn't.

'I know that she killed my friends too,' Ryker said. 'And she's trying to kill me.'

Yasmin kept her eyes on Ryker though didn't say a word for a while. 'Sit down.'

Ryker did so. The short guy went over to Yasmin and they had a hushed exchange. Then the two guys moved off, over to the pool area, where they remained lurking, watching, though out of earshot. Ryker noticed there was a crate by the pool filled with various toys and inflatables. No sign of the kids here today though.

'So?' Yasmin said.

'I'm sorry for what happened,' Ryker said.

'Did you know Mo?'

Ryker shook his head.

'And you don't know me. So how can you be sorry?'

'The woman who killed–'

'The woman who killed my husband came to my home. She tied me up. She threatened to kill me. She tied wire around my arm and nearly sliced it right off my body.'

She lifted the sleeve of her tracksuit top to reveal the circular gouge in the skin on her wrist. Ryker clenched his teeth.

'Why would she do that?' Ryker said.

Yasmin didn't answer.

'Did you know her?' he asked.

'I'd never seen her before.'

'Do you know anything about her at all? Her name? Why?'

Yasmin's eyes narrowed a little now. 'I hoped that was why you were here. To help me. If not, then why have you come?'

'I will help. I want to find her, and I want to stop her. Anything you can tell me will help me with that.'

Yasmin said nothing for a good while. Ryker looked around the grounds. To the pool, to the two men who weren't being discreet in the slightest with their eyes constantly on him.

His eyes settled back on the villa. Yasmin's arm was outstretched as she played with the purple flowers of the vines that rose up all along this portion of the back of the house.

'Do you like this?' Yasmin said.

'Yeah,' Ryker said. 'Bougainvillea.'

She nodded. 'Pretty, isn't it?'

'It is.'

'But it's also full of thorns. Every time I try to take the dead flowers out I get spiked and scratched all over my hands and wrists.'

She carried on twiddling, Ryker's gaze focused on the grim scar on her wrist.

'Interesting, isn't it?' she said.

'What is?'

'That something so beautiful can also cause so much pain.'

Ryker held Yasmin's eye for a second. What was she getting at?

'You mean the killer?' he said.

'Have you met her?'

Ryker shook his head. 'But I know she killed my friends. Three so far.'

He cringed just a little each time he referred to his ex-colleagues as friends, but it was simply a more easy to understand term for Yasmin than any more realistic alternative.

'She's certainly beautiful,' Yasmin said. 'But deadly too. The worst possible combination.'

Ryker said nothing.

'Do you know the story of bougainvillea?'

'I don't,' he said, a little confused now.

'It was named after a famous explorer. Louis-Antoine de Bougainville. He sailed all around the globe.'

Ryker nodded. 'Actually I've come across that name.'

'But you probably never realised he named this flower after himself?'

'No.'

'Typical man.'

'Typical in what way?'

'The thing is, he didn't even discover this flower. He had a botanist on board his ship. Philibert Commerçon.'

'So it should be called Commerçon.'

Yasmin's features lifted a little. Not a smile, but something resembling life at least.

'Doesn't sound right at all, does it?' she said as she looked at the flowers.

'Not really.'

'So the famous explorer trumped his botanist and named the flower after himself. An age-old story about the big man taking the glory from the little man.'

'I've definitely heard that one before.'

'Except that isn't all.'

'What isn't?'

'Some people believe it wasn't even the botanist who discovered the flower, but his lover. I don't even remember her name, she was so inconsequential, the poor thing. Nobody cared about her at all. Did you know at those times women weren't even allowed to travel on these ships? It was bad luck to have women on board. She was likely only on the expedition because she sneaked on disguised as a man.'

'Interesting story, but I have to admit you've lost me a little.'

'Well,' she said, finally taking her hand off the flowers. 'Think of Mo like our dear old botanist.'

Ryker nodded now. He got it.

'And you're his lover,' he said. 'In the background, because women aren't supposed to be at the forefront of... whatever it is you and your husband... did.'

'Exactly.'

Was she basically admitting that she was the master behind her late husband's criminal empire?

'Yet you've still no idea why this woman came after you?'

'And that's where this story gets... complicated. Because I know Mo, and I know our business. But I have no idea why this woman targeted us. Mo got involved in something I knew nothing about. Something I still know nothing about. Do you know how frustrating that is? How agonising? I want to miss him, I do miss him, but I'm also so fucking pissed off with him.'

Ryker nodded but said nothing.

'What you have to realise is, I also understand where we are in the order. Mo and I... neither of us was the big one, you see, neither of us was Louis-Antoine de Bougainville.'

'So who is?'

'I think you'll figure that out yourself soon enough.'

A strange answer.

'You won't tell me?'

'You've given me nothing, so I don't see why I should.'

A fair point, in a way.

'I still don't understand why she came after you,' Ryker said.

'Because my husband betrayed her. She wanted money that he owed her.'

'And did she get it? Is that why you're still alive?'

'No. I'm alive because of my guardian angels.'

She looked up to the sky as she said this.

'Your guardian angels?'

'I'll be very honest with you now. I have tried to find out who they are, just as I tried to find out about her, and I found absolutely nothing. A helicopter arrived here when she was with me. That's why I'm alive. Not because I was spared. They saved me. They took her away. That's the last I saw of her.'

Now Ryker was seriously confused.

'But you've no idea who they were? The people who saved you?'

She shook her head. 'I hoped they'd killed her, but...'

'No. She's not dead. Not yet.'

'Then I was mistaken. Perhaps they weren't my angels after all.'

No. And Ryker really had no clue what he was stumbling over here. He looked to that mass of purple flowers as his brain whirred. Then he got to his feet.

'Thanks for your time.'

He turned to leave.

33

Honestly? Ryker felt more than a little perturbed by Yasmin Khaled's cryptic clues. Why hadn't she just blurted whatever she knew?

Still, he'd come away from the villa with a vastly different impression of the woman from when he'd first laid eyes on her. Yes, she was in mourning, and her grief was clear, but she hadn't been an accessory spouse to Mo Khaled's criminal life. She'd been a key part of a mini empire. Was now the queen of what remained of that empire.

But who sat above it? Were they the reason that Grichenko was now dead, and that a female assassin was after Ryker and his crew from Doha?

Ryker headed back to the Range Rover, but he didn't go anywhere. Anyone coming from or going to the Khaleds' villa would pass by this spot. The conversation with Yasmin echoed in his mind.

'*...neither of us was the big one, you see, neither of us was Louis-Antoine de Bougainville.*'

'*So who is?*'

'*I think you'll figure that out yourself soon enough.*'

Cryptic? Maybe, maybe not.

Ryker had been sitting for less than an hour when the convertible, top down, whizzed by. Her sunglasses on, Yasmin's hair flapped wildly in the wind. She was alone in the car.

A nice simple choice. Go back to the villa, tackle the two chumps and take a better look around, or follow.

Follow. For whatever reason, he had an inkling Yasmin was helping him out here. Though that didn't mean he wouldn't be discreet. Had Yasmin spotted him? If she hadn't, would she expect him to be there, following her? Either way, he kept well back as he trailed down the mountain to the coast. She headed on through Marbella town, and to the even more exclusive Puerto Banús – a marina world renowned for the celebrities and rich people that frequented it.

Yasmin drove into a multi-storey attached to a designer shopping complex. Ryker followed in and took up a parking spot on the ground floor. He had no clue if she was going into the shops, or to somewhere outside. He banked on outside. More hoped really. If she'd only come out for a spot of shopping then he'd made a mistake and he wouldn't hang around.

No. No mistake. As he waited by a palm tree on the corner by the car park entrance, he spotted her thirty yards away, coming down the steps of the complex and to the road. She was smartly dressed now – low heels, a floral dress and denim jacket. Aviator sunglasses covered most of her face.

He waited until she'd crossed over then set off behind her. She made a beeline for the marina, past trendy and expensive shops, bars and restaurants. A few cheap ones, too, whose owners made a living by playing off the area's renowned high-end vibe, and catering to the 'normal' folk who flocked to gawk.

It wasn't long before Ryker moved on to the busy pavement

that wrapped around the marina like a walkway at an aquarium. Ninety-five per cent of the many pedestrians idled at a snail's pace as they ogled the array of luxury yachts. At least the busy street meant Ryker could keep a better watch on Yasmin without fear of being rumbled.

Halfway along the marina, she headed onto the bustling terrace of a seafood restaurant. Ryker kept going. Took a left at the corner of the marina and then took a seat at the café terrace there, where he had a decent view back to where Yasmin had gone.

She wasn't alone. She was seated with her back to Ryker. Across from her was a man. Louis-Antoine de Bougainville, Ryker presumed. He was in his late fifties, perhaps early sixties, with a shaved head and sun-weathered skin. Ryker would've guessed from his features, his dark eyes, his complexion, that, like Khaled, he was of North African or possibly Middle Eastern origin. He wore a striped designer shirt, had shimmering sunglasses propped on his forehead.

But it wasn't the man himself who Ryker took a keen interest in, but the entourage around him. Yasmin had gone to the restaurant alone, but as Ryker scanned he counted three, four, five, six men seated around who he was sure were keeping watch over the man Yasmin was with.

A waitress came to Ryker and he ordered a soft drink. Over the next twenty minutes he kept a close watch on Yasmin and the man as other people came and went, both on the terrace, and all around. Neither Yasmin nor her companion ate. Ryker tried his best to discreetly take photos with his new phone, but he hadn't bought the cheap burner for its lens, and at a distance the pictures were likely next to useless.

Finally, movement. Not from Yasmin or the man, but from the stooges around them. Three of them left the terrace, one by one, scanning all around like secret-service agents protecting the US President. Except these secret-service agents wore shorts and flip-flops. Next, the man himself got to his feet. No shake of the hand with Yasmin. No embrace, or kisses on the cheeks. Everything was cold and perfunctory.

The man headed out of the restaurant with his crew. Some of them close by him, others ahead and behind. That was the problem. Two of them remained behind. Standing just outside the terrace as the boss walked further away from Ryker. He wanted to follow but he'd have to go straight past those two to do so.

Yasmin got to her feet. She moved out to the pavement. She glanced in Ryker's direction for a split second. He froze. But moments later she was walking away.

The two men were still standing in wait. Watching. Ryker had to at least try.

He put a five-euro note on the table then got up. He headed back onto the street, then cautiously walked along the pavement toward the restaurant. Yasmin turned left down a side street, back toward her car, and was out of sight. Up ahead the boss was still in Ryker's view, but only just.

The two men remained in position, on the opposite side of the pavement to Ryker. He kept one eye on them as he neared. Neither was paying him much attention. Ryker was almost alongside them when one of them whistled. An ear-piercing, fingers in the mouth whistle. Several people turned to see who it was and why. Ryker did too. The whistler was staring at Ryker with a smug grin on his face.

'Yeah, you,' he said to Ryker.

Ryker stopped and faced him, said nothing.

'Come on, follow me.'

The man turned and went to walk away. In the opposite direction to the boss.

Ryker didn't budge and the man soon stopped.

'So?' the guy said, facing Ryker again. 'Are you coming or not?'

What did he have to lose?

'Yeah,' he said, moving into the road to cross over to them. 'Show me the way.'

34

The three of them walked side by side, Ryker in the middle, back the way he had just come from, past the café where moments ago he'd been sitting. His empty glass and the money he'd left remained on the table.

'Where are we going?' Ryker asked, glancing to each of the men in turn.

'Just walk,' the one on his right said. Not the whistler. It was the first time this one had spoken.

'Your boss went the other way. No offence, but I'd rather be speaking to him than you two chumps.'

The insult got Ryker nothing more than a grunt. They carried on in silence, away from the marina, into the narrow streets of the town that surrounded it. There were less and less pedestrians out and about all the time. Soon the street they were walking down was deserted, barely even a murmur could be heard of the hubbub behind them.

The man to Ryker's left turned.

'Down here,' he said, moving into a cramped lane.

Ryker glanced over his shoulder as he stepped behind him.

Then he stopped just inside the lane when he saw another two men already there, waiting a few yards ahead.

He was grabbed from behind. Two men. The one he'd walked with plus one other? They twisted his arms behind him and marched him a few steps further forward. He struggled against the hold but the grip was strong and purposeful.

That was fine. For now.

Ryker scanned the group gathering around him. The three men in front, plus the ones holding him. Five in total. The three crowded around Ryker in a circle, their hands down by their sides at the ready. No weapons in sight. One of the reasons why Ryker hadn't already jumped into action and fought them all off.

'You don't have to do this,' Ryker said.

The man who'd whistled at him stepped forward.

'We don't have to. We want to.'

He threw a fist into Ryker's belly. He'd tensed his abs to protect himself but it was still a strong and painful blow. The blow of someone who knew how to fight.

Perhaps this wasn't as straightforward as he'd hoped.

'You should have brought some weapons,' Ryker said, through laboured breaths. 'You're going to need them.'

'Weapons?' The guy smiled as he looked to his chums. 'We don't want to kill you. We want to break you. We're gonna turn your body to mush.'

His balled fist flew forward again. Into Ryker's belly again. Then a shot to the kidney. Then another. Ryker concentrated on the pain. Channelled it deep within. Focused on it as much as he could, tried to turn it into energy and fight that could explode back out of him.

Another gut shot knocked the wind from his lungs. His body went limp.

Five on one. But only one was taking the shots. Ryker was sure the others wouldn't stand by. They'd all want in.

Sure enough a few moments later and the grip on Ryker's arms relaxed. One of the men behind flinched as though he was about to shove Ryker to the ground. Ryker peeled out of their grip, grasped the man's arm, spun around, dragged the man's arm downward as he twisted. He threw his knee up as he yanked down harder and the man toppled over Ryker's leg and was heading for the ground.

The man hit the deck and Ryker stomped on his leg. *Crack.* That was him done. Four to go.

But the other four weren't just waiting around for their turn. They all descended on Ryker at once. He took a blow to the head. He ducked and spun and sent a crushing uppercut. Another man down and out. Three to go.

A blow to the kidney again. So hard it sent tears straight to his eyes and a wave of pain rushed through his body.

Ryker swung his elbow back, made a solid connection. Swivelled and delivered a punishing hook which caught the guy there in the temple. He went down. But not out. Ryker was too disorientated for it to be a killer blow.

One of them jumped onto Ryker's back. Grasped him around the neck. A tight hold. Choking. Ryker's eyes bulged as he tried to breathe. He bucked and went to toss the guy over his shoulder, used his elbows to try and strike him, but the man held on tight.

Ryker raced back. As fast as he could. Slammed the man up against a wall. Did it again. Again. Finally the hold on his neck loosened. Ryker grabbed the arm around his neck and threw himself forward. This time it worked. The man holding him went head over heels, over Ryker. Both of them landed on the deck. Ryker's fall was cushioned. The man landed with a horrific smack on his spine.

His arm flopped next to him. He was out of this fight.

Two left.

A flying foot caught Ryker full-on in the face. Blood spurted from his nose and his lip. He reeled back, scrambled to his feet. The two remaining fighters were both in front of him. One of them was Mr Whistle. The other was the guy Ryker had already floored with the hook. He looked woozy and wobbly. Mr Whistle was snarling.

They both charged forward to Ryker. Probably the stupidest thing they could have done. Fuelled by anger rather than good sense.

Ryker went for the groggy guy. Grabbed his arm as it flew through the air. He twisted the man around, using him as cover. Lifted his knee and arced his foot forward – a front kick that at least helped to fend off Mr Whistle. He twisted the arm into a hammerlock. Pulled until he heard the snap. Shoulder dislocated. He lifted his elbow and drove it down into the back of the guy's neck. He crumpled.

One left.

Mr Whistle.

But he was a quick mover. Literally flying through the air toward Ryker with a spinning kick aimed for Ryker's head. Ryker could do nothing. The connection was solid. He was going down. Somehow he had just enough focus to avoid crashing head first, though his forearm scraped painfully on the tarmac as he landed in a heap. A boot to the groin caused Ryker to see stars but he fought against it.

He turned over. Grabbed the flying foot as it headed for his face for the killer shot. Ryker burst up. Pulled the foot with him. The guy had nowhere to go. He toppled back and Ryker added insult to injury by following him down to the ground. He landed on top, and the man groaned and winced in pain. His eyes rolled. A pool of red circled out from underneath his head.

Blood dripped from Ryker's face onto the man's. He was still conscious, but he wasn't getting up in a hurry.

'Where is he?' Ryker said.

The man shook his head. Or was it just rolling?

'Tell me where your boss is.'

Nothing. Ryker fished in the man's pockets. Wallet. Phone. Key. Not a car fob. Just a basic key with the word Yamaha engraved.

'What's this?' Ryker asked. 'A motorbike?'

The man shook his head again as he murmured incoherently.

Ryker thought for a moment.

Got it.

Ryker used the man's thumb to open the phone. Scanned quickly through the call and message list.

'Gerardo?' Ryker said. 'That's your boss?'

A slight twitch in the man's eyes. Good enough for Ryker.

He pocketed the phone, then got to his feet. He looked around the fallen men. Two were out. The others were awake and glaring, clutching the stricken parts of their bodies. Ryker thought about searching them all. Then he heard a siren pulsing over the rooftops.

Who had called the cops? It didn't matter. He was done here.

Key in hand, it was time to go and find his boat.

35

One bullet hit the man in the shoulder. The other hit the woman in her gut.

'Leia, my sack!' her dad shouted. 'Take it off!'

Leia thrust herself forward to him, yanked the sack from his head. He only took a second to survey the mess around him, then he hobbled-cum-fell forward and threw himself down on top of the man. He raised his bound hands and smashed them down onto the man's face. Did it again and again until blood was pouring. Leia flinched each time he struck. She wondered if her father would ever stop.

The man went from bucking and writhing to barely moving. Barely moving. But he was still moving. His hand was moving. For the gun which lay just out of reach.

'Daddy!'

He didn't have time to react. The man grabbed the weapon. Brought it up. Right below her father's chin.

BOOM.

His head erupted. Blood and brain and skull splatted across the room. Leia's heart thudded in her chest. It felt like it had exploded inside her just like her father's head had.

Yet despite the shock she found herself on her feet. Found herself racing toward the carnage. The man was covered in blood and thick dripping flesh. He was trying to pull himself out from underneath the corpse.

He didn't realise Leia was gunning for him until it was too late.

She screamed – an intense, gut-curdling battle cry – as she crashed her foot down onto his arm. She wrestled the gun from his faltering grip. Took aim and fired.

Now he wasn't moving.

Leia stood there, gun in hand, staring down at the mess, the blood, the body of the man and her father. Her chest heaved, her heart thudded and ached, her brain was on fire. She didn't know whether to sob or to scream, to go into a frenzy or to collapse in numbness.

Slowly she turned. The woman was across the other side of the room. Propped up against the wall, one hand clasped over the wound in her gut. She'd taken off her balaclava. Her face was ashen, her eyes bleary. She was breathing in short, shallow bursts.

'I'm sorry,' she said.

Leia edged toward her. The gun remained in the woman's right hand. Yet Leia didn't see her as a threat. She continued on then kneeled down by the woman's side. Her brain was in turmoil, the inner noise of it churning was deafening.

'Thank you,' the woman said before grimacing in agony as blood oozed out around her hand. 'You saved me.'

It was true. Leia had. And she still couldn't understand exactly why. If she'd just let the situation play out, what would have happened? It was clear to her that Remi, whoever that was, wasn't really coming. Didn't that mean that the man had taken the decision to accept her father's offer? That he had planned to kill this woman and let Leia and her father go in exchange for two million dollars?

Leia had prevented that.

But then her father's first instinct had been to attack the man too.

Not the woman. Somehow, in all of this it was the woman who felt like the more noble and just of the captors.

'Please,' the woman said. 'Help me.'

Leia reached forward and took the gun from the woman's grip. She didn't resist at all. Leia slid the gun across the floor, out of reach. The man's weapon remained in her hand, just in case.

'Let me see the wound,' Leia said.

The woman nodded and slowly, agonisingly, took her hand away. Leia reached forward and carefully lifted up the edge of the woman's top. Blood oozed and gurgled out of the small, dark, round hole.

'I need help,' the woman said. 'Stop the bleeding.'

But Leia's brain continued to rumble. The man had been the one who was going to take the offer. Leia had stopped that. Yet her father's first instinct had still been to tackle the man...

Leia pulled her hand back.

'You have... to help me.'

Except the point was, she didn't. Her mother and father were both dead because of what this woman had done.

Leia got it now. Her father's words, his bargaining. It wasn't an offer. It was a test. A trap. He'd never planned to let either of these two live.

Neither would she.

'Please,' the woman said, her voice even more weak than before.

Leia reached forward. Balled her fist. With her fingers clenched, all of her energy, all of the confusion and the turmoil and the grief in her mind was channelled away, through her arm, into her knuckles.

Leia screamed with rage as she slammed her fist into the woman's gut. She ground her pointed knuckles in deep. The woman jolted and spluttered. Her eyes looked like they would pop right out of her skull.

Leia pulled back her fist and thwacked it into the sticky mess a second time. Twisted left and right, grinding further and further. The woman's mouth was wide open in a silent, pain-filled scream. Leia pulled her now bloodied fist back and pushed the gun's barrel past the woman's lips. She tried to shake her head away but she was already too weak. Leia used her other hand to steady her.

'Please,' the woman said. Or at least that was what Leia thought she was trying to say, but it was hard to tell with the gun stuffed in her mouth.

'This is on you,' Leia said. 'You deserve this.'

She pulled the trigger.

Devereaux was busy eating a burger and chips in the run-down bar, staring at the text message on her phone – giving James Ryker's whereabouts – for what felt like the hundredth time since she'd come here.

Marbella. That's where she should have been. Full circle. Almost. Ryker was one of only two of her targets remaining before she completed the list that Paulo and Kyri had given her. Would she be free from them then? No, she didn't believe so. Men like that didn't believe in keeping their word. Only in constantly bettering their own positions in life, regardless of the destruction and misery to others.

Which explained why Devereaux remained in Copenhagen, rather than in Spain.

The trick had been relatively simple. There was no doubt, based on recent evidence, that Paulo was good at tracking Devereaux. She didn't believe he'd followed her across Europe and back directly on her tail. She would have noticed. It would have been too obvious. Yet still he kept appearing in the same city as her almost at his convenience. Which she had determined most likely meant he was remotely tracking her. Given that she travelled so light, regularly ditched and restocked clothes and other basic belongings, it was obvious that he was using her phone to track her. She'd known that for days now. She could have changed devices to make life harder for him, but really what would have been the point before now?

But now it was time to turn the tables. She'd cloned the phone. Was now using the one hundred per cent clean copy. The original phone was currently in Spain, ever closer to its final destination in Andalusia. A simple mailed package to the Khaleds' villa. Would Yasmin understand when she opened the box?

One thing she did know for sure was that Paulo was no longer in Copenhagen, because over the last few hours she'd turned the cat-and-mouse scenario on its head. She'd tracked him. To his hotel. Out of his hotel. To the train station. Most likely, he was tracing a similar path to Spain as Devereaux's phone. But he'd left something behind in Denmark.

Which was why Devereaux had come here.

She kept watch on the street outside as she ate. It was early afternoon and the area, on the fringes of the city's relatively small financial district, was busy enough, though not exactly bustling. Devereaux took her time with her food. There was no rush. She saw nothing of interest out of the window as she sat and ate.

Finally, she was done. She paid for the food and the glass of wine then headed to the street outside. She looked across the road to the Grande Hotel. It didn't look too grand. Perhaps it had done so a hundred and fifty years ago, but now the eight-storey building's grey stonework had turned a mucky-brown colour and even at a distance the paint of the windows looked cracked. The banner outside the hotel suggested it was a five-star establishment. Perhaps the customers liked the worn-down look. Or maybe Devereaux was being harsh.

She walked over to the hotel, ignored the bellboy and headed to the gold-look revolving doors – the gold paint was bubbled and peeling in places revealing the grey steel below. Shoddy.

Devereaux moved through the reception area, past the two lifts where there was even more spray-on gold, and to the door for the stairs. She walked up. All the way to the top floor. She moved out onto the corridor. The once plush carpet felt a little tacky underfoot. All in all she was pretty disappointed. This place was basically a five-star for people who were so very desperate to be five-star, but couldn't really afford it. Not the impression she had of the man she'd come to see.

She reached the last door in the corridor. There weren't many on this floor, which was taken up by suites of varying sizes. Judging by the shape of the building, and the distance between the doors on this level, the suite beyond here was likely the smallest of them. Another disappointment.

She took out the key card. The one she'd pilfered hours earlier from an unsuspecting maid at the end of her shift. Fingers crossed it still worked.

It did.

As Devereaux swiped the card against the lock a little green light blinked and there was a click somewhere inside the mechanism as the lock released. She pushed the door open. A smell of stale sweat, fried food. The sound of a TV. Devereaux silently closed the door then continued through, past the door for the bathroom, past the door for the bedroom where the sheets on the king-sized bed remained a mess, and to the lounge area.

A football match was playing on the TV. A half-eaten tray of food lay on the coffee table. Wearing nothing but a white robe, which was partly open to reveal a hairy thigh and an even hairier belly, was a man.

'Hello, Kyri,' Devereaux purred.

～

There was no fight. Devereaux was mildly impressed by that. By the fact that Kyri recognised the dire position he found himself in, nothing he could do without his warrior by his side. Ten minutes after interrupting his football match, he was hog-tied on the floor, no robe now, just his boxers. Two pairs. One to cover his modesty, the other stuffed in his mouth to gag him.

'Did you really not expect that this would happen eventually,' Devereaux said, sitting on the sofa as she played with the knife, testing the sharpness of the point by digging it into her fingers in turn.

At her feet, Kyri moaned and groaned. Devereaux rolled her eyes and reached forward and pulled the boxers from his mouth.

He took a few seconds to compose himself. 'You stupid woman. You have no idea what you're doing.'

Was that the best he could come up with?

'Don't I?'

He squeezed his eyes shut for a few moments, as though trying to think of something. 'H-how did you find me?'

Devereaux frowned. 'You really want to know? Or are you just trying to buy time?'

He smiled a little now. A crooked, forced smile. 'I admit, I underestimated you.'

'You did. But how did you really think this would end?'

No answer to that one.

'Paulo's not coming to save you,' she said. 'Most likely he's already in Spain. Looking for me. Trying to keep an eye on me to make sure I stick to the deal. And, I'm guessing, so that he can kill me the second I've finished my work for you.'

Kyri shook his head. 'No. Why would he kill you? Why would either of us want that? Look at you. You're brilliant.'

Despite herself she was strangely flattered by his words. 'But before we move on...'

She straightened up and moved to her bag and took out the wire cutters.

'Oh, wait, you might want these again.'

She kneeled down and stuffed the boxers back in his mouth. He whined and moaned and tried to shout out, even before she grasped his hand and pulled his fingers open. He fought it, but it was no use. She took hold of the index finger on his right hand, pushed the blades of the cutters into position and... *crunch.*

His whole body shuddered as the severed digit bounced to the carpet. He choked out a muffled scream. Devereaux clasped the bloody stump with a flannel from the bathroom. When she took the stained fabric away thirty seconds later blood continued to pulse out of the open wound. Hopefully he wouldn't lose too much too soon.

'That's better,' Devereaux said, stooping down to catch his eye. 'I feel like we're more equal now. Though certainly not even.'

He was moaning again. Trying to talk. She pulled the boxers back out. He was breathing heavily. Sweat dripped from his face to the floor.

'Please, Leia. Not like this. You don't know what you're doing.'

'Really? But I thought you were utilising my skills for the very fact that I definitely do know what I'm doing. You on the other hand... do *you* know what you're doing? Like, what are you doing in this shithole of a hotel. Honestly, I expected more from a man like you.'

Somehow Kyri managed to smile and laugh at that. Though the laugh was more like a cackle, and despite his predicament, Devereaux sensed sarcasm and mocking.

'You really have no idea about me, do you?'

'I know you're just like all the others. A rich man who uses violence to achieve his aims. A rich man who uses others to do his dirty work for him. I should know. My own father was one. Just like you.'

He shook his head, his demeanour more solemn now.

'You're so wrong,' he said. 'Think, Leia. Think what you really know of me.'

'Hmmm,' she said. 'You know what helps me to think? When I'm concentrating on my work. So just let me...'

She reached out and took another of his fingers and unravelled it despite Kyri's attempts to keep it curled and clenched.

'No, no!' he shouted.

Yes. She snapped the cutters together and the finger plopped to the floor next to its friend. Kyri roared through gritted teeth, doing a decent enough job of holding back a scream. Perhaps he didn't need the boxers.

'You were saying?'

He puffed and panted, but that was the only response she got.

'"Think what you really know of me". That's what you said, right? Okay, so this is what I know. Once upon a time you were friends with a Russian gangster. He faked his death and was living a new life in England. Years later I was paid to kill him. You took issue with that so came after me. But rather than kill me, you whisked me off in a helicopter to Cyprus with a couple of commandos and your psycho friend. Once there, you threatened me in front of a family you'd just had butchered. I lost a finger so you could better make your point, and you made clear to me that if I didn't kill the people you wanted me to, I'd suffer a horrible death. Have I missed anything out?'

That strange smile was back.

'No,' Kyri said. 'You didn't miss anything out. But you did make a few mistakes.'

Devereaux raised an eyebrow.

'I didn't kill those people,' he said.

'In Cyprus? No? So Paulo did. Like I said, you have others do your dirty work.'

He shook his head. 'No. Neither of us killed them.'

'But you told me–'

'Now I'm telling you different. We didn't kill them. And that helicopter? The commandos, as you called them? They were soldiers. Real, legitimate soldiers. Now what kind of person would have access to them? To that equipment?'

Devereaux grit her teeth as his words rumbled in her mind. No, this was all a trick. He was playing her. A desperate attempt to save his life. It wouldn't work.

'Ask yourself why I'm here now,' he said. 'Why I'm still in Copenhagen. Still busy trying to cover for you.'

She didn't want to hear this. She hadn't come to play his games.

She took out the knife.

'You kill me and–'

She grabbed his hair and pulled his head back and drew the knife effortlessly across his neck. A gaping wound opened up and blood flowed out like a waterfall. His panicked eyes met hers as he gargled hopelessly. Was he trying to talk or just to breathe?

'And what?' she said.

But Kyri said nothing.

Moments later the only noise coming from him was the slosh of blood flowing. She let go of his hair and his head flopped to the carpet with a squelch.

Devereaux rose up and stared down at the corpse and the widening pool of blood. She sighed. She thought she'd feel satisfaction in this moment. She'd been playing Kyri's demise over and over in her head for days.

Instead, she felt a little empty inside.

She knew why.

Kyri's words still flickering in her mind, she turned and headed for the door.

36

With the sirens descending, Ryker's first instinct was to get away from that alley. But soon after, happy he was safe, he found a quiet spot a few streets along where he used his jacket to do his best to wipe the blood away from his face, and to compose himself.

Luckily, there was no serious damage, though his face was swollen and would be badly bruised within a few hours. Wasting no time, he headed back toward the marina, avoiding the more congested area where the superyachts were located. He was looking for a much more modest affair, and there were only a small number to choose from as he walked along the jetty. Two crafts with a Yamaha motor, and only one that looked like it could be wedded to a multimillion Euro yacht; a shiny silver, grey and black dinghy.

Soon he was heading out into the open Med, and steadily building speed now that he was past the restrictions of the marina. His destination was clear. There was only one boat moored within sight. A gleaming yacht – its slick colouring exactly matching the dinghy. The yacht was big, but not so big that it wouldn't have fitted into the marina. Either the owner, who Ryker was hoping was Gerardo, was a cheapskate, or, more likely, he liked his privacy. That was fine by Ryker.

He was about halfway between land and the yacht when he heard a cascade of whining engines behind him. He turned to see another boat following out of the marina. But that wasn't making the high-pitched racket. Then he saw them. Off to the right, coming from the beach? Three jet skis, in a row, racing toward him.

He was still a good half mile from the yacht. He was already going full throttle. He looked around. Everywhere else the sea was quiet. It was low season after all. As he glanced behind again he could already see he wasn't going to make it.

But who was driving the crafts? Surely not the same guys he'd just hammered. At least not all of them.

The jet skis were coming in fast. Ryker could hear the guys on them shouting. At each other, or to Ryker?

As they neared, two went to his left, one went to his right. Still going full pelt, Ryker yanked on the rudder a second before they came side by side with him. The dinghy swooshed right, turning and sinking down in the water from the sudden change of direction. The jet ski rider swerved to try and avoid the collision. He didn't manage it. The jet ski side-swiped the front of the dinghy and the rider went over the handles and into the water.

Ryker released the throttle until the dinghy had righted itself, then pulled again and shot off. The other two jet skis were to his left still, turning to come back at him a second time. Ryker only had a few seconds before they reached him, and he wasn't sure he'd get away with the same trick a second time.

No, he definitely wouldn't. The jet skis both stayed to his left, but gave him a wider berth this time, heading around the outside, right past him. Then they turned again to head directly for Ryker's side.

No. Not the side. They were aiming in front of Ryker's path. What were they doing?

When they were just a few yards away they split up, one going to the front, the other to the back. Ryker twisted the rudder, aiming to go left, but the dinghy simply wasn't as fast, or as manoeuvrable as the jet skis. As the one at the front approached, the rider stood up from his perch and launched himself forward, knife in hand, aiming directly for Ryker.

Ryker squirmed back, but in the cramped space there was nowhere for him to go and he lifted an arm as the man clattered down onto him. They both ended up on their sides. They grappled, the man trying to get enough space to stick the blade into Ryker who fought furiously to keep the weapon at bay. Another thud on the dinghy. The boat rocked and swayed. The other jet ski rider was on board.

Ryker needed to end this. He craned his head back then delivered a crushing butt to the man's nose. Blood poured, but the man still fought. Perhaps it was the earlier fight that had drained Ryker, but he wasn't sure how long he'd be able to hold the knife off. And what about the second man?

There he was. Ryker saw the shadow. Saw the foot coming down toward his head. Ryker let go of the knife hand and rolled away as quickly as he could. The man's foot stomped down onto the deck with a thump. The knife plunged down, too, to the spot where Ryker's chest had been a split second before. The blade sank straight through the wall of the dinghy.

Air hissed and the torn fabric flapped and the boat wobbled and nearly toppled. Ryker clambered to his feet. The knife man was still trying to get up. The other man was facing away from Ryker, hunched over as he tried to stay on his feet while the dinghy bobbed violently. Ryker lunged forward and grabbed him around the neck, kicked his legs out and tossed him over the side. There was a splutter and a slurpy churn and a scream as the man's arm or leg or something crashed against the propeller. Bad luck really, Ryker hadn't intended for that, though he doubted the rotor of the puny engine would do too much damage.

The knife man was back up. Beneath Ryker's feet the boat was all but underwater. No point in staying on here. He charged for the man and grabbed him around the waist like a rugby player and both of them flew off the side of the sinking boat. They splashed down. Under the water, as the man flailed, Ryker pulled the knife free and slashed it across the man's shoulder, then used his feet to propel him away and thrust himself back to the surface. The man bobbed up several feet away, shouting in pain and writhing as he tried to stop his injured body from sinking.

Ryker turned and front-crawled back to one of the jet skis. The engine continued to purr away. He jumped on and looked around. It was a scene of carnage. Wrecked boat, blood streaks in the water, three men splashing around trying to get to something to keep them afloat.

He pulled on the throttle. Found the yacht. All of a hundred yards away now. The next moment there was a booming gunshot and a splash of water inches from Ryker's left. He ducked instinctively as he looked to the back of the yacht where two men were standing facing him.

One was the man Yasmin had met earlier – Gerardo? The other Ryker didn't recognise. He was holding an assault rifle, pointed at Ryker.

He let go of the throttle and the jet ski slowed to a crawl.

'That was your warning,' Gerardo shouted over as Ryker stared into the barrel of the gun. 'The next one goes in your head.'

37

Ryker continued to stare over at Gerardo as the jet ski drifted forward. The gun remained trained on him. Neither of the men on the boat said anything more.

'You're Gerardo?' Ryker shouted over.

'I am. And you must be James Ryker.'

Curiosity flashed in Ryker's mind. Did Gerardo know his name only because Yasmin had told him earlier, or had he already known?

'We need to talk,' Ryker said.

'You have a funny way of asking for something so simple.'

Ryker raised an eyebrow. 'You didn't make it easy to ask.'

He looked over his shoulder to the mess in the sea.

'Fair point,' Gerardo said. 'You owe me a new boat.'

Ryker said nothing to that. The jet ski nudged up against the side of the yacht, right next to where the word 'Princess' was neatly stencilled.

'So am I coming aboard?' Ryker asked.

After a pause, Gerardo answered the question with a nod. Him and his henchman both stepped back and Ryker clambered off the jet ski and onto the immaculately polished deck.

'You should–'

Ryker never finished the sentence. The dumb idiot with the rifle decided to make a move on him. He lurched forward, swinging the rifle through the air so he could swipe the butt against Ryker's skull.

Ryker reeled back. Grabbed the rifle. Pulled the man toward him. A second later he'd wrapped his arm around the man's neck and his other hand was wrapped around the rifle's grip, the barrel pointed to the floor.

He squeezed the trigger. A booming shot echoed out across the sea. The bullet thwacked into the wood of the deck, less than an inch from the man's foot, sending splinters flying.

'That was your warning,' Ryker said into the man's ear, glancing to Gerardo as he repeated the earlier warning. 'The next one goes in your head.'

He unwound his arm from the neck and used his heel to drive the man forward and away. The guy rolled into the fall, sprang back and whipped around on his haunches as though ready to attack again. He paused when his eyes rested on the rifle barrel, now aimed at his head.

'Okay, that's enough,' Gerardo said, sounding less than impressed. 'You've already cost me plenty this afternoon. I don't want you wrecking my yacht too.'

'Then it's about time you got your man to stand down,' Ryker said. 'Him, and any others.'

Gerardo sighed. 'Go and tell Leo to get us moving,' he said to his man.

The guy slowly straightened up, never taking his eyes from the gun.

'And call the others,' Gerardo added. 'Tell them to clean up the mess out there themselves.'

The man nodded and went to move off.

'Stop,' Ryker said. He did. Ryker turned back to Gerardo. 'How many people have you got on board here?'

'My captain and DJ here,' Gerardo said. 'That's it.'

Did Ryker believe him? Or was this guy – DJ – about to go and round up some more troops?

'And where exactly are we planning to sail to?'

'I thought you'd appreciate anywhere other than here right now? As well as I know the coastguard, they rarely take kindly to gun battles at sea.'

'Let me make this clear to you,' Ryker said. 'Either of you tries something stupid–'

'Save your threats,' Gerardo said. 'They're lost on me. Come on. You wanted to talk, let's talk.'

He nodded to DJ who walked off to the right, where steps led up to the top deck – presumably where the captain, Leo, was located somewhere out of sight. Ryker watched DJ for a few seconds before Gerardo turned and headed toward the doors to take them inside.

'No,' Ryker said. 'We talk out here.'

Gerardo sighed and turned and glared at Ryker. There was a perceptible shudder across the yacht as the engines were turned on and a frothing behind Ryker as the propellers whirred to life. The craft effortlessly glided forward across the water.

'Very well,' Gerardo said. 'Please, take a seat.'

He plonked himself down on the cream leather bench that stretched across the deck, under the canopy of the upper level. Ryker moved over and hovered for a moment before he took the seat opposite. He still held on to the rifle, although a little more casually, the barrel pointed to the floor.

'I think I know why you're here,' Gerardo said.

'Good. That'll save me some effort.'

'Leia Devereaux. You're on her kill list.'

Ryker ground his teeth but didn't say anything. He assumed Gerardo was referring to the assassin, but he hadn't yet come across that name.

'It seems that way,' Ryker said. 'But I don't know why.'

'You don't?'

'Do you know who I am?' Ryker asked.

'Of course I do. And I knew a long time before Yasmin Khaled called me earlier to say you'd been to see her, asking questions about her husband's murder.'

'His murder at the hands of Leia Devereaux.'

'Precisely.'

'How do you know me?'

'I didn't say I know you. But I do know of you.'

'How?'

'Let's just say our interests have been aligned more than once in the past.'

Ryker could only assume Gerardo meant during his time in the JIA, but he wouldn't seek to clarify yet.

'And now?' he asked.

'I'm not so sure.'

'Which is why you sent heavies after me?'

'Better safe than sorry, no?'

Ryker humphed. There was something about Gerardo's nonchalance, his passiveness, that riled Ryker and unsettled him a little.

'We've only been speaking a couple of minutes but you seem to revel in the fact you know more than I do about the mess I'm in. So what's happening?'

'What do you want to know about?'

'Let's start with Pavel Grichenko.'

Gerardo set a steely glare on Ryker now. 'I was there. Ten years ago.'

Ryker knew what he meant. 'Doha.'

Gerardo nodded. Who was this man? A gangster? An agent? A bit of both?

'Why?' Ryker asked.

'Like I said, our interests were aligned. I was one of the key reasons why Grichenko was your target that night.'

'You work for the UK government?'

'Does it look like I do?' he said as he swept his arm around his yacht.

'So you were working *with* them?'

'Let's put it this way. I wasn't working against the UK government. Your superiors.'

Ryker chewed on that for a few moments. It wasn't unusual for intelligence agencies to work alongside businessmen, politicians, others from all walks of life. Anyone who had something to give was game. Clearly, Gerardo was a rich man. Well connected too, by the sounds of it. Was that how he'd come to be in bed with the UK intelligence services? The JIA? At least in Doha ten years ago. What about since?

Ryker's mind took him back to that night. The palace. The faces. Had he and Gerardo crossed paths back then? Unwittingly on Ryker's part. Knowingly on Gerardo's. The thought made Ryker all the more uneasy. And just a little vulnerable and foolish.

'I had plenty of friends in UK intelligence,' Gerardo said. 'In the wider government and diplomatic circles too. I still do. Grichenko on the other hand, had gotten into bed with the wrong people, one too many times.'

'You knew we'd been sent in to kill him.'

Another nod.

'And I'm guessing you knew that we failed that night.'

'Yes.'

'I didn't,' Ryker said. 'I was told he was dead. I was told the cover story of his disappearance was simply Russia trying to save face.'

'And I'm sure you simply moved on to the next assignment unquestioningly. It wouldn't have mattered to you.'

Ryker said nothing to that, even if what Gerardo had said was true. But Ryker was different now. Now he questioned everything.

'Don't beat yourself up,' Gerardo said. 'You had no need to know the truth.'

But apparently Gerardo had a need to know. How far up the chain did his influence reach?

'Did you know of Grichenko's new life?' Ryker asked.

'I only knew he survived that night. I didn't know of his new life until a few weeks ago.'

A short pause as Ryker's brain whirred. 'Did you order the hit?'

Gerardo didn't answer, but the look on his face suggested the answer was yes.

'So why is your assassin now after me?'

'She's not my assassin.'

Ryker shook his head. 'I understand, for someone like you, the need to operate at arm's length. So let me take a guess. You quietly got your runt Khaled to order the hit, rather than do it yourself.'

Gerardo looked pissed off at that. 'He was more than a runt.'

'You paid him to sort it out. To find someone to do the hit.'

No reaction from Gerardo now.

'I'm right, aren't I? And I'd also guess that Khaled didn't know someone like Devereaux. *You* gave him her details, and let him sort it all out. Khaled was a middleman to keep your nose clean. So what happened? Why is he now dead and Devereaux trying to kill me and my team from ten years ago?'

Gerardo took a long inhale as he held Ryker's eye. 'Kyriakos

Anastopoulos happened.'

Another name Ryker had never heard of before. The flicker in his eyes must have told Gerardo this.

'Don't worry,' Gerardo said. 'I wouldn't expect you to know Kyri. But you can think of him as a peer of mine. An equivalent. Like two sides of the same coin. A mirror image. You get the idea.'

Ryker felt he did. Most likely another rich and corrupt man, with tentacles extending into political life. But Kyri's extended into Russia rather than the UK.

'He's a friend of Grichenko's?'

'Very close. For ten years I knew Grichenko was alive but had no clue as to his new life. For ten years I think Kyri knew and hid the truth. When Grichenko was killed... let's just say my Cypriot friend wasn't very happy.'

'Stop beating about the bush. Just tell me straight what's going on.'

Gerardo sighed. 'I honestly don't know exactly how this played out, because, of course, I have no contact with Kyri, and Khaled is now dead. But somehow, Kyri got to Devereaux. She killed Khaled, and under Kyri's order she's now after each and every one of you who tried to kill Grichenko ten years ago. Kyri is going to make you all pay.'

'That makes no sense. I've not been a target of his before.'

'But you didn't know about Grichenko surviving before. Now you do and what? You're on a warpath to find who wronged you. That's why you're a target.'

'What about you?'

'Good question. And another reason for my tentativeness earlier. I know this woman. I've seen her handiwork. She doesn't care for morals. She lives for killing. If someone's paid her to come after you, then there's nothing you can do.'

Ryker looked away from Gerardo, beyond him and to the

rippling water. They were still hugging the coast, but had moved way east of Marbella which was disappearing in the distance. Other small craft were dotted about across the water though no sign of the police or the coastguard coming to accost them about the mess in the sea by Marbella. What had happened to Gerardo's cronies? Had they simply headed back to shore?

'I need a drink,' Gerardo said as he got to his feet. 'A strong one. What's your poison? Whisky? Brandy?'

'Whatever you're having.'

'Good answer. Come on.'

Gerardo headed toward the doors again. This time Ryker followed. They moved on through to a grand lounge area, about as opulent as Ryker had ever seen, whether in a mansion, palace, or hotel, never mind on a boat. He didn't outwardly react despite the knowing look on Gerardo's face – pride at his display of overt wealth.

'We're basically part of the same team,' Gerardo said, handing Ryker a glass with a good inch or so of caramel-coloured spirit. 'Yet our lives couldn't be more different.' The way he said it made it clear that he pitied Ryker. 'Ever get the feeling you could have worked smarter?'

Another comment designed to rile. Ryker held it in. 'All the things I've done, it wasn't for the money.'

Gerardo smiled. 'I see that. I don't understand it, but I see it. You think you're a moral crusader, is that it?'

It wasn't the first time someone had said those words to Ryker recently. He took a sniff of the drink. Whisky. A damn good one too. A large sip confirmed it.

'But what have you got to show for it?' Gerardo said. 'You could have just had a good life instead.'

'Who set us up in Doha?' Ryker asked. 'I still don't get how Grichenko ended up in England if the people you were working with wanted him dead.'

'What's there not to get? No government is controlled by one person. There's opposing factions everywhere you look. Every country has its own enemies operating from within. I thought a man like you would be well attuned to such matters.'

'So who set us up?'

Gerardo's phone pinged in his pocket. Bad timing. Or convenient timing, perhaps. He took the phone out and put it to his ear but didn't say a word. When he pulled the phone away his face was etched with anger.

'What is it?'

Ryker heard it before Gerardo answered. The hum of a helicopter. Approaching fast.

Ryker put down his glass, grasped the rifle in two hands and pointed the barrel at Gerardo's head.

'I didn't do this,' Gerardo said, even more angered.

'Maybe not. Who is it?'

There was a perceptible shift in the yacht's momentum. They were slowing.

'Who is it?' Ryker said again, with more force this time.

Gerardo took no notice. He slapped his glass down and brushed past Ryker. Ryker spun and followed him, the barrel pointed to his host's back.

'Stop!' Ryker demanded, but Gerardo didn't heed the warning.

Ryker followed. The noise of the helicopter grew with each step they took. They passed back onto the outer deck. No one there. There was a thud somewhere above. The next moment a hefty object dropped down from the upper deck and landed in front of Gerardo with a booming crash that shook the wood Ryker was standing on.

Gerardo and Ryker both froze. It took Ryker's brain a half second to figure what he was staring at.

A body. A twisted, bloody body. Definitely dead. DJ.

38

Ryker looked up. He couldn't see the helicopter beyond the overhang of the upper deck, but could hear it hovering somewhere above. Was there a gunner on board? No. He didn't think so. He'd heard no shots fired. Which meant someone – possibly more than one person – from the chopper was now on board the yacht.

'Wait here,' Ryker said to Gerardo.

'Fuck you,' Gerardo said, spinning around, his face like thunder. 'This is *my* boat.' He stormed past Ryker, heading back inside. To where? For a weapon?

Ryker heard creaking above.

He hesitated for only a second before rushing for the stairs, gun held out and at the ready. He bounded up. Spotted the black-clad figure when he was only halfway to the top. Opened fire. A burst of three bullets. All hits to the man's legs. Non-fatal. Ryker had no clue who he was firing at here. The man went down with a guttural growl of pain.

Was there more than one person up there? Ryker slowed a little, moving the rest of the way more cautiously, step by step. He was still four from the top when through the open cabin doors he spotted the crumpled figure of another man. His white shirt was dotted with blood. The captain, Leo, Ryker could only presume.

The attacker on the floor in front of Ryker was writhing in pain. A sub-machine gun lay out of his reach, though Ryker was sure that hadn't been used yet to kill either DJ or Leo. Which meant most likely there was at least one more person up here. But where?

He continued up, even more cautiously now. Looking, listening.

There it was. Nothing more than a flicker of a shadow, off to the left of the downed man. Ryker ducked and raced up the final steps so he was out in the open space and not confined on the stairs. He swung the gun around and fired.

A volley of bullets erupted as Ryker arced into the space. Another black-clad figure was there, but he was out of the line of fire, and was himself pointing a pistol to Ryker's head.

Ryker dove for the deck as the man opened fire. He didn't let up, coming for Ryker and shooting at the same time as Ryker scurried back and tried to readjust his hold on the rifle. Almost there, but the man was already on him. Magazine empty, he tossed the gun at Ryker's head then pulled back his boot and crashed it into Ryker's jaw.

The blow sent Ryker's head rocking. He tried again to manoeuvre the rifle but it was wrenched from his hands. A fist hurtled toward his head. He had just enough focus to block the shot. Then, roaring with effort, he bucked, lifting himself and the attacker up.

The guy had a knife in his hand now. Ryker drove forward, taking the man with him. Three, four steps, then...

Right over the balcony railing.

Ryker held on as they fell. They landed with a thud and an

oomph on the lower deck, Ryker on top. The knife clattered away. Ryker was dazed. The man beneath him even more so.

Ryker balled his fist and sent a punishing shot to the man's head. Then he reached up and dragged off the balaclava.

He almost wished he hadn't. It took his confused brain several beats to calibrate and realise who he was staring at.

Wes Aldern.

39

Distracted, Ryker was unprepared for the uppercut to his jaw. Aldern squeezed out from underneath and clambered to his feet. Ryker was up, too, and edged back, both of them crouched down and at the ready to attack or defend. Aldern's knife lay a couple of feet from him. Both of their guns lay somewhere on the upper deck. Ryker didn't dare take his eyes off Aldern for a second, but somewhere above he could still hear the circling helicopter.

'So?' Ryker said.

Aldern glared but said nothing as a dribble of blood wormed down his chin from his lip.

'Back from the dead,' Ryker said as his brain put together the pieces of this man's deception. 'Do your wife and son even know?'

Still nothing from Aldern. But then his eyes flicked to Ryker's right. Gerardo. A bang as he kicked open the doors. Ryker glanced over his shoulder to see him brandishing a heavy-duty carbine.

Movement to the right. The helicopter swooped into view.

Ryker spotted the glint on the open deck. A gunman. Then another glint in the sea. A speedboat approaching.

For what seemed like several beats, but was probably not even a quarter of a second, Ryker's eyes met Aldern's. His ex-colleague smiled.

Then all hell broke loose.

Gerardo opened fire first, but within an instant there were booming gunshots coming from two other directions. The helicopter, the boat. Ryker didn't even know who was aiming for who, but he had no choice but to dive for cover by the side of the plush cream leather bench. Bullets raked the yacht all around him. Wood and plastic splinters flew through the air.

Gerardo's burst of fire was short-lived as a series of bullets thwacked into his midriff. His body pulsed with each hit before he collapsed in a pool of his own blood.

The carbine was a few yards from Ryker. He went to crawl that way but a bullet splatted into the wooden deck right by Ryker's arm and sent a two-inch wooden splinter deep into his wrist.

He slid back into his corner, grimacing in pain, hunkering down to avoid the barrage of gunfire and debris. He yanked the wood out as he stared across to the other side of the deck where Aldern was similarly hunkered. But then he looked up, to the helicopter, nodded and jumped to his feet.

A fresh wave of bullets smacked into the yacht – from the boat – aiming for Aldern as he dashed for the opposite side of the yacht. He took a bullet in the shoulder a moment before he hurled himself up and over the side and into the water.

Then came a moment of serene calm. An eerie ceasefire, at least on deck. It didn't last long, and when it was broken the shooting was no longer toward the yacht. The gunmen in the boat and on the helicopter were firing at each other.

Staying as low as he could, Ryker edged forward. Above the

gunfire, the sound of the helicopter bobbing up and down, twisting left and right, filled Ryker's ears. He grabbed for Gerardo's weapon. The strap was caught under his body. Ryker yanked and the body jostled and the strap came free.

Ryker spun around, laying almost flat on his back as he raised the weapon up.

He was pointing it at thin air.

No sign of the helicopter. In fact, the sound of its rotors were dying down by the second.

Then the gunfire stopped altogether as Ryker moved into a crouch. The helicopter's din quickly faded. He cautiously moved out into the open. Pointed the gun out to the boat that was all of ten yards from him and closing in. Four people were on board. Ryker recognised three of them. The only one he didn't know was the driver.

'You can put that gun down,' Yasmin shouted out.

Either side of her were the two men she'd had at home with her earlier. Both of them were holding assault rifles. Both of the guns were trained on Ryker.

He glanced up and behind him. The helicopter was steadily flying up and away. He could only assume Aldern had somehow gotten safely back on board.

He faced Yasmin as the boat edged even closer.

'Put the gun down,' she said again. 'You really don't have much choice.'

She wasn't quite right about that. Two against one were far from the worst odds Ryker had ever faced, yet something about this bizarre situation told him he should play along.

He lowered the weapon and moved toward them.

40

The boat bobbed up and down, jostling over the rippling waves of the Med as they raced back to shore.

Ryker had been disarmed of the carbine the moment he'd stepped aboard. Voluntarily, kind of. Yasmin's two grunts still held on to their weapons though they weren't pointing them at Ryker.

He and Yasmin were seated at the back of the cramped space. Her hair flapped wildly in the breeze.

'Thank you,' Ryker said. 'If you hadn't turned up–'

'Don't believe that I came out here to save you,' Yasmin said, shooting a cold look Ryker's way. 'That may be what has happened, but it wasn't my intention.'

Ryker said nothing to that as he held her eye.

'You want the truth?' she said. 'I came to help Gerardo. I came to kill *you*, if I had to.'

Ryker shuffled a little uneasily.

'I heard what happened in Marbella. One of Gerardo's men called Hierro.' She nodded over to the goon on the left. 'He told Hierro what you did. Gerardo was my friend. A good friend.'

Those last words were a little choked though Ryker wasn't feeling sympathetic, even if her friend was now dead.

'You set me up,' he said. 'You knew I'd follow you from your villa. Gerardo had a team ready and waiting to attack me.'

She shot him another look. Anger, above her dismay. 'What did you expect? Turning up in our world, asking questions like you were.'

Was that a fair point?

'You said you came out here to kill me,' Ryker said. 'So why haven't you?'

'I said I came out to help Gerardo. To help him against you. But I wasn't expecting those others.'

'You know them?'

She didn't speak for a few moments. 'Remember what I told you about the day that... woman came for me.'

'Her name is Leia Devereaux,' Ryker said.

Her quizzical expression suggested she hadn't known that. But Gerardo had. What else hadn't he told her?

'The day she came for me, the day she tortured me, I told you my guardian angel saved me.'

'You said a helicopter turned up. They took her away.'

She nodded.

'And you said you at first thought they'd taken Devereaux because they were helping you. They were taking her away to kill her. Or at least that was what you hoped.'

'Now I realise it was the opposite. They are the people she's working for. That man you were fighting with? He was on the helicopter that day too.'

Ryker let that one sink in. Wes Aldern. Not only was he still alive, but he was somehow behind everything. He was running Devereaux. Together, he and the assassin were hunting down Ryker and everyone else from Doha.

Why?

To keep his own beak clean.

For all the searching Ryker had undertaken, all the questions he'd asked of the others, it was now clear that Aldern was the reason the Grichenko assassination had gone wrong a decade ago. He'd sabotaged it. Had helped Grichenko escape. Most likely had helped him set up his new life.

How long had he been a double agent? And what about his fake death? Ryker still didn't get that.

Gerardo had ordered the hit on Grichenko. Nothing more than settling an old grudge. But in doing so he'd alerted Kyri Anastopoulos, and Aldern had crawled out of the woodwork. Those two were surely working together. Devereaux had been plucked away and given her new task; killing everyone involved in the Doha debacle. Not for moral revenge, or anything as justifiable as that, but because Aldern must have realised that the likes of Ryker would start asking too many questions about the past once the truth about Grichenko's new life came out.

'Are you okay?' Yasmin asked.

Ryker was shaking with rage. 'Yeah,' he said.

'Do you know who he is?'

'Yes.'

'And?' she prompted him when he didn't say anything more.

'And you can be sure I'll find him.'

Half an hour later Ryker was back in the stolen Range Rover, blasting up the motorway north, toward the French border. Yasmin had been kind enough to escort him straight to the car, rather than to the police or to a group of waiting henchmen. A surprisingly positive outcome really, even if she had confiscated the carbine he'd taken from Gerardo.

She'd sent him on his way with a clear instruction. Find Wes Aldern, and make him pay.

Ryker had rarely been so happy to take an instruction from someone, even if he was far from convinced that Yasmin – or her dead friend, or her dead husband for that matter – were in any way good people.

He called both Lange and Diaz as he drove, but got no response from either. Were they already dead too? Or were they just ignoring the calls because they didn't recognise the number it was coming from? Either way, he didn't leave them a voice message, though he wasn't really sure why.

He only stopped to refill with diesel. The Range Rover was a guzzler, but it also had a huge tank. After umpteen hours on the road, Ryker was drained and weary, but he wouldn't stop and rest.

He finally decided to leave a message for both Lange and Diaz. They had a right to know about Aldern.

Or had one or both of them already known? Was it even possible that one of them was somehow in cahoots with Aldern?

No, that would be a revelation too far, surely.

Copenhagen was Ryker's destination. As far as he knew Diaz remained there, and if Lange was still on the case of tracking down the Doha crew, perhaps she was there too. And if they and Ryker all congregated in the same place, then he had to believe that sooner or later so, too, would Aldern, and his new killing machine Devereaux.

He was still at least half a day from the Danish capital when he received the text message. Lange.

Can't talk. I know where she is.

Ryker glanced back and forth between the screen and the road. *I know where she is.*

Devereaux?

A few moments later another text came through. Nothing but a string of numbers. Ryker needed only a few seconds to realise what it was. Co-ordinates. Driving with one hand he put the numbers into Google. Bingo. The location was in the French alps. Only a few hours' drive.

He put the new destination into the GPS. Then sat back for the rest of the ride.

41

'*T*ake *my offer. Two million dollars... I know I'm asking a lot of you. A betrayal... Weigh it up. Two million and you live. Or you get nothing and you die... I can tell you love him. He loves you too. But let me put it another way. How much for him to betray you instead?*'

Somehow she always came back to those moments. Her father's words. The meaning behind them, the insinuation that trust was such a malleable, or perhaps even non-existent construct, had stuck with Devereaux ever since. How many people had betrayed her in her life? How many people had she betrayed?

She shut down the car engine and looked out across the frozen lake. A thin layer of snow covered the surface. Abandoned rowing boats were dotted here and there, their bows wedged deep in the ice. There were no houses in sight, just coniferous trees and the odd boathouse. The closest was thirty yards away, directly along the lake edge from where she was parked.

One other car – a little silver Audi – was already here, by that boathouse.

She got out of her car and moved around and opened the boot lid. Two bleary eyes peaked out at her.

'Don't worry, this will all be over with soon.'

She slammed it shut without waiting for a muffled response. Then with a flicker of a smile on her face she headed over toward the boathouse.

She kept one hand in her coat pocket as she approached, her fingers encircled around the handle of the hunting knife. The only weapon she had on her. It'd be enough if she needed it at all.

Still, as confident as she was, she moved with caution, looking around her as she went. This place was as remote and deserted as you could get. Pretty much the exact reason she'd chosen it.

She reached the wooden entrance to the building. She turned the handle, pushed the door open and spotted him crumpled on a chair in the corner. He held a hand up to the opposite shoulder. His face was creased with pain.

'Hello, Paulo.'

He glared at her.

'Where the hell have you been?' he said, his anger evident from his bared teeth.

Devereaux chuckled.

'Such a hostile reception,' she said.

'Where's Kyri?' Paulo said.

A good question. And one that Devereaux was pleased to hear. After all, the fact he was asking likely meant Paulo had no idea his boss was dead. She hadn't tidied the hotel room up much. She hadn't had time. But she had hung the do not disturb sign on the door, and set up a tiny camera hidden in the room's air-con grate so she could keep watch on anyone coming and going. There'd been no sign of Paulo having done so. Not that he would've had the time. He was fresh back from chasing James Ryker in Spain. Which apparently hadn't gone too well for Paulo, judging by the state of him.

Had Ryker fared better?

She'd soon find out.

'I said where is he?'

'I don't know,' Devereaux said. 'Drinking wine and eating olives in the sun most likely.'

'He's not answering his phone. I know something's wrong.'

Devereaux shrugged.

'You think this is a game?'

'You have, so far. What happened to you?'

'I got shot trying to do your job for you.'

'Ryker? Except he's not dead, is he?'

A flash of uncertainty on Paulo's face, though Paulo didn't question how she knew.

'So what now?' he asked.

She took a couple of steps toward him.

'I have a surprise for you,' she said as she approached him.

'Yeah?'

'In my car.'

'Lange?'

'Just for you.'

'Is she dead?'

'Not yet.'

'Why not?'

Devereaux shrugged again. She was only a couple of feet from him. Even as anger diffused from his body, his pheromones tickled her nose and caused her blood to race.

'You wanna see?' she said.

He didn't say anything but shuffled as though about to get to his feet. Devereaux smiled.

'You need a hand?'

She reached out to him.

Paulo shot up like a flash. He'd had a hand clasped over his bleeding shoulder, but the arm had kept his other hand covered. Now she knew why. The gun came out. She had the knife in her hand, but he kicked the blade from her grasp.

The knife clattered away. He grabbed her by the throat and pulled her off her feet and threw her up against the wooden wall. The whole structure wobbled and shook from the force and Devereaux let out a yelp of pain. Or was it surprise? Or anger? Or delight?

He forced the barrel of the gun into her temple, pushing so hard her head was forced down to the side, into her shoulder.

'You really aren't as clever as you think,' he said. His face was just inches from hers. 'One mistake too many for you.'

'So you're going to kill me? Just like that?'

'No. I won't. Not until you've served your purpose.'

He pushed the gun harder still and she squirmed. It felt like her neck was about to tear open, her head was bent at such an angle.

'And which purpose is that?' she said through the discomfort.

A pause. The pressure was released slightly. Then a little further. Soon her head was near upright once more and she was staring into the abyss of his eyes.

Then he leaned forward and planted his lips onto hers.

It wasn't long before they were deep in a passionate kiss. The gun remained in place, the barrel skimming her skin, somehow making the moment all the more enjoyable for Devereaux as Paulo pushed his body into hers.

Her arms were wrapped around him when she heard creaking wood.

Two men burst in.

Paulo jumped back. His eyes on Devereaux. A sickly grin on his face.

42

Ryker contemplated ditching the car before he got to the location. Thought about circling around and heading in on foot from the north side, opposite to the most obvious route which Lange would surely assume he'd approach from.

Instead, he just kept on going, following the GPS directions, largely because as he closed in on the destination, he became more and more curious – suspicious too – as to why he was out here at all. The last houses of the nearest town were miles behind him. All he could see outside the car windows was the twisting road and the thicket of trees either side of him, in front, behind. The chequered flag was in view on the GPS screen but there was no indication of anything out here. No town or village, no place or road name. No amenities. Just blue and green shapes, indicating the outline of forested areas and water, plus three thin snaking black lines, intercrossed over the map to indicate the only roads in this barren area.

Ryker took the final turn. Less than a mile out. He kept going, and was soon emerging from the woods into a huge clearing. A frozen lake. Up ahead were two parked cars. Not far beyond them a boathouse. A single storey, not big enough to fit anything in it other than a couple of basic rowing boats or dinghies.

He slowed the Range Rover right down, cut the engine off and used its momentum to roll to a stop a few yards from the other parked cars.

He stepped out into the bitter cold. It'd been several hours since he'd last been out of the car and the temperature had dropped significantly in that time. A far cry from the positively balmy Spanish coast.

He edged toward the two parked cars, his eyes busy as they worked the area; the cars, the boathouse, the iced-over lake, the woodland that surrounded him in every direction.

A biting wind blasted across the open space, whistling and howling in his ears. Serene, but hardly quiet. Yet as he approached the cars, hunkered down in a lame attempt to keep the chill at bay, he was sure he could hear a noise. Banging? Clattering? Intermittent, and not particularly loud or forceful. But it was definitely there, just somewhere beyond the wind noise, and growing more distinct with each step he took.

The sound was coming from the Mercedes. From its boot. Ryker reached the car. He carefully, subtly, tried the boot lid. Locked. He edged around to the driver's door. Unlocked. He opened the door and reached in and found the button for the boot. A click as the lid popped open. Then moaning.

Ryker moved back around, ready for a surprise attack.

He peeked over the edge.

'Lange?'

She was bound and gagged.

Ryker moved with more purpose now. He reached in and grabbed her under the armpits and hauled her out. He untied the rope on her wrists and ankles, ripped off the tape that covered her mouth. Her legs were weak and wobbly and for a few seconds he had to hold her to stop her from toppling over.

'What happened?' he said.

'It's... her.'

A tear escaped her eye.

Her. Devereaux. Ryker's beady eyes darted about, but he could see no one else here. He knew where Devereaux most likely was though. The boathouse. A simple trap?

'Where's Diaz?'

Lange looked confused. 'Diaz? Ryker, she's dead! Everyone's dead apart from me and you.'

'No,' Ryker said. 'Not everyone.'

He rooted around in the boot. Lifted the false bottom to reveal a spare tyre and toolkit. He took the wrench. When he straightened up he saw the pleading look in Lange's eyes.

'We have to go,' she said to him. 'Kaspovich is still in Copenhagen. I have to tell him what's happened. What's happening.'

The Range Rover was right there behind them. He didn't have enough fuel to get them to Copenhagen, but he did have enough to get them to a town. He had his phone too. He took it out of his pocket. No signal. But if they travelled away from here there would be soon enough.

Then a scream cut through the pummelling noise of the wind. Ryker could pinpoint it exactly.

He looked to Lange. 'Go if you have to, but I can't.'

She didn't say anything, but he could see the doubt in her eyes.

He took his keys from his pocket and held them and his phone out to her. She only hesitated for a second before taking them.

'I'll get help,' she said.

Ryker didn't say anything, just nodded before she turned and rushed over to the Range Rover. She was in the midst of a hurried U-turn when another scream – even more panicked than before – cut through the air.

He turned to face the boathouse, then set off toward it. His eyes darted about. No one in sight. But as he edged forward he was sure he spotted movement just beyond the treeline to his right. He stopped and stared but saw nothing more, other than the thick branches of the firs which swayed this way and that, non-stop in the wind.

He continued to the boathouse, the wrench held out at the ready. A clatter came from inside the flimsy structure. A surprised shout. Then another. Then a gunshot. More banging.

Ryker rushed forward. Crashed open the door. Two bodies down. One was a man he didn't recognise. Glugging his last breaths, his eyes wide, as he held a hand to a gaping wound on his neck. Next to him was a woman. Devereaux. Crumpled and grasping her side. Her hands were covered with blood. Her eyes met Ryker's and he was sure she very nearly smiled.

'You,' she said.

A gun lay on the floor between the two of them. It wasn't clear who had originally had it, though neither of the wounded had the strength to go for it now.

What on earth had happened in here?

Ryker crouched down and dropped the wrench and picked up the pistol. Movement caught his eye again. Beyond the partially open doors at the end of the building that led out onto the lake. Gun in hand, Ryker stepped over there and pushed the right-hand door further open.

Two men on the ice. Heading away. One hobbled along, the other had his arm wrapped around the injured man's shoulder, helping to drag him.

'Aldern!' Ryker shouted out.

The men stopped and turned. Sure enough the one on the left, carrying the other, was Aldern.

'Ryker,' Aldern shouted back. 'Good to see you again so soon.'

'Just tell me why.'

'Why what?'

Ryker continued to edge forward, gun held out.

Aldern said nothing.

'Was it just money? Is that all it took?'

Aldern scoffed as though Ryker was talking nonsense. 'You make it sound like a bad thing. I only did what was best for me. What? You've worked the last twenty years for another reason? The greater good? But who gets to decide on that?'

Ryker was reminded of what Gerardo had said to him on the yacht. Gerardo and Aldern were two men who'd found themselves on very different sides, yet apparently both had the same outlook; money trumped morals. Trumped pretty much everything.

'I've seen men like you my whole life,' Aldern said. 'You think you're moral. You think you're superior because of it. But you're no better than me. We've both done horrible things. And why? Because someone in an office in England says it was okay?'

Ryker wasn't about to argue that one. A key reason why he'd left behind his life in the JIA was because he could no longer correlate the actions he was being told to take with the justification that he needed. But he hadn't simply headed after money instead. He still wanted to make a difference, somehow, however small.

'I saw your wife recently,' Ryker said.

That got a flicker on Aldern's face.

'Her life's been destroyed because of your lies.'

'You know nothing about that.'

Except the way he'd said it told Ryker exactly how Aldern felt. Ashamed. For all his bravado, he knew he'd let his family down.

'You left them alone.'

Nothing from Aldern now.

'All so you could carry on your shady life.'

'I did it to protect them!'

Aldern's hand twitched. Ryker fired.

Somehow, Aldern had already decided to use his injured comrade as a shield and hunkered behind him just in time. The bullet hit the man in his back before Aldern tossed him to the ice and whipped out his own weapon. He unleashed several shots and Ryker dove to the ice which creaked and cracked under his weight.

Aldern didn't let up as Ryker scuttled away and he was soon out of ammunition. Ryker got back to his feet as Aldern turned to slink away. He lifted the gun to fire again.

Another crack in the ice. Behind him. Not from his weight.

Ryker spun and saw the man lunging for him, slicing a serrated knife through the air toward Ryker's throat. Ryker reeled back, pointed the gun up and fired. The bullet shot upward through the man's chin. Blood spattered onto Ryker's face as the dead body thudded down.

Another man coming at Ryker from the right. Had they come from the trees?

Ryker sank down to his knee, readjusted his aim and fired off two shots just before the man had a chance to unload his own weapon. Neither were hits. Ryker adjusted again and pulled again. Once, twice, three times. The first two were hits. One in the belly, one in the chest. The third pull resulted in nothing but a sorrowful click. The magazine was empty. And Ryker had no more on him.

He turned back to where Aldern had been. Except rather than running away, he was now bearing down on Ryker.

Aldern launched himself forward. Ryker sidestepped as Aldern barged into him and they both clattered onto the ice. A deep crack this time. The sound splintered outward. Water dribbled up to the surface.

They grappled on the flimsy ice. Ryker took a blow to the chin. He delivered one back in kind, then pummelled Aldern's sides as they twisted and turned on the ice. He grasped hold of Aldern's shoulder, the one with the bullet wound from Spain, and squeezed as hard as he could. Aldern roared in agony and his grip loosened and Ryker pushed himself away and then rose to his feet. Aldern did the same, albeit more gingerly.

Movement off to Ryker's side again. But this time he was unarmed and there was no quick solution as he turned to see Leia Devereaux edging across the ice. Despite the glistening patch of wet on the side of her coat – bullet wound, or knife? – she walked unimpeded, an almost satisfied look on her face.

'What do we have here?' she said. She came to a stop. The three of them in a triangular stand-off. There was a gun in her hand. From where, Ryker didn't know. She was wafting it about casually, like it was a toy. 'Are you two fighting over me?'

Her voice was warm and her tone... Ryker didn't know how to describe it, but it didn't fit the mood here on the ice at all.

'Come on, Leia,' Aldern said to her. 'You're so close. Finish him, then we're done. You get your life back, just like we agreed.'

'Oh, Paulo, he won't be my last though, will he?' Ryker glanced between the two of them. Paulo? Aldern's new identity? 'I've saved that honour for you.'

She lifted the gun to fire. A leg shot. Aldern sank down to the ice, growling in pain through clenched teeth.

Devereaux winked to Ryker then continued forward to Aldern. She stopped not even a yard from him and leaned over.

'But you can be damn sure, my sweet, that I'm not going to let you off easily. Not after what you've done to me.'

Then she turned to Ryker. Pulled the gun up.

Ryker flinched.

But the shot never came. Instead, there was a crash and a chunk of ice, eight feet square, disappeared into the water. Aldern and Devereaux both went with it. Ryker flung himself back and scuttled a few feet away as he stared aghast.

Devereaux and Aldern both flailed about in the water, trying to grasp the edge of the ice. Conflicting thoughts tumbled in Ryker's mind. What was he supposed to do? Leave them both to die in there? Head over and make sure they stayed under?

He didn't know. Before he could talk himself out of it he was flat on his stomach sliding across the ice toward the hole. But who was he going to save? Even he didn't know.

By the time he got there Aldern was clinging onto the broken ice, trying to haul himself out. Ryker reached out to Devereaux who was still flailing, her head only intermittently above water. She tried to grasp his hand but couldn't. Moments later she was gone.

Ryker used his arm like a brush to sweep the snow off the ice. He spotted the shadowy movement underneath; Devereaux floating away, desperately banging on the ice to try and break it from beneath. Ryker hammered down on the frozen surface. The ice creaked and strained, but didn't break.

He slid along the surface, following her movement. An even bigger creak beneath him this time. He soon realised why. Aldern was out of the water and right next to him. Bad move. The added weight was once again too much and the ice gave way and both of them were soon under.

Ryker's heart thudded erratically from the sudden shock of the icy water. He gasped for breath as he tried desperately to keep afloat. He managed to push himself to the edge and grabbed the brittle slab of ice, but as he went to haul himself out another chunk broke away and he was under the water again.

Something further beneath brushed his leg. Aldern? Or just a piece of broken ice? He kicked out, thrashing about. Grasped the ledge once more. No, that wasn't ice below him. The arm grabbed him around the waist. Dragged him under once more. He and Aldern tussled under the water. Ryker did everything he could to pull himself free as Aldern slipped further and further down.

Ryker managed to wrench a leg free from Aldern's grip. He hammered it down. Aldern's head? Whatever he hit, the contact was solid, and Aldern's arm finally came loose. Still, Ryker hit down again, then again. The next time he did so he connected with nothing.

He pushed his body back up, broke the surface of the water and took a desperate gasp of air.

He grasped the edge of the ice once more. His body was leaden and depleted. His heart felt like it would explode from his chest. His body quivered from the cold. He wasn't sure he could hold on to the ice, never mind haul himself out.

A sound caught his attention and gave him focus. Sirens. Not too far away. Then the clatter of a helicopter. He saw it a moment later. Racing in, low down, just above the treetops. For a flash his mind took him back to Spain. The Med. The yacht. The helicopter with the gunner on board. What would he do? Dive back under the water for safety?

But a few seconds later he spotted the insignia on the side of the chopper as it came in to hover above him. *Police.*

That somehow gave Ryker the strength he needed. He clambered out of the hole. Pushed himself across the ice until he was clear of the sloshing water, then rolled onto his back to stare up to the sky as he continued to gasp in heavy breaths.

The sirens got louder by the second. The helicopter disappeared from above, but the sound of it hardly dulled. Ryker lifted his head a little to see it landing over by the boathouse where two police cars were racing in past the woods.

Ryker found the strength to lift his torso and then he sat

there on the ice watching the cavalry descend. Half a dozen officers, all armed. Within seconds there were a dozen. They were shouting over. It took Ryker's brain a couple of confused seconds to determine what they were saying.

Don't move. Stay where you are.

Or something like that at least. But were they shouting at him, or...

He turned to look back to the hole.

Devereaux. Out of the water. On her knees, shivering violently as she coughed water from her lungs. When she was done she lifted her head and caught Ryker's eye.

She smiled.

There was a splash of water by her side, by the hole, and as Ryker glanced there, a body bobbed to the surface, face down. Aldern. Or Paulo, or whoever the hell he was.

'Ryker?'

Lange. Ryker turned to her. She was warily heading across the ice toward him and Devereaux, police flanking her on both sides.

'Are you okay?' she shouted.

He didn't answer that. He couldn't. He really wasn't sure what the answer was.

43

One month later

Winter remained in full swing, though at least now the days were beginning to lengthen once more. Spring would arrive soon enough, and as Ryker approached the stone bench overlooking the Vltava river, he was glad the sunshine was out to at least help against the chilly temperature.

Lange was already waiting for him, a steaming paper cup in her gloved hand. She gave him a half smile as he took the space on the bench next to her.

'You're alone,' Ryker said.

'You weren't expecting me to be?'

'I thought Kaspovich might have come to snap some cuffs on me and whisk me back to London.'

He noticed the quizzical look on her face.

'I know you two have some sort of history,' she said, 'but I actually think he's one of the good guys.'

Ryker raised an eyebrow. 'Wait, he's not listening to this is he?' He looked around theatrically. 'He's going to jump out at any second...'

'Very funny.'

They went silent for a few moments. Ryker looked over the riverfront. Not many people were out and about, though a few eager tourists idled over the arched bridge a hundred yards further down, heading toward the historic centre.

'So, Prague,' Lange said.

'Yeah.'

'Any particular reason why?'

Yes. This was where he'd been right before he found out Grichenko had been murdered. He didn't like to leave a place before he was properly ready to, before his business was done.

'No,' he said.

She stared at him for a few seconds. It was clear she didn't buy his answer. 'Can you believe I've never been here before? All the years I've worked in the field, and this is my first time to one of Europe's capitals.'

Ryker didn't have much to say to that.

'I like it,' she said.

'You wanted to talk to me?'

'I thought you'd be interested in an update.'

He was, even if for some reason he had a hard time admitting it.

'Devereaux is out of hospital. She's in a maximum security cell somewhere in France. We're not yet sure what will happen to her. The French authorities are trying their best to keep everything quiet, given how events played out so badly on their soil.'

'Gone are the days of keeping something like this quiet.'

'You'd think so. Although I'm sure you agree that in many ways it'd be in all our interests for that to be the case.'

'Maybe.'

'Anyway, we're working hard behind the scenes to get Devereaux to the UK.'

'What do you know about her? Who she really is, what she's done?'

'Not as much as we'd want to.'

The way she said it was odd. Ryker wasn't sure he believed her, but he didn't bother to pry. The main thing was that Devereaux was locked up. Ryker didn't need to know her history.

What he was more concerned about was the likes of Kyri Anastopoulos. Wes Aldern. Gerardo Silva. Because the wrongs of all of those men had shaped the events of Doha ten years ago, one way or another, and Ryker wanted to understand how and why. Many people were dead because of them. Each of those three had paid the ultimate price, but – most worryingly – those men weren't operating alone. How many governments were tarnished by their actions? How many people within those governments were complicit and remained in positions of power? Ryker was sure the answers would never come out fully, nor timely, and that was what bothered him the most.

'Do you know who turned Aldern?' Ryker asked.

'No.'

'What about his paymaster, Anastopoulos?'

She shook her head.

'Do you know who he was working with? There must be someone in MI5, MI6, the UK government, who helped with Grichenko's new identity. And that means they worked against us in Doha.'

'I know, but it's not that easy.'

The troubled look on her face suggested she genuinely meant her words.

'Isn't it?' Ryker said.

'If you care so much, why don't you come and help me? I'm

sure we could work something out that's unofficial enough for you. It probably won't surprise you to know I've had Peter Winter on the phone asking the same.'

'Not going to happen.'

He'd said goodbye to Winter, his old boss, for good, and that's the way it would stay. As much as he wished, corruption would never stop. He couldn't solve every problem.

'You don't want to right the world's wrongs anymore?'

He didn't answer that.

'Then why did you get involved in this at all?'

'Perhaps you misunderstand why I do what I do,' he said. 'I didn't start this. It all started from one man's personal grievance. Gerardo Silva. He was the one who set in motion Grichenko's death in England. Nothing more than petty vengeance on his part. Everything else flowed from that.'

Although Ryker realised that was a very simplistic way of looking at things. Did the British authorities know Aldern had faked his death? Was Aldern simply hunting down his ex-colleagues to hide the fact he was a double agent, and scared that Grichenko's death would lead to his secret being exposed somehow? Who exactly were Kyri and Gerardo in league with? Which governments? Which intelligence agencies?

It was all so murky it made Ryker's head hurt.

He wished he knew the answers. But the fact was, it wasn't his fight now.

'You could have just stayed in the shadows and watched this all unfold,' Lange said. 'You didn't and–'

'How could I with someone like Devereaux on my tail?'

He glared at her now, as though she were badgering him unnecessarily. But which one of them was it that really didn't get the point?

'Sorry, Nadia, but I did my bit for you,' he said, 'and now we say our goodbyes. You won't be able to contact me again.'

He got up from the bench. As he looked down at her he struggled to read the look on her face. Disappointment? Apprehension? Fear?

'But you'll always know how to contact me,' she said.

'I will. But I won't. Stay safe.'

Ryker turned and walked away.

Two hours later Ryker was walking past the Golden Angel building. Today, the etched angel, looking over the square, glistened in low winter sunlight, and the entire area felt more positive for it. He carried on across the two blocks to the smaller and quainter square. The bar was right in front of him. He paused for a few moments before moving across the street and heading inside.

It felt like an age since he'd been here, yet it was less than two weeks. Still the place was abundantly familiar as he switched his gaze from the table with the two young, rough-looking men to the bar where Simona was standing playing with her phone.

She looked up and frowned then very nearly smiled. Ryker walked over and took a seat on a stool.

Simona stared at him for a few moments as though she wasn't sure what to say or think.

'*Dobrý den,*' Ryker said.

'You're back,' she said. 'I'm surprised. After you left me like that.'

'I'm sorry.'

She looked at him but said nothing to that.

'You want goulash?' she asked.

'Only if you'll eat it with me.'

Now she smiled, just a little, as she held his eye. But Ryker could hear the shuffling behind him. Footsteps. He swivelled on the stool to see the bearded man up on his feet.

'I told you to stay away.'

'Yeah, about that–'

The man lunged forward. Ryker jumped up from the seat, grabbed him, twisted his arm behind his back then smashed his face down onto the corner of the bar. His legs wobbled, nearly gave way. Ryker pulled the arm up more tightly behind his back and all resistance was gone.

'Let go!' a voice behind Ryker shouted out.

He glanced up to the bar to look at the man behind him in the mirror, but was left looking at Simona instead. She shook her head. A shocked look was plastered on her face. Fear, but also something else. Optimism?

'Do you know what you've done?' she said. 'They'll come for you.'

Ryker smiled. 'I hope so.'

He drove the man's face down onto the bar again. The guy crumpled to the floor.

Then Ryker turned and launched himself at the next one.

THE END

ABOUT THE AUTHOR

Rob specialised in forensic fraud investigations at a global accounting firm for thirteen years. He began writing in 2009 following a promise to his wife, an avid reader, that he could pen an 'unputdownable' thriller. Since then, Rob has sold over a million copies of his critically acclaimed and bestselling thrillers in the Enemy, James Ryker and Sleeper series. His work has received widespread critical acclaim, with many reviewers and readers likening Rob's work to authors at the very top of the genre, including Lee Child and Vince Flynn.

Originally from the North East of England, Rob has lived and worked in a number of fast-paced cities, including New York, and is now settled in the West Midlands with his wife and young sons.

Rob's website is www.robsinclairauthor.com and he can be followed on twitter at @rsinclairauthor and facebook at www. facebook.com/robsinclairauthor

A NOTE FROM THE PUBLISHER

Thank you for reading this book. If you enjoyed it please do consider leaving a review on Amazon to help others find it too.

We hate typos. All of our books have been rigorously edited and proofread, but sometimes mistakes do slip through. If you have spotted a typo, please do let us know and we can get it amended within hours.

info@bloodhoundbooks.com

Printed in Great Britain
by Amazon

63376360R00199